THE SNOWING AND GREENING OF THOMAS PASSMORE

Something strange has happened to Thomas Passmore. Waking from a warm Australian beach, he finds himself at Heathrow Airport on a winter's morning, only he can't remember getting there. Burdened with emotional baggage and a sense of déjà vu, Thomas pieces together fragments of his life by walking through the shadows of his past. Haunted by his father's suicide, his mother's rejection and by memories of his first love, his increasingly bizarre journey takes him into a world where one man's struggle to live again, as timeless as the battle of the seasons, becomes a choice between loss and life.

PAUL BURMAN

THE SNOWING AND GREENING OF THOMAS PASSMORE

Complete and Unabridged

ULVERSCROFT
Leicester

First published in Great Britain in 2008 by
Legend Press
London

First Large Print Edition
published 2009
by arrangement with
Legend Press
London

British Library CIP Data

Burman, Paul.
  The snowing and greening of Thomas Passmore
  1. Fathers- -Death- -Fiction. 2. Suicide- -Fiction.
  3. Memory- -Fiction. 4. Psychological fiction.
  5. Large type books.
  I. Title
  823.9′2–dc22

  ISBN 978–1–84782–702–9

Published by
F. A. Thorpe (Publishing)
Anstey, Leicestershire

Set by Words & Graphics Ltd.
Anstey, Leicestershire
Printed and bound in Great Britain by
T. J. International Ltd., Padstow, Cornwall

This book is printed on acid-free paper

For
Gwil, Lowri and Siân

1

A car blossoms into flower twenty metres ahead. Petals of twisted metal in orange and red unfurl towards the memory of a distant sun, and green doors sprout out across the road. Winter one moment and spring the miraculous next; then back to winter.

★　★　★

Sleep. Let me sleep. Let me drift with the flow of a rising tide.

My lips are shredded paper-bark glued tight with dried blood and resin. Hush. My swollen eyelids are sealed with sand and salt to shut the blinding brightness out. *Keep out!* Sealed tight against a storm of raining glass, shards of ice, the rending of metal. Sealed tight against a winter morning torn asunder, the hail of blood and bone, a day disembowelled. Something has happened, sometime, somewhere, but these lips, these eyes, are sealed by resin, sand and salt. Glued shut.

Hush. Just let me be and let me sleep. Forget the bags of blood and bone.

ROLL UP! ROLL UP! SEE THE AMAZING ABERCROMBIE MAN DISAPPEAR. WHOOSH! LIKE A RABBIT IN A HAT! ABRACADABRA!

SEE THE FLYING CYCLIST PERFORM CARTWHEELS THROUGH THE AIR!

This beach is a place beyond me; of surrender. My body is flotsam — broken timbers lashed with frayed rope, studded with rusted nails — but my mind is jetsam.

Wrecked. Beached.

This wind's a hot breath across my back, my neck, my driftwood-head, and the crashing of surf is a sleeper's lullaby. Ssh. My once-hands, my once-feet, are flowing into numbness, but the blanket of water slides warm against my thighs, and I think I might've pissed myself. Or if I haven't, that I will. That I can, and it won't matter. Not here.

Let me flow into numbness and dissolve here, as rocks are ground to sand, and let me drift. Let me drift with glued lips and sealed eyes and stopped ears.

Sleep. Let me sleep.

Grumbling in from an outstretched arm of reef rolls the echo of a roar, and I know the tide is turning. I know this explosion of sound and what it signifies. I know this place. I know how the sea rises and falls, rises and falls. There's a shell in my ear and I listen to the suck and sigh of the surf.

So, when the sea turns to tuck me in with satin-slippy sheets of kelp, I try ripping a smile to thank her, except this fickle mother changes her mind and pushes me forward and out, untucking me across a pillow of rock. And the tide slip-slaps against me, tapping me on the shoulder, in what's a gentle rhythm at first, but soon becomes insistent.

'Time to wake up, sir,' it says. Slip-slap. 'My, you're a deep sleeper. It's time to wake up, sir. We've landed.'

Landed? Let me drift, let me sleep. Fingers of seaweed, pebbles for toes.

Wrenched from the beach, I open gritty eyes to see a flight attendant leaning over me, rows of seats, open baggage compartments, the anonymous backs of passengers crowding down the aisles, clutching coats, bags, passports, pressing forward. Among them, the backs of three figures are momentarily familiar: a businessman wearing an Abercrombie and a bowler hat, a young mother cooing to the baby she's cradling, and an elderly man with his trousers tucked into his socks. The attendant smiles and her smile is anchored in lip gloss and eyeliner; she's on

3

board her uniform; her colours are Chanel No. 5.

'I'll stay on the beach a while,' I say.

'Pardon?'

'There's a café. Have to get to the café.'

'We've landed,' she says. 'There's several in the terminal.'

I shake my head, rub my eyes. Try yawning, but can't. Am numb all over.

'Are you alright, sir? Did you take something to make you sleep?'

'Where are we?'

'London, Heathrow.'

'Where from?' I say. 'Where have I been?'

'Pardon?'

I shake my head again.

I've woken on a plane at Heathrow airport, at five-thirty on a winter's morning. Sleeping on the beach was more welcome than this — and there's a chance I'll prove this is a dream by finding myself naked.

'Would you like a hand with your luggage, sir?'

Poking out the side-pocket of my flight bag is a small, crumpled packet of thin, white card, with a prescription label on the front in my name: Thomas Passmore.

'Sleeping tablets,' I tell the attendant, who nods, although I'm stuffed if I remember getting the things. They're not the sort of

4

thing I'd mess around with. Not these days. But somehow they've caught up with me. Somehow.

From the cabin speakers comes a tinny rendition of *Fly Me to the Moon*. The flight crew are waiting at the cabin door for me; they smile and thank me for flying with their airline. It's still night-dark outside and, from a gap between the boarding bridge and the plane, comes a rush of cold air so sharp its knife-edge slashes at me before I pull my coat tighter. The sunken eyes, hollow cheeks and flinty smile of one of the pilots reminds me of someone — and it isn't good — but I'm dopey with sleep.

'Enjoy your stay,' the bastard says, and his stony eyes are laughing at me. Then he mumbles something else I can't quite catch.

If only I could yawn and clear my head.

In the Arrivals Hall, I dig into my pocket for my passport wallet and its plastic edge slices across my finger.

'Shit,' I say and pull out two passports.

One is burgundy and documents my British citizenship; the other is dark blue and records that I'm Australian. In both I'm Thomas Daniel Passmore, born in Nenford. But there's something else I feel I should know. Something important. And yet, while there's a familiarity about this entire pattern

5

of events that creates the most profound sense of *déjà vu*, it doesn't help me remember what in pity's name that something is. What am I doing here? What am I really doing here? As soon as I see a bin, I'll dump that packet of mind-fucking mogadons where they belong.

The customs official looks at my British passport and smiles. At this moment such reassurance is exactly what I need. She speaks to me and smiles again, but I must be half-deaf from landing.

'Thank you,' I say. 'Thanks.'

★   ★   ★

In Heathrow's bus station the December freeze has another stab at me and I catch my breath. The air rasps against the back of my throat, condenses and becomes an icicle growing in my lungs. All the same, I'm soon playing with the fog of each breath of air I exhale.

Inhale.

Exhale.

Draw in.

Blow out.

When we were kids, walking to school, we'd pretend we were smoking on mornings such as this. We'd put two fingers to our lips and take drags from invisible cigarettes, and say things like: 'Ah, darling, the first smoke of the day is absolutely divine.' Or: 'Would you care for a cigarette, old chap?'

Breathe in.

Breathe out.

As I limp towards the coach bay, tugging my suitcase behind me, I rest a moment to glance at my watch. Almost nine-twenty. Can't be. I tap the face to see if it's stopped, but the second hand's moving, moving, moving, and for one crazy instant I'm slipping out of this early dark towards a different time zone. With a jolt, I snap properly awake again, take a long drag of the icy air, pull out the winder and adjust the time.

The coach circuits the airport before heading to Watford, where I'll catch a train for Northampton ... I think; I hope. Somehow I know to do this, as if I've done it before. Hitching up my coat collar, I shove my hands deep into my pockets and stare out of the window.

I remember the orange sky-glow from years back. There's no sign of sunrise yet, but with the jumble of road lights and fluorescence streaming from the buildings, dripping off advertising hoardings, it's easy to see how things are.

7

Too small a country for so many people. Too much busyness and too little sky.

Military Personnel Carriers are stationed in sand-bagged compounds close to each terminal. I see armoured cars and, not quite hidden, a couple of tanks.

WELCOME TO LONDON HEATH-ROW is emblazoned across a huge sign that spans several lanes of carriageway.

On a concrete pillar beneath, someone's daubed another slogan in black paint: *FUCK OFF!*

I would if I could. I don't want to be stuck here.

Heat begins filtering through the coach, and the driver turns on his windscreen wipers against the winter drizzle that's almost sleet, but I can't stretch the numbness from my leg.

A vast tract of industrial estate adjoining the airport is under redevelopment. Block after block, surrounded by miles of cyclone fencing and plywood panelling, littered with warnings: *HARD HAT ZONE, SAFETY GOGGLE ZONE, KEEP OUT, TRESPASSERS WILL BE PROSECUTED, PATROLLED BY SECURITY DOGS*.

'Yeah, sure it is,' I murmur, thinking of childhood and Gazza, and I let my head fall back against the seat and close my eyes. Can't keep them open any longer.

Thirty seconds later, the driver slams on the brakes and I'm thrown forward. A car horn to the side of us blares, and two lanes of night traffic slew to a halt. From where I'm sitting, I can't see what's happened, but the coach driver pushes open his window, leans out and shouts: 'Learn to drive, moron!'

* * *

Gazza and I break into the building site on a dull Sunday afternoon. The world's snoring after a morning of car-washing, Sunday roasts, church and all that other Sunday crap, but we're after life and adventure. We're both ten and in Year Six at St Giles' Primary School, and although Gazza's often in trouble with the police I don't figure that what we're doing is wrong.

Life's for living, not sleeping. Sleep's a snippet of death, and you're a long time dead, just stuck there, ain't you?

'Too easy,' I say, tugging back the bottom corner of chain link fence for him to crawl under.

Above the gap I've created is a sign that reads *NENE VALLEY SECURITY CO*, with a picture of a German Shepherd and a security guard. Both have pointed noses. Below, there's another sign in red letters:

9

TRESPASSERS WILL BE PROSECUTED.

'Hook it back to this,' Gazza says, twisting a strip of wire onto the fence, 'so we can scramble out if we need to. In a hurry, like.'

'D'ya reckon we'll need to? Do they really have dogs?'

'Nah, not them. They only patrol at night. Some old busy-body walking their poodle might see us if we're not careful though.'

It's a new estate of fifteen semi-detached houses. About eight houses on one side of the road are almost complete, but the remaining seven only have foundations laid, and a network of deep trenches extends from each into a deeper trench, which runs the length of the estate. Pallets of bricks and roofing tiles are stacked all over the place, several wheelbarrows and planks have been abandoned, and a bulldozer is parked over the top of one of the trenches, its caterpillar tracks straddling the pit.

'It's bloody great,' Gazza says, running up one plank and standing on another that bridges two pallets of bricks. He bounces on the plank as if it's a trampoline. 'I was here yesterday. I made this.'

There's nothing wrong with being here. The fence is round the site to stop little kids from getting in and hurting themselves. It's not like we're gonna steal anything — a new

10

house, a bulldozer or a brick or something. Besides, before they ripped all the trees out, there was an orchard on this land, and we used to sneak through a different fence when we walked down Wights Lane to scrump an apple or two in autumn, and no one minded much then.

'Fan-bloody-tastic,' I agree, clambering down into a trench.

This is the day Gazza — Gary Fletcher — finds a lump of flint the size of a small axe head. He might have the wrong sort of smarts for school (and Mr Walters sure has it in for him), but he's sharp enough to spot the truth behind a piece of flint caked with several tons of earth, halfway down a new sewerage line.

He's pulling off gobs of claggy red mud when he calls me over. 'Look at this, Tommo.' Crouching down, he rinses it in a puddle until it shines clean, then holds it for me to see, but won't let me take it.

'What is it?'

'Don't throw it. Promise.'

We've just fought a ten-minute war, tossing 'grenades' of soil and half-bricks from trench to trench. I'm still grinning and my hands are the colour of clay.

'Why not? What is it?'

Rounded smooth across the top edge of two flat sides, it's been chiselled down to

11

form one long, razor sharp edge. The following day, the curator at Northampton Town and County Museum will tell Gazza's mum and him that it's a side-scraper — part of a Stone Age tool kit — for cutting hide off meat thousands of years back. He'll have to lie about where he found it, of course, but he'll offer it to the museum, so they can label it and shove it in one of their rows of boring glass cabinets, as long as he can take it to school for Show and Tell first.

In answer to my question, he says, 'I reckon it's old.'

'How old? It's not a fossil, but we might find some here.'

'Cavemen-old. I reckon it's an axe. You know, Stone Age, like we did in those projects last term. They probably hunted woolly mammoths with this,' and he swipes it through the air, nearly slicing my bloody ear off. 'Or sabre-tooth tigers.'

'I've got a spearhead at home,' I remind him. 'You know, you saw it. I used it in my project. Found it in the garden.'

Only then does he let me hold it.

Gazza will take it to school and impress the hell out of Walters. He'll get Gazza to stretch a sheet of paper as tight as he can between two hands and, in one pass, old Waters will slice it in two with the flint — the straightest and quickest of cuts. Sharp enough to shave with, he'll tell the class, still beaming. The old fart won't be able to help but turn Gazza into an assistant at his own Show and Tell.

Gazza will remain a hero for a few days, all the teachers going out of their way to tell him how observant he's been and wanting to show their own classes the paper trick. His popularity won't last long though; only until the next playground brawl or until some kid forgets they've left their lunch money at home and points the blame at his infamously light and sticky fingers.

Beneath the concrete that smothers Nenford, there must be thousands of Stone Age implements buried. I've got two myself, though neither beat Gazza's. I found the first when I was seven, one shitty Christmas Eve, at the bottom of a hole I'd dug for a most important tree — a few days after Dad's funeral. It had the shape and size of a spearhead, with two sharp and slightly curved sides of a triangle coming to a point. The shape caught my attention, as well as its whiteness against the dark soil.

When I took it to school to show my teacher, she took it to the museum to show the curator. It was called a point, and was probably used to work hide or get meat off bone, or to craft wood on a dull Stone Age

13

Sunday afternoon. Along its edges I could see, as if they'd been done the day before, where each scallop-edged fleck of flint had been chipped to create a serrated and keen edge, sharp enough to score a tight line, or fashion a hole in a cured skin, to separate the hunger of boredom from the satisfaction of food in the stomach and robes to wear.

A couple of weeks after Gazza's find, I keep my eyes peeled when Mum asks me to dig the last of the spuds for dinner. I'd like to outdo Gazza and find the foundations of a complete Neolithic village under our vegetable garden, but know the chances of discovering even a seventy-year-old penny is thinner than slim.

'If you want to earn extra pocket money, you can turn the whole bed over for me,' says Brian, my step-dad. Brian the fuck-wit. I haven't heard him walk down the garden, but he's standing on the path with a colander for the spuds. 'Get shot of these weeds, eh? It'll save me a job later,' he says. 'But don't dig the parsnips, mind. They need a good frost to give 'em flavour. Alright?'

'Yeah.'

I don't really expect to find anything but, just before Mum calls me for dinner, I unearth a second point. Coarser, less smooth, but still a point. What are the chances of that?

I can't know it at the time, but one day I'll

keep them in a little red tin on a shelf in a house that I'm glad to call my home — in Australia. I can't know it at the time, but perhaps it's the discovery of these that'll kindle my interest in trying to understand the past.

Sometimes, in my head, I see two cavemen sitting on my mother's lawn. They're hammering away, underneath where the almond tree used to be — planted by my father and sawn down by Brian the fuck-wit — or under the Norway spruce (*Picea abies*). Around where they sit, as they knap the flint, there are so many shards scattered it looks as though they've been shelling nuts.

There's comfort in knowing, I think, that this place was inhabited long before Nenford grew into a farming community close to a shallow stretch of the River Nene. There were settlements in the valley long, long, long before the invasions of the Romans and the Danes and William the Conqueror, before the civil war of the Roundheads and the Cavaliers, before the agrarian and industrial revolutions, before the Space Age in which I grew up saw the village of Nenford in the county of Northamptonshire (as far from the sea as a place can be) become yet another boring suburb to yet another over-populated

15

English town. There's comfort in understanding our continuity with the past, that it stretches back thousands upon thousands of years, through all ages, and that we're rooted to the land and the elements much deeper than we're rooted to the concrete of ring-roads and motorways and housing estates, or to the detritus of modern civilisation with its choked rivers and its orange-glowing sky and its choking politics, its choking religions and its choking banks and, and, and . . .

We're connected whether we know it or not.

For my two Stone Age flint workers, the garden was an edge of forest or heath of course. But what's the point of so many points? Unless there was sweet fuck-all to do except make one and throw an old one away, like inventing disposable goods. Maybe they were dissatisfied with their lot in life — *Neolithic ennui*. Perhaps they were looking for hunkydory, hoping to make the absolute, ultimate point, or discover metal, and thereby introduce a new age.

'Hey folks, welcome to the Bronze Age.'

Maybe Gazza and I were just dead lucky in what we found.

★   ★   ★

16

I hang out with Gazza a fair bit for a couple of years. We're best mates for a while. We make a trolley in his driveway, his mum teaches us how to make doughnuts, and one warm, windy Saturday we catch the bus to Northampton.

We wander about, pressing our noses against shop windows, pushing the lift buttons at Walkers Department Store, playing guerrilla fighters between the maze of aisles in Woolworths, and he asks me whether I want to nick stuff, but I shake my head.

'Not even sweets? A choc bar?'

'Nah.'

He laughs.

Crossing Market Square, he says, 'In here,' and leads me into Thorby's Hardware & Garden Supplies.

'Wait here,' he says, leaving me in front of two carousels of seed packets: several varieties of pumpkin, cucumber, courgette; a thousand varieties of tomato.

Perhaps he's after weed killer, I think, and we'll be making fireworks in his bedroom later, and I almost miss seeing him lift the tube of greenhouse fumigators off the shelf and stick it in his pocket. He's that quick.

'Follow me,' he mutters as he strolls out the shop.

We walk a few yards and then run down

the nearest alley, out the other end into a car park, and I'm looking behind all the time to see if a store detective is chasing us.

'We're okay now,' he says. 'You can stop looking. You look like you've done something wrong. No one saw me. I'm too good for them. Don't worry.'

'You got a greenhouse in your garden?' I say, looking at the shiny tube, prising the plastic cap off.

'Nah. These are great smoke bombs though. You got any matches?'

I nod. Of course I do; I always carry a box. And I love the idea of smoke bombs.

'Here, watch this,' he says. 'And be ready to run.'

He takes the lid off a dustbin and places a tablet inside, then lights it. From the other side of the car park we watch smoke billowing upwards into a genie, and a middle-aged couple begin walking over to investigate. They're lugging their shopping bags and looking around to see who's set it off, and we scarper.

Dashing down a back lane, kicking and scattering a raked-up pile of autumn leaves, we pause to drop a smoke bomb in an empty milk bottle and Gazza dares me to lob it over the wall into someone's garden. We peer through a crack in the fence to see the smoke

18

streaming across a pocket handkerchief of lawn and up into bedsheets on the washing line.

Thick, acrid smoke.

We wander down to Midsummer Meadow, where old folks are resting on park benches, tapping the ground with their walking sticks, and where a pregnant woman pushes a screaming baby in its pram to and fro, to and fro, trying to rock the thing back to sleep. At the river, two young lovers are walking their dog on the opposite bank, so we run to the next bridge, light three fumigators and scarper. The wind pushes the smoke downstream, makes the bridge impassable for a few minutes, and we cack ourselves laughing until our sides hurt.

I stick one in the exhaust pipe of a car, parked at the side of the road, but lose the flame when I try lighting it, and don't notice the driver of another car a few spaces back. He must have been watching us.

'Oi! You little brats!' he shouts. 'What the hell do you think you're ruddy doing?' He's striding toward us, all red in the face like I've lit his fuse instead, and the miserable sod gives me no chance to light a second match before we have to run hell for leather.

When we've got fifty yards on him, Gazza turns and sticks two fingers up in the air.

'Stupid old git!' he shouts, and we run laughing across the rush of traffic.

Perhaps he thought we were letting tyres down, but we're just having fun. That's all. It's not like the old rust-bucket would've gone up in flames or anything.

There's a demolition site we find our way to. Northampton's full of flattened cinemas, theatres, factories, tenement housing, sitting there year-after-year, awaiting redevelopment, making the town look like the shit's been bombed out of it. On this one, all that remains of where people's houses once stood are slabs of concrete, lead pipes and ceramic toilet waste outlets hacked off at ground level, a few areas with broken floor tiles still attached and the suggestion of where a bath might have sat, as well as a mass of broken beer bottles, bundles of weather-wrinkled newspapers, and piles of bin liners spilling their guts of household rubbish. The only sniff of hope in so much crap is where weeds have begun growing through cracks in the concrete.

Gazza comes across a paper bag that looks full and is neatly sealed. He has a way of finding things and knowing what they are. He points to it and I'm about to kick it open, but he shakes his head and picks up a stick.

'Don't,' he says, 'not unless you want gunk

on your shoe. Bet I know what's in here.'

'A dead kitten,' I suggest.

'Nah. Wrong shape. And it's a chemist's bag.' Then he prods it open with the stick and says, 'Jam rags. Used jam rags.'

I reckon it must be a sort of cake somebody's thrown away, until I realise it's blood, not jam.

'Women's rags,' he tells me.

Later, it might seem an appropriate setting to learn about the scheme of things — birth, life, death, decay — and Gazza might've told me more, except I pretend I already know.

'Oh them,' I say. 'Yeah.'

We're blood-brothers for a year or two, Gazza and I, but will drift apart at the end of primary school. He'll go to secondary school in Nenford and I'll go to Northampton Grammar. At first we'll nod when we see one another down the village shops, but we won't talk. He'll fall in with a group of older kids who'll have nothing to do with the likes of me, not unless I've robbed the Post Office, tried burning down the school or stabbing some poor bugger.

★ ★ ★

Gazza dies when he's seventeen. He's tearing along in a stolen car, being chased by the

21

police; lights flashing, sirens screaming.

Afterwards, it seemed it was bound to happen and I felt no surprise at the news. He was often in trouble with the cops, getting into places he shouldn't have been, doing things he shouldn't have done, which maybe he did just for the kicks. Maybe he was the wrong type of smart for the world he'd found himself in and that was the only way he could push himself to meet new challenges. Perhaps, in his own way, he was chasing hunky-dory too.

$\star$ $\star$ $\star$

Gazza says, 'When you die your whole life flashes before your eyes. In the time it takes for your brain to shut down, you relive everything — the whole bloody deal.'

'Yeah. All the good times and all the bad times,' I reply. It's a regular conversation piece. Almost everyone talks about this stuff at some-time. 'Or perhaps you only see those parts you properly remember, or want to remember.' And I'm thinking about my dad, and I'm wondering whether you might relive all your best dreams too, or whether this curtain-closing flashback would be one sick nightmare.

'Faster than the bloody speed of light,' Gazza adds.

22

'That's enough language, Gary Fletcher,' his mum tells him. 'It's not needed, thank you very much.'

We're trying to make half-decent dough-nuts; deep frying the dough, laughing as they swell to size, engorged with air; rolling them in sugar, sticking them in our gobs, burning our lips, our tongues. We experiment at piping a mess of jam into them, before cooking them, after cooking them, but it never properly works.

'It's like when you dream,' he carries on. 'How it seems that hours have passed, but really it's only a few seconds.'

It's a small kitchen and his mum hovers in the background, wandering through, peering over our shoulders, giving encouragement. She lets us get on with it, while making sure everything's okay. Seems like a good mum to me.

Me: 'Yeah.'

Gazza: 'Time doesn't always happen at the same speed. It's been proven.'

I drop a ball of dough into the pan and the hot oil roils and spits like a crazy ocean in a crazy storm, spattering two splinters of heat across the back of my hand, and we laugh.

Me: 'Jesus! Look at the size of that.'

'Fan-bloody-tastic,' he whispers.

'Hush now. Ssh,' his mother says. And the

sea settles to a gentle slip-slap to focus upon. And my eyes grow heavy and lined with grit. Then she says, 'Enough now. Hush now.'

And rather than Gazza's talk of death, I listen to the sea instead, breathing in, breathing out. In, out. In, out. The shell to my ear.

2

Sheltered by a backbone of reef, the shallows are emerald green with the translucence of old glass. The beach is soft, white sand, free of seaweed and driftwood, and stretches in a broad, boomerang curve to define its bay. Fifty metres back from the lapping of a low tide, a fringe of dunes, sewn together with pigface and spinifex, rises and dips in a ribbon of peaks and troughs.

Slap, slap, slap.

Except for the patterns created by wind and recent rain, and the contoured tracking of this gentle, slapping tide, there isn't another mark on this world. It's unblemished. And there's something delicious about kicking through the water, keeping pace with a shoal of minnows and their shadows (more shadow than substance), and planting my footprints, one after the other, across the wet sand, to watch them wash away again as if I've never been.

If I walk this beach forever, then I'll be sculpted by the elements into a new pattern. I'll be the driftwood sanded smooth.

I look back and see my trail erased, and all

I am is what's left standing here. To lie down and sleep — wouldn't that be sweet?

The sky is a cerulean blue with fingers of cloud drifting in. Beyond the reef the waves are bigger, darker, and I strain to make out what might be fins from a pod of dolphins, or the tail of a whale breaking the surface. Not sharks.

A ripple of wind slides across the surface of the shallows, and then another and another. It whips a skittering of sand along the beach and I blink too late. Sand in my eyes, grit in my mouth. And, in this moment of half-blindness from a flurry of sand, I recollect the image of a man on a bicycle cartwheeling backwards through the air, feet pedalling furiously through a similarly sandy moment. The absurdity of the memory makes me smile, and I wish I could place it: circus performance, photograph, film scene, or dream.

Looking down, away from the wind, an abalone shell washes up and taps against my foot. Tap, tap, tap. The tapping becomes harder, more insistent, and the sand in the wind becomes glass . . . something solid . . . a window, vibrating against my head . . . against the chugging stink of a diesel engine. And I'm wrenched from the beach onto a train.

'Thomas! Thomas!' Her hand raps on the

other side of the glass, and the jolt this and her voice gives me draws a brief crease of pain across the back of my eyes. 'Get off! Quick! Wake up!'

'What?'

'I think you've gotta get off here, mister,' a passenger across the aisle is saying. 'D'ya wanna hand with your bags? Else you might not get off in time, like.'

'What? Oh, yeah. Thanks.'

Dopey with sleep and suddenly nauseous, I'm hurried out of the rail carriage onto the platform, to the feigned disinterest of other passengers. I'm glad of this help, but here's the thing: I'm stuffed if I remember transferring from the coach to the train at Watford. The last thing I remember is letting my head sink back against the seat as we left Heathrow. All the same, I know where I am and why I'm here.

Annette has stepped back on the platform, to the safe side of a yellow line. Her arms are folded now and she's stamping her feet against the piercing cold. She wears a long, black overcoat, buttoned all the way, and a matching white scarf, hat and gloves. I smile even though I'm tired, but her smile freezes mid-way into a grimace. She looks like an impatient liquorice Allsort, which was never a favourite sweet of mine.

27

The air is cold, thin, sharp, like a frozen razor blade, but it clears my head, tightens my stomach, helps me recover. The nausea passes.

The brief hug she gives me is awkward and brittle. The last of the carriage doors slams shut, a whistle blows and the train pulls out in a series of jerks. We watch it leave. The frost across the sleepers hasn't yet thawed.

'If I hadn't woken you, you'd have gone on to Birmingham,' she complains.

'Wouldn't be the end of the world,' I say. 'Although on second thoughts — Birmingham — shit!'

'I'm serious.'

'I know you are.'

'And I'd be wasting my time, standing on a freezing platform, waiting for you.' She wraps her arms tighter around herself, and I'm frightened she might implode if we don't move on.

'Hello, Annette,' I say. 'It's good to see you.'

She sighs and unwinds a little. 'Hello, Thomas. I suppose you're tired?'

'Beyond tired,' I say. 'Well beyond tired.'

She looks down at my suitcase and flight bag, then back at me. 'Does that mean you need to sleep before you see Mum . . . or what? Perhaps it'll wake you up if you freshen up first, have a bath.'

'We'll go see her first,' I say, picking up my luggage.

We make our way along the northbound platform, across the bridge, and down the southbound platform towards the entrance. It was a summer day when I waved Kate on her way to France. It was an autumn day when I waited for the train to take me to London to see her those few weeks later. I've hated Castle Station and Euston for two decades.

'I can take you to the hospital,' Annette tells me, 'but I have to be at work this afternoon. I've taken too many days off recently. I can't keep leaving them in the lurch. They'll sack me.'

'That's alright. You do what you have to do. I'll catch a taxi to Nenford afterwards. Just give me a key.'

'You can stay at mine tonight if you want. It's a bit cramped, but it's closer to the hospital. Andrew did. He's had to drive back to Scotland today. There's only an old sofa bed and I might wake you up when I get ready for work in the morning and — '

'Thanks, but I was planning on going back to Nenford. For old time's sake and all that . . . '

'If you're sure.'

'I am.'

She loses more of her stiffness and takes

29

car keys from her pocket, but makes no move to step into the gritty drabness of the car park. 'Bitter weather for December,' she says. 'We might even get snow before Christmas.'

'That'd be nice.'

'No, it wouldn't. Aren't you cold with your coat undone?'

'Numb,' I say. I've done something to my leg. Pinched a nerve or something. But she doesn't appear to notice.

She looks at her watch and hesitates. 'It's not really visiting time, but I'm sure the nurses won't mind if we explain . . . '

I look at my own watch and frown: nine-twenty. Didn't I adjust it? Perhaps I didn't. The second hand is still moving. And I jiggle my wrist to see if that'll fix it. 'What time is it, Annette?'

'It's not visiting hours until — '

'Stuff visiting hours, Annette. I've just travelled ten thousand miles to see my sick mother. Tell them that.' And I step towards the automatic doors.

'This isn't Australia,' she says.

★　★　★

My mother's asleep. And she looks a decade older than her sixty-three years. Her stick-arms poke from the blanket, and her head,

30

with its thinning net of grey hair, barely makes an indentation on the pillow. In looking at this woman, who I feel I must love even though I've found her hard to like, I see a woman whose skin now hangs a size too big. She is less than she was, which surely means she can hurt me less than she has.

Also, under this harsh lighting, the starched whiteness of the hospital linen has leeched the colour and substance from her, so that her baggy skin has the sheen and texture of a wrinkled sheet of soft wax. Or maybe these are symptoms of her illness and its treatment. Observing her like this from the end of her bed, I'm reminded of a candle nearing the end of its wick, and I don't know whether I sigh with relief or anxiety. Or both.

She half-opens her eyes.

'What are you staring at? I'm not asleep, you know. Aren't you gonna give your mum a hug?'

'Did we wake you?'

'I was just having a catnap,' she says, and begins struggling to sit up until Annette presses a button on a remote control, automatically raising one end of the bed. Her voice is weak and rasping. 'It's too hard to get a decent night's sleep in this place, what with the racket — the hacking cough of her over there, all these machines blipping and clicking away, and the constant fussing of nurses wanting to know whether you're alright or not. I would be if they'd only let me get a blooming night's sleep.'

If it's cold outside, then it's stifling hot inside. Annette takes off her coat, hat, scarf and gloves, but, with her pink jumper and blue skirt, is still a liquorice Allsort — just a bit more sugar-coated. I throw my coat onto a chair and peel off my jumper, realising my mother might melt into a puddle of wax on the floor if she stays here too long.

'How are you?' I ask.

'Ready for a good night's sleep, that's how I am. What on earth are you doing here? It was Andrew yesterday and you today. Someone told you I'm on my deathbed, did they?' She glares at Annette, who moves closer to her, sits on the edge of her mattress and smoothes a wrinkle from the blanket.

'Something like that. But I thought it was time for a visit anyway. Seemed like a good time to come.'

'You're a liar,' she says, and almost smiles.

'How're you feeling today, Mum?' Annette asks.

'How are my grandchildren? They'll be almost grown-up now. Tamsin, Elspeth . . . '

'And Daniel,' I add. She's always refused to use his name — my father's name. 'They're

32

fine. They're good kids. Very Australian. Very outdoors, gregarious. They'd have liked to come with me — I'd have liked to bring them.'

'How are you feeling today, Mum?' Annette asks again.

'Tired,' she says. 'Tired of being asked how I am. I feel like everybody expects me to drop dead any moment.'

'Don't say that.'

'As if I should be feeling a lot worse. It's a mystery why I've been brought here in the first place. It's that blooming doctor. He needs his head read. They just needed to give me some tablets, that's all. Maybe he gets a bonus for every patient he shoves in here.' And she begins laughing, until that brings on a fit of coughing, which makes her wince and gasp, and Annette reaches over and brings an oxygen mask close to her face. She waves it off at first, but then, when she can't catch her breath, nods and takes a few pulls from it.

Annette raises her eyebrows at me, as if to say: told you so.

It's too hot in here. If we take all the white hospital sheets and spread them across the ward — across the beds, drips, monitors and floor — it'd look like snow, and it'd be cooler and fresher then. I undo a couple more buttons on my shirt.

★ ★ ★

The house is cold and dark, and seems to have grown again now that I'm alone in it. After my last visits all those years back, I thought it'd be like squashing into a dolls' house, but it isn't. There's even room, I suspect, for my childhood ghosts to have squeezed back into the darkness of cupboards and into the shadows under beds, or to be perched along the beams in the attic — now that I'm here.

Too many ghosts.

My earliest memories are rooted to this house and its garden, even though there was a time I'd thought to leave them all behind. Or to supplant them even, with memories of my children's childhood, from a different time and a different place.

Wandering from room to room, turning the lights on and off, plugging in a couple of heaters to take the stagnant chill from the place, I remember going through this routine as a nervous kid, whenever I was home by myself. Except now I'm doing it with a sleepwalker's momentum, room-by-room, until the route leads me to the kitchen, where, instead of standing on a chair to raid the biscuit tin, as I once did, I now fill the kettle and look for Mum's jar of teabags. The mugs are in the cupboard where they've always been kept, but the milk's a rancid green liquid with yoghurt-like sediment.

However, I'm putting off the most inevitable move of the lot, even though it's the gravitational pull towards this that, seemingly, is becoming responsible for the momentum behind everything else. It's too soon and I'm dog-tired, and how can I justify it? I wish I knew. Even so, I'm letting myself get drawn in. I'm letting it happen. As a diversion, I work out that, with eleven hours difference, it'll be eight o'clock before I can phone Elin and the kids to tell them I've arrived. That I've arrived and have visited my mother in hospital. Mission accomplished. Almost.

Sipping bitter, black tea, I stare at the tidy suburban bleakness of the back garden before snapping the Venetian blind shut.

'What the fuck,' I say, and head into the lounge to unzip my suitcase and start rifling through my clothes for wherever I've tucked the address book, but the case is open and the book's on top.

I might have returned to see my sick mother, but I'm also here for this. I know I am. After nineteen years, I'm going to find Kate again. I can't help it. For reasons I can't fully fathom, I need to know she's okay and that my loss hasn't grown any bigger. Just this. I can satisfy this, if nothing else. The momentum's too strong to resist. Perhaps this is one ghost I can lay.

Kate.

Twenty-two years ago, when I phoned her that first time, her dad told me she was having a saxophone lesson and asked me to phone back later. I'm half-expecting the same conversation as I dial the numbers now.

I dial the first three numbers, then pause too long before dialling the rest and have to start over.

It rings once — too loud, too clear — and I hang up.

By four o'clock, night is a shroud being lowered from the sky, wrapping the day in long sleep, that snippet of death. Peering through the lace curtains, every house in the street has a Christmas tree in its window or coloured lights and tinsel. Mum has nothing. Her decorations are the dozen Christmas cards standing in a row on the sideboard. Christmas has always been a lonely and cold season in this house. Maybe, tomorrow morning, I should go to the shops and buy a small tree, a Norway spruce, and decorate it for her return from hospital.

I picture her walking into the lounge, seeing the tree in front of the French windows and having a final seizure on the spot. Night-night, sleep tight.

★ ★ ★

She stands over me at the kitchen door — Mum — tying the strings of a cotton sun hat under my chin, and it's a bright summer's morning. I feel her fingers working the bow, but pinching when she pulls it tighter.

'For goodness sake, hold still, child,' she says. And: 'Now, don't you just look handsome in that.' She leans forward to plant a kiss, but the garden's a world of light and bird-song, and the world beckons.

Tottering down the path, I stomp through the shadow of a young almond tree, trying to splash it apart, and then jump from the path to the grass — hoppity-hop — to break into a dizzying run, round and round, discovering how to make the world spin faster, faster, faster, until tripping over the sun and landing in a heap with the world still spinning. Looking up and up and up — stretching up — and discovering a blue, hypnotic vastness that's the sky above. An ocean.

This garden is divided into a vegetable plot and a square carpet of lawn, with a border of plants and rocks between. Mum will always like masses of colour dancing together here:

the yellow of jasmine spilling in cataracts over moss-softened stones, pools of pink and mauve aubretia swimming with bees, green fountains of gladioli spurting orange and red spears. It's forbidden to walk on the border — by my dad, my mother and, later, my step-father — but there's a short path of stepping-stones which steal a passage through the waves of leaves and stems and flowers, linking the land of lawn with the land of lettuces, marrows, potatoes, rhubarb.

If, as a toddler, this garden is paradise then it's a serpentless Eden at that. And of the sprawling housing estate being built beyond the creosote-stinking fences, which border the garden's length and breadth, I don't have the faintest idea. It remains a flat world with walls.

My head still spinning, I'm scooped up and thrown into the air like a bird, then caught and perched on my dad's shoulders. Daniel Thomas Passmore. I can't see his face, only the top of his head, but I can feel the roughness and strength of his hands, and can smell the sweetness of tobacco in his clothes and hair.

He sets me down on a patch of lawn and then he's gone again.

Dad.

The arms of the honeysuckle stretch along

the trellis, tying it in knots, and it's laden with clusters of knotted red berries, which I begin to pluck and squeeze between my fingers — the colour of thin blood — before wiping their stickiness across the grass. Knowing they must be delicious, I long to plant a cluster in my mouth, but daren't.

Next to the honeysuckle, a cluster of crimson pæony drowse languorously. There's a richness to their colour, texture and scent which I'll always find sensuous, and their languorousness and sensuousness will one future day put me in mind of the sexuality of beautiful women. Some petals, already dropped, lay wilting on the soil; other stems are expectantly heavy with tight balls of bloom bursting to unfurl and deliver their display. Each pregnant ball is a tight furl of unbloomed secret, and I begin prising with clumsy, untrained fingers to unravel the buried passage and core of one flower. When it rips, I move to an open blossom and am about to bring it to my mouth when several petals of the fleshy velvet fall at my touch. Broken that easily.

Startled and guilt-ridden, I retrieve the petals, then bring them to my mouth and bite with my front teeth, but the scent's too strong, so I tear each of the fallen petals into strips and bury the evidence of this dissection in a hollow of dirt I've scooped out. This will become my first remembered experience of sensuality and brutality; my first experience of death, guilt, burial.

Playing with the crumbs of dry soil, it's amazing that such juicy berries and soft, crimson wafers and giant honey-suckled beanstalks can be created from dirt and fed by it. I stroke my fingers through the dust and lumps — ploughing, then harrowing the soil into a new dusty fineness — then pick up a chocolate-sized crumb, sniff it, and pop it in my mouth.

Yuk! I spit and dribble the grit from between my teeth, rubbing my lips and tongue with the fingers of a dirty hand. Cheated, but wise enough to keep quiet about it, I run inside to the kitchen, where Mum's baking a cake. I wait at her side, tugging her apron, urgent to lick the mixing bowl.

'Wash those grubby hands first,' she says, not knowing where my mouth has already been.

3

My dad was in glass, as they say, but got smashed when I was seven. He turned sand into glass, white light into a rainbow of colours, but was careless with himself.

My mother won't tell me what his job at the glass factory involved. It's one of the subjects she won't allow to be broached. As a teenager though, I'll discover several books stacked in a dark corner of the attic, which she's somehow failed to find and throw away, and I'll guess from a couple of these that he worked in the accounts department, balancing figures, income and outcome, positives and negatives, black ink and red. But he could've been a draughtsman or a glassblower. My dad could've been anything.

There's the time he gives me a glass prism, when we spend the whole evening shining a torch beam through it at different angles, creating spectrums of colour out the other side and doing experiments. And there's the time I think of as Our Best Day Ever, shortly before the day of his dying.

It's a Saturday morning and we're sitting at the kitchen table. There's a loose edge of veneer at one corner of the table, and it's my habit to pick at this with a thumb nail. The breakfast dishes are on the draining board, and Mum's standing to one side of the small kitchen, slightly separate to the scene, but smiling.

'Come on, Tommo,' he says, 'it's that time of year. Sling your coat and hat on. We'll walk down the village. You can help me choose our Christmas tree this year.' And he unhooks my black duffle-coat from where it hangs and drapes it over my head.

The previous night's frost hasn't thawed, and my fingers and toes, my ears and my nose, ache with the sharp cold as I run to keep up with him — stride, stride, stride — but it doesn't matter. Two of my steps to one of his.

There's a crowd at the greengrocery and the floor is damp and dirty. As Mr Hall scoops Brussels sprouts and carrots, or tosses King Edwards onto the scales, his breath creates foggy clouds and his bulbous red nose has a drip on the end. Dad sorts the stack of Christmas trees — Norway spruce, *Picea abies* — and pretends to seek my advice.

'We should get one with roots and a clump of soil on, Tommo, do you reckon? It'll last longer.'

'Yes,' I tell him, and make a show of

examining and rejecting the trees he's passed over. There's the slish of tyres on the salted Main Road and the grumble of motors caught behind the town bus.

'It wants to have a good shape. Not one of those spindly things. One that's a bit taller than you, I guess. Can you see one, Tommo?'

And I point to the one he's holding apart from the rest, which he hasn't yet appeared to properly notice.

'That one,' I say.

'This one?'

'Yes.'

He lifts it off the ground, turns it round, inspects it from several angles. 'I think you're right. Yes, he'll do brilliantly. Excellent choice. I'm glad you came. You know a good tree when you see one, that's for sure. We'll have to get you on this job every year.'

It may be a day of icy coldness, but the sun is bright.

Back home, we find a bucket and place a couple of clean half-bricks at the bottom, to stop the tree from toppling. The soil in the vegetable garden is frozen and, though Dad hacks at it until he's red in the face, he only manages to chip away a few crumbs and to bend one of the fork tines. He rolls a thin cigarette and lights it, and I hold onto the fork for him. I'd hold his pouch of tobacco

43

too if he let me, and secretly sniff at its snug, honeyed aroma.

'There's not much joy in this,' he says, letting smoke drift out his mouth with his words. 'We'll never fill the bucket at this rate. We could boil a couple of pans of water, I expect, to thaw it out,' but then he remembers a bag of sand stored next to the dustbin.

Together we carry the tree through to the lounge and place it in front of the French windows. He helps me decorate the bucket with red crêpe paper and the picture of Father Christmas I'd painted at school.

'That'll do,' he says. 'Now for the real fun.'

From upstairs he fetches a large box of decorations and initiates me in the ritual of dressing the tree. First he strings the lights, spiralling them between the layers of branches, working from the tree's tip to its base; he plugs the lights in, switches them on, isn't disappointed when they don't illuminate, but fiddles with each tiny, coloured globe — twisting, tightening them in his large fingers — until they all light up. Then he introduces me to the baubles and the birds. There are about twenty glass spheres to hang — some gold, some blue, some green, some pink, but mainly silver — and half a dozen birds to clip on.

'These are very old,' he says, holding one of the glass birds and brushing a finger along the fine bristles that represent tail feathers. 'I'll put these on. They belonged to Granny Potts — my grandma, your great-grandma.'

And when we've done that, he tugs out streams of gold and silver tinsel, which we layer from branch to branch.

He stands back and squints his eyes. 'Just like snow,' he says.

I copy him and can see it myself. 'It is,' I say. 'It's like snow on the branches.'

'But it's not finished yet.'

'The star,' I announce. It's wrapped in tissue in a separate box, but I can tell from the shape what it is.

It has a long point at the bottom and shorter ones all the way round, suggesting rays of light, and again it's made of glass and is coloured silver, gold and blue. Dad pegs it to the tip of the tree, and there's a different light to the room now, and the air is rich with the scent of spruce sap.

'How about that?' he says. 'Perfect. Shall we call Mum?'

'There's one more thing,' I say.

'What? We won't fit anything else on.'

'Just one thing. Please.' I run upstairs and fetch my prism. 'If you tie some cotton round it, we can hang this too.'

'No, Tommo. I think we've got enough. We don't want to overdo it, do we?'

'Please.'

'Why? It's not a decoration.'

'It'll catch the light, if you tie it in the right place, and make a rainbow.'

'I don't think — '

'Please, Dad.'

'Well, alright. But only this. Nothing more. Let's see how we can do it.'

And then it's time for Mum to admire the magic.

★ ★ ★

Christmas is just four days away and he's late home. Not so late that Mum's anxious or angry, but for some reason I'm standing on a dining chair waiting at the window, pressing my forehead against the cold glass. Perhaps he's told me he'll bring back sprigs of holly or mistletoe from the market, or balloons.

'Come away from there,' Mum says. 'Find something to do, for goodness sake, child. He'll be home when he gets here.' And she mutters something about a traffic jam or a flat tyre.

The village bobby arrives as she's taking mince pies out of the oven. I watch him cycle up the street, take note of our house number and clamber off his bike before it's properly stopped, the way I've seen cowboys dismounting a moving horse in films. Leaning his bike into the privet hedge, the policeman blows his nose on a big, white handkerchief before crossing to the front door.

'Mum!' I shout, running to fetch her.

She wipes her hands on her apron as she moves towards the bulky shadow, which fills the glass panel and spills darkness down the hallway. I stand behind her, not wanting to miss out.

'Mrs Passmore?' the policeman says in a voice that's deep, but which he softens in a way that makes it sound misplaced.

'Yes.'

'It's about your husband. I wonder if I might come in.'

She stands a moment, unmoving.

'Go to your room, Thomas.'

I scramble upstairs and lay on the freezing lino, hoping to hear from there, but can't. All I hear is the murmur of a deep voice, which sounds like water burbling over rocks from where I am, and then a silence, followed by my mother saying, 'Thank you.'

Only that is clear: 'Thank you'.

There are no tears or screams to remember.

I find her sitting in my dad's armchair. She

doesn't see or hear me at first, but is looking down, staring at her clenched hands, pinched tight and frozen.

'Why did the policeman call?' I ask. Twice. 'Mum?'

'Weak,' she mutters. 'So weak.' And I wonder whether she's talking about the policeman, me, my father or herself.

Extending an arm to draw me to her, she then withdraws it and folds her arms, squeezing herself in and upright.

'Go to your room, Thomas. Go straight to your room. No, wait; come here first. Stand here. I have to tell you something.'

To begin with, my childhood imagination paints a simple picture of his death. I imagine a cartoon-like collision between two cars, similar to scenes from my favourite comics. Kerpow, bang, crash! The smash snaps something vital in his body, like the filament in a light bulb, the snuffing of a candle, but everything else remains intact. Kerplonk! Dead. No blood, no gore, no disembowelling agony; no chest-embedded steering wheel, no shredded limbs or dismemberment; no ebbing, waning, draining of consciousness among shards of plastic, chrome and rubber littering the bitumen; no expanding puddle of oil, petrol, brake fluid, blood, piss.

Our house becomes crowded with visitors,

relatives, well-wishers, busy-bodies, who suffocate Christmas with their shrouded whispers and morbid clothes, and their stink of eau-de-Cologne and mothballs. There are aunts I've never seen before, who expect me to sit still or play in silence without toys, and when I ask if I too can go to the funeral they ignore me so furiously that I daren't suggest it again. So I find pleasure where I can, and it sits in a bucket, decorated with red crêpe paper and a painting of Father Christmas.

Each morning I turn the tree lights on and leave the rest of the room to winter darkness. Sitting cross-legged in front of our tree, I soak up the warmth of its brightness and the richness of its scent, until Mum comes in and switches them off again.

On the second morning, she says, 'Leave the lights alone. I don't want those bloody things on.'

Someone calls and delivers a clear plastic bag that contains Dad's 'effects'. Mum thanks them and leaves it untouched, unopened, on the cabinet near the front door, at the bottom of the stairs. When she's not looking, I stare at the contents: keys, his wallet, some coins, his wristwatch on its brown leather strap, his tobacco pouch and his comb. I want to open the bag and touch these things, but daren't.

On Christmas Eve, I know everything's gonna be okay again — we can't forget Christmas, even if there's no presents under the tree yet. And I turn the prism by its cotton until one of the lights shines through, although I can't find the rainbow among the baubles and tinsel, among the shadows behind the needles. It's the first day the house doesn't fill with visitors by lunchtime and the first day I don't have to squeeze my nostrils against the stink of their mothballed Sunday finery.

I sit in front of the tree until mid-morning, building a farm out of wooden blocks and stocking it with pigs, two cows, a carthorse, one sheep and a few hens. I drive a tractor through the yard, build a shed for it, with a book for a roof, and then decide to people it with my collection of cowboys and Indians . . . after which the slaughter begins.

Mum walks into the room, holding my coat, scarf, hat and gloves. Both gloves are attached to my coat sleeves with elastic, so I don't lose them.

'I want you to go to the shops, for milk and bread. But be careful on the pavements — they may be icy. Don't try sliding. I won't be pleased if you skin your knee again or break a leg. Oh, and Brussels sprouts and spuds too. I'll write it down for you.'

'I don't like Brussels sprouts,' I tell her. 'Do we have to have them?'

'Your father likes them,' she begins, and then drifts into a poisonous quiet. 'Just go.'

When I get back from the village, the tree has gone. There's a telltale trail of sand on the carpet and the step by the French window, which she hasn't yet swept up. Across the lawn is a scattering of broken baubles and a strand of tinsel; across the patio lays the broken shards of glass birds, the star and fragments of my prism, and at the end of the garden, dumped on its side, with several decorations still draggled around it, is the tree.

'I hate you!' I shout, and run to the kitchen where she stands at the stove. 'I hate you!'

But she doesn't shout back or smack me, or send me to my room, or even turn and look at me, so I slam the kitchen door and crawl under my bed to cry among my toys.

That afternoon, when she's fallen asleep in front of TV Christmas carols, I grab a cardboard box and pad down the back garden to the tree, picking up baubles and tinsel along the way. Dragging the bucket off the root ball and sand, I shove the tree upright against the fence. The decorations have lost their glow outside, so I begin undressing it, untangling the gold and silver

51

tinsel, unclipping the remaining birds, taking off the baubles and unwinding the lights.

The soil is rock-hard, so I run a saucepan of hot water in the kitchen and pour it over the spot I've chosen. I find Dad's spade in the shed and scrape away an inch of topsoil before hitting the freeze again, so hurry back to fill the saucepan once more and put the kettle on to boil. Mum's in the deepest of sleeps, curled like a baby, but with her mouth wide open and her hands tucked beneath her chin. She should be in bed. I'm about to sneak past her and turn off the TV — the King Singers are beginning *The Holly and the Ivy* — until I realise the sudden quiet might wake her.

The afternoon light is fading, but the boiling water sends up a massive cloud of steam that fills half the garden. When it clears, there's a slush of stones, grit and a twitching chrysalis, which I shovel to one side. I pour more water and probably scald a few worms to death, but I'm creating the hole. It'd be good to dig all the way to Australia and leave this mess behind, but night is drawing in and the ground's too hard. When I'm about a foot down, and ready to drag the Christmas tree over, among the washed stones is a piece of white flint which, I'll learn before too long, was knapped into a point thousands of years previously, and it's waiting to be noticed and picked up.

I pick it up.

My hands are numb with cold, but the sharpness of the point, the keenness of its edges, can still cut through that. Holding it in the palm of my hand, examining it from every angle, I draw its sharp edge across the fleshy heel of my thumb, then drop it into my pocket and continue planting my Christmas tree the best I can.

When I've finished and my gumboots are caked in mud from pushing the soil down around the roots and the base of the trunk, I stand back and admire my handiwork. It's almost dark, but my eyes have adjusted as the light's dissolved. And I no longer care about the hiding I'll get.

However, the tree seems too empty now, and cold, so I kneel down and sift through the box of decorations. Pulling out three of the glass birds, I peg them on different branches, and the tree is happy again.

* * *

Later, heading upstairs to my bedroom, I stop to look at Dad's 'effects', still sitting on the cabinet in that horrible plastic bag. Having

53

planted the tree, I'm feeling reckless and brave and so I unfold it, take out his wristwatch, put it to my ear, listen to the soft tick of it: the gentlest of movements. It's still going. Though it's too big for me, I strap it to my wrist, and then, before refolding the bag the way it was, I take one last, long heady draught of the smell of his tobacco. My dad. My tree. My watch.

★   ★   ★

Our home withers and the house acquires a smothering quiet about it; soil-heavy and pressing down. Living there is like being buried alive. And something between my mother and me withers too.

★   ★   ★

Another visitor comes casting a shadow through the glass of the front door about a week after Christmas. The visitor is *all* shadow, even though it's dark outside.
    'Hello, young man,' it croaks.
    Dark-suited, dark-browed and sunken-jowled, I recognise Reverend Lofton, even though he's not wearing his black frock. Visible between the lapels of his coat is a black vest and white collar, while craning

down from this is the craggy face of a gargoyle, beaking forward with a lop-sided grin and hollow eyes. His likeness is chiselled in stone, perched along the roofline of St Giles' church, facing the school. At Harvest Festival and Christmas and Easter each year, he leads the school in morning assembly, chanting sentences that bubble and stew around the hall, which already reeks of stale school dinners, as he preaches about flesh and blood and corruption, bread and wine, life and death, salvation and damnation.

He brings a cloying scent into the house, which pervades the lounge and hallway, but beneath it is the centuries-old dampness and mildew of crumbling stone. I walk past the doorway several times and notice him sitting forward in the chair, balancing a teacup and saucer on its arm. The best china. He may be offering sympathy and solace, the busy God's-body, but even at seven I recognise how proud my mother is. She sits opposite, in my father's chair, and holds her teacup with her little finger poised uncharacteristically in the air.

'Why was that man here, Mum?' I ask afterwards. I'm in my pyjamas and I've even brushed my teeth, but my dressing-gown won't button up anymore.

She's sewing. Lengthening a hem or mending something.

'Reverend Lofton? To see if we're alright, I suppose.'

'Are we?'

'Of course we are.'

'Why don't we go to church, Mum?' And I expect anything from anger to delight.

She carries on with her sewing. 'We just don't.' Blunt. As hard-edged as her thimble.

I move closer to her sewing, stand in her light. She looks up.

'Some of my friends do.'

'What?'

'Go to church.'

'You want to go too?' She pricks her finger with the needle and puts it to her mouth.

Although he's a man who scares me (partly because he's more gargoyle than man — a bogey-man — and partly because everything about him stinks of death), I'm also curious.

'I don't know,' I say, knowing that I do, and realise in the same instant that my dressing-gown is inside-out.

'Why on earth would you?'

I shrug.

For the following Sunday, she asks Mrs Davies, an elderly neighbour, to take me to church with her. I've learnt enough at school to know it's a house of ghosts and souls, and that maybe Dad's ghost or soul might find a way there too.

The Reverend Lofton is cloaked in the softness of white and purple — surplice and silk stole — but he can't mask his gaunt face. Escorted by a dozen choirboys, he slides from the vestry, up and down the gloomy aisles, snaking through the eleventh-century church towards the chancel, illuminated by candles burning gold and brilliant against the burnished brass. My skin prickles and, at first, I'm sure it's because ghosts from all the way back to the Dark Ages are pressing against me, hanging off the backs of the oak pews, kicking their hallowed heels to every chanted response in the ritual. While the sermon is boring beyond anything I'd ever imagined, everything else is part of the dark mystery: the foreign language, the wine and the slivers of bread, the hymns, the sitting and standing, the kneeling and praying — the mumbo-jumbo of magic. Hocus pocus; abracadabra.

Sanctus, sanctus, sanctus.
Our Father.
Our Father who art.
Hallowed be Thy name.
Forgive us our trespasses as we forgive those who trespass against us, and give us this day our daily bread.

Forever and ever and ever and ever.
So be it. Amen.
Sanctus, sanctus, sanctus.

But when I walk out, nothing's changed at all. If there're ghosts in there, then Dad's isn't one of them. I'm further from him than ever before, and drifting towards learning that death is the premature extinction of a light, along with all the possibilities of its hidden colours, replaced by the dark vacuum of winter night. For all time.

Old Lofty — the Angel of Death — visits once more, about a fortnight later, but not after that. I've been playing at a friend's house, but I can smell him and the best china is sitting on the draining board. This time, I ask nothing of my mother and don't go to church again either.

★   ★   ★

A respectable year and a quarter passes before Brian Taylor slithers onto the scene — or before I meet him, let's say. Outside, it's a cold, spring day, with daffodils in bloom, shivering yellows in the wind, hurrying-up the sun. Inside, the atmosphere is tense with the odours of purple Windowlene, polish and purple hyacinths.

'This is Mr Taylor,' Mum says. The visitor

she's made me wear a crummy tie for. 'Say hello to Mr Taylor.'

Her eyes are shining, probably from polish fumes.

'Hello, Mr Taylor.'

He stretches out his hand to shake mine, man-to-man. I'm eight. He has a dark moustache and thick, horn-rimmed glasses, and he has the smell and slip of Brillo in his hair and on his hands.

'You can call me Uncle Brian. He can, can't he, Margaret?'

'He can.'

There's a celebratory smile between them, which I catch, but pretend not to. If it was a butterfly, I'd put it in a glass jar to see if it'd lay eggs . . . and it'd die there.

All the same, it's good to be made a fuss of. For a while.

Brian Taylor is listening to the radio with Mum when I'm told: 'Say night-night and get yourself ready quick-smart for bed, young man.' He's absent the next morning, but rings the doorbell an hour before lunch. I know he'll reappear because the smell of roast beef and Yorkshire pudding hasn't filled the house since the accident.

'We used to have Sunday dinner every week when Dad was alive,' I say by way of polite, man-to-man, lunchtime chit-chat.

'Didn't we, Mum?'

'Ssh,' she says. 'I've told you before I don't want to hear you talk about that. If you've got nothing useful to say then don't say anything.'

'How about we go to the park this afternoon?' Mr Taylor says, stabbing the roast potatoes and cutting the beef with a fierceness that's been missing from meals for too long.

We go that week, the following week, and the week after that.

It doesn't matter at first because I like hearing her laugh again, even if he grips her hand in his own slippy paw; even if it's him that makes her laugh — not me, not Dad. There's been times when she's spat bitter words at the memory of my father, and I've felt guilty, as though some of this was my fault and because her sense of loss was bigger than anything I could replace it with.

'Do we have to do the same thing every week?' I ask one time.

'It's a kindness,' she tells me from the bathroom mirror, pursing her lips to achieve symmetry of lipstick. No longer the same person. 'He doesn't have to take you to the park.'

'We could go by ourselves,' I say. 'You and me.'

'We could, but we never did though.'

60

This is true. And whose fault is it?

I try running circles around their conversation as they walk the village pavements arm-in-arm, expecting me to skip ahead. I imagine I'm the string on a kite tying their words up in a tangle of interruptions, so they'll have nothing left to say to one another, but they're quicker than that.

Several months after, following a brief appointment among the red carpets and plush government furnishings of Northampton Registry Office, we're officially made a family. The frequency of the man's visits and the ease with which he's settled into Dad's chair puts the event beyond surprise.

And the memory of my father as a person recedes. With it goes part of who I am — my link with who I've come from, my connection to our past. There's nothing else to hold onto except his name — the smallest of fragments — and the knowledge of his death.

Until they try smashing that too.

I've been sent to bed early after something I've said, but, unable to sleep, I pad downstairs quietly, politely, in the hope I'll be forgiven and allowed to watch TV. When I'm in the hallway though, I stop to flick my hair into a parting, the way Mum likes it, and I hear them talking about me.

'Tell the boy, Margaret. You've got to tell

him sooner or later.'

I move to the doorway of the kitchen and stand there with my arms at my side, thinking they'll see me waiting politely, but she's got her hands on the edge of the sink, facing the window, and he's standing behind her, talking to her back.

'Not yet. I can't.'

'The longer you leave it, the harder it'll get, and he'll keep on saying these things. What happens when some busy-body tells him his Dad killed himself? What then?'

'Ssh,' she spits, 'don't you dare. Don't you ever dare.' There's a pause, before she adds in a softer tone: 'He might hear.'

'For crying out loud, Margaret, the boy's asleep, thank God,' he says, and turns away from her to see me standing there. The clock ticks. The water gurgles down the sink. 'Well, there you go. Why the hell aren't you asleep like you were told?'

My mother turns then and, at the sight of me, covers the round 'O' of her mouth with one hand, as if she can shovel their words back in.

'Why aren't you in bed?' Her hand straightens and tenses, ready to slap.

'I couldn't sleep. You're talking about Dad,' I say. It's an accusation. 'You can't talk about Dad,' I tell Brian. 'Mum doesn't like it.' Now

I'm parroting the day's lesson back at him.

He seems to expand several inches when I say this, like an angry red balloon, and I'm ready to duck if he explodes.

'This is bloody ridiculous, Margaret. Tell him. You have to ruddy tell him.' In two steps, he pushes past me and then I hear the front door slam.

We're alone in the kitchen now and, with both hands, she beckons me. I think she's going to hug me, because I've stood up for her against Brian, but she puts her hands on my shoulders and grips them hard, digging her fingers in, clamping me in place.

'Your father killed himself,' she hisses. 'He put a rope round his neck. Do you understand me?' Her face is hard; she isn't crying.

I stand looking at her and can't speak or blink. She might as well have hit me.

'There, is that what you wanted to know? I hope you're proud of yourself. Does that make everything better, does it?'

I try taking a step back, but she grabs me tight again and I lose one of my slippers. There'll be red marks under my pyjamas. 'He was in a car crash,' I say. 'I saw the policeman come round. You told me he was.'

'Now you damn well listen to me and listen well.' And she begins shaking me backwards and forwards. Her fingers are pressing in and hurting, and when I try shaking them off she shakes me harder. 'He hanged himself. Put a rope round his neck, rather than . . . couldn't . . . the coward . . . He was weak.'

'He was in a car crash.'

'I sold the car to pay the bills.'

'No!' I shout. 'No!'

And now she lets me go. She takes a step back and turns to face the window.

'Yes,' she says. Quietly. 'He gave everything up, including you. That's how much he cared.' She turns from the window and begins tidying her hair. 'Don't you ever ask about him again. I don't ever want to hear him spoken about. Not ever. I forbid it.'

'Why? Why shouldn't I?'

'Get out of here. Go to bed this minute.'

* * *

The year after that was the year the twins were born. Annette and Andrew. A half-sister and a half-brother, but too young to be fun.

* * *

I begin digging my way to Australia, I suppose, and twenty-odd years later we arrive.

64

* ⋆ ★

Beyond the runway and airport traffic, is a vast, dry plain and, on the distant horizon, an eruption of hills. There's a clear, sharp light and a cloudless, soft, deep blue to this morning sky, which is wider and higher than anything I've ever met before. I almost trip over with looking up.

'Birdie,' Elspeth says, tottering towards some kind of honeyeater.

A line of ants trails across the red brick pavement and up a palm tree, but the taxi rank is empty.

'We'll have to phone for one,' Elin says.

'The phones are yellow,' Daniel announces. 'I saw one in there, didn't I, Mum?'

Jingling a few foreign coins in my hand, I hold them out as if I've minted their foreignness myself. No longer pounds and pence, but dollars and cents — the small currency of a new everyday life.

Daniel, Tamsin and Elspeth chatter like a flock of excited birds; chattering to me, to Elin, to each other. And the trees are busy with the birds chattering too. And I think of the subdued silence of our British garden, with only the drone of the motorway in the background.

'It's hot already,' Elin says, 'and it's not

even eight o'clock.'

Instinctively, she leads the children under the shadow of a tree — long, pendulous, grey-green leaves; strips of bark dangling like brown snakes — and we draw our gaggle of cases and hand-luggage into the fringe of it. But, after so many cold, anaemic years, I stand in the sun and let it warm me. I want everything to be different, to leave my ghosts behind. I'm ready to begin a new day.

Closing my eyes, it seems only an instant later that we're paddling though the shallows of a low tide, just a hundred metres or so from the apartment we're renting. The beach is a wide belt of sand that stretches on and on and on in both directions, holding the Southern Ocean up on one side and everything that's the city on the other, and it's all but empty.

'Look, you can see the bottom!' Daniel declares. 'See-through sea.' Reaching down, he picks up a shell, then another and another. Perfect spirals. 'Can I keep these?'

'They'll still be here tomorrow,' I point out.

But Elin nods and he slips them into the pocket of his bathers, and Tamsin reaches down and chooses a couple herself.

'Birdie!' Elspeth squeals, pointing and stepping backwards out the water.

'Fish!' Elin shouts. 'I can see fish. Over here. Hundreds of tiny fish!'

'Fish!' we all shout.

'See-through sea,' I repeat, picking up a shell too, tracing its whorls with one finger.

And Daniel throws himself down and starts splashing about, and Tamsin joins him. Elspeth reaches up and holds onto my hand, and I scoop her up and hold her horizontal so that, when I spin around, she becomes a bird flying in circles across the sea. I stop when she screams too loud, swinging her instead onto the perch of my shoulders, where she grips hold of my hair and kicks her wet feet against my chest, and giggles.

'Dad,' she giggles.

'Dad,' I say.

An elderly man wheels his bicycle along the sand, watching the ocean, a couple of swimmers cutting broad strokes, the endless churning and chasing of the surf perhaps, and he stops. His trouser cuffs are tucked into his socks, and he wears bicycle clips on top of these; his shirt is unbuttoned and he wears a white vest beneath.

'Beautiful — no?' he says.

He can only be talking to us.

I nod. 'It certainly is.'

'Beautiful, for sure. Yes?'

He looks Greek or Turkish. I like his accent, his lyrical intonation. He makes me smile.

'Yes.'

'You swim — yes?' He points the stump of a finger at Daniel and Tamsin who are now building a sandcastle with a moat leading down to the waves.

'The water's so warm,' Elin says.

'I not swim,' he laughs. 'I look, I like, I fish, but not swim.' For each phrase, he mimes an action, but at the end he pulls a face to emphasise he's not a good swimmer. 'A stone — yes?' And he points downwards.

Elin and I laugh, the kids stare.

He pauses a moment. 'On holiday — yes?'

'We've emigrated,' I tell him. 'Arrived a couple of hours ago. Thought we should have a paddle. This is our first day.'

'Ah. Big move for *pehdheeah* — childs.' And he leans down to adjust his bike clips.

'For all of us,' Elin laughs, but there's an edge to her voice.

'We flew here on a big plane,' Tamsin chips in.

'For sure, is long way to swim. Is long time to dig,' he tells her, and winks.

For sure. I look at him closely, waiting for something else, but the moment passes, and he climbs onto his bike and cycles along the sand, waving at us with one arm, waving at the sea.

'Have good day,' he calls.

And the waves drift in, draw out.

In.

Out.

4

The first time I notice Kate Hainley is at a New Year's Eve party given by a friend of a friend of a friend. I'm seventeen, insecure and incomplete, while she . . . well, she's something else.

The party takes place in a sparsely furnished flat above a down-at-heel shoe shop in the centre of Northampton, and I'm one of the early desperate dozen to arrive. Having arranged to meet friends in The Lion's Head — a fine establishment for scoring a tab or two of acid — I'm late and they're nowhere among the crush of pissed New Year's Eve revellers. I figure they've moved on already, but they're not at the party either. As a result, I begin the evening pretty much how I'll end it: leaning against a wall in the hallway, smoking too much and listening to people crap on about nothing I give a shit about, and staying because there's nowhere else to go this New Year's Eve, and because it's sleeting outside.

She blows in with a group of eight or nine. They're laughing and exuberant and, straightaway, half-fill a room that's garlanded, I now notice, with sprays of holly and sprigs of mistletoe. With her at their centre, they begin dancing to the very next song and the party isn't half-empty and dull any longer, the flat is no longer cold, and the bleakness of winter grows more remote. After a few steps, she kicks off her clogs, peels off her jumper, and begins pirouetting.

Beyond the main rhythm picked up by her feet, her fingers pull threads of music towards her and she spins them into something new with each gyrating sway of her neck, shoulders, hips. Fanning her fingers across her face, then flowering them into an arch above her head, she cascades them down her body, outlining her waist and hips, and I think of flamenco dancers I've seen on TV. My foot taps to the music and I inch along the wall to keep her in view as she turns and twirls and turns some more.

After three or four songs belting from the amplifier, she stops, flicks her hair out of her face, picks up her bag and slips on her clogs.

'Excuse me,' she says with an open smile, stepping in front of the guy standing next to me, but she doesn't glance in my direction.

Five minutes later, she's got some bloke by the hand, pulling him to where her friends stand drinking, and he's pretending to resist, but loving every second of it. They cheer and she makes him dance too.

Because of the embroidered gilt patterns on her skirt, the cut of her blouse, her long, dark hair, and the seductiveness of her dance, there's something Latin or gypsy-like about her. More than anything though, she radiates a wholeness and vitality I'd love to possess. She shines with it, is a light because of it. She's alive, awake, fresh. If I knew her, or someone like her, then my life would be richer too — but I don't and I'm just some hollow nobody leaning against a wall with a beer in one hand, a cigarette in the other and a pocket of over-cooked cannabis cookies.

'Hello, my name's Tom,' I should say. 'There's something about you I . . . Something about you makes me feel . . . well, I don't really know because . . . Can I dance with you? Will you dance with me? Please.'

As if.

In one of Dad's old books, which Mum doesn't know I've found, there's a passage by a guy called Bede, who in 731AD compared life with a sparrow's flight through a banqueting hall on a winter's day. Bede wrote: *'In the midst there is a comforting fire to warm the hall; outside, the storms of winter rain or snow are raging. This sparrow flies swiftly in through one door of the hall, and out through another. While he is inside, he is safe from the winter storms; but after a few moments of comfort, he vanishes from sight into the wintry world from which he came.'*

Watching her reminds me of that image. Life is fleeting and there are too few opportunities to snatch happiness. Perhaps this is the lesson the old suicide, my old man, learnt too late.

And it pisses me off that this might be the only truth he left me.

What happiness did he fail to grasp and hold onto? What loss or regret had been impossible to live with? How do I know I won't inherit the same miserable, shitty defeat?

Someone says, 'It's almost time,' and I glance at my watch — his watch — tap its glass, as several people start counting down: 'Ten, nine, eight, seven . . . ' And every clock in the country is ready to chime twelve.

'Should old acquaintance be forgot, And never brought to mind . . . '

Everyone is singing and I'm lip-synching along, and taking two or three steps closer towards her group, and wishing. I'm wishing that she'll dance in my direction, find herself facing me and end up kissing me under the mistletoe. She'd wrap her arms around me and learn to know who I am.

But she doesn't and I can't do anything about it, weak bastard that I am, so I grab my damp coat and sidle out into the bleakness of an icy night to trudge the five bitter miles to bed.

*   *   *

She had the widest eyes of glistening burnt umber that ever smiled, a flow of hair that was deep chestnut brown and lips of rose, but more than that she glowed, and sometimes when I'm at other parties or sitting in a pub or listening to a band I look for her.

*   *   *

When I see her two months later at the Spring Dance, chatting with a friend of mine, and without the other moths clamouring for her light, it's so far beyond all probability it's as though a greater force is in play — a syzygy. Sometimes, the yoking of the sun and moon to the earth creates king tides and bizarre cross-currents, which wash up exotic treasures, the flavours of other worlds. Everybody has some luck once in a while.

It's the first Saturday in March and the first day in ages it hasn't slashed down with rain from morning to night. All the same, the sports field next to the Students' Union Hall is flooded and I've had to weave between vast puddles in the car park to get to the entrance. Even though the forecast promises a week of brighter weather, spring doesn't feel any nearer and, at that point in the evening, it's impossible to imagine winter ever coming to an end.

'How ya going, Andy?' I say, unwrapping my scarf, unbuttoning my coat and letting him punch me on the shoulder. 'You managed to get across then? I didn't think you were going to make it.' He lives twenty miles away, and Saturday night buses aren't reliable.

'Jez decided to come — the DJ's a friend of his — and he's giving us a lift back to Abetsby, so everything's hunky-dory.'

'Hunky-dory,' I repeat and laugh. I've never heard this old-fashioned expression used by someone my age before, but it sounds good. They probably think I'm stoned. 'Everyone's fishing for hunky-dory,' I say and laugh some more.

She's looking at me and smiling, so I shrug and say, 'Hello.'

Andy makes a joke I don't hear, then says: 'Kate, this is T.P; he's — '

'Hunky-dory,' she says.

'Gone fishing,' I say.

Andy winks at me. 'Fly fishing.'

'Teepee?' she says. 'Like a wigwam?' She tucks a lock of hair behind her ear.

'Tom,' I tell her. 'Tom Passmore.'

'I've seen you somewhere before, Tom. D'you live in Northampton?'

'Nenford,' I say. 'But I saw you at a New Year's Eve party last . . . well, last New Year's Eve. I don't think you'd have noticed me.'

'Oh. I wish it had been some other time. That wasn't a night to remember.'

'You looked like you were having fun.'

She shrugs. 'Not really. I drank too much. It wasn't good.' She looks at Andy and then says to me: 'Will you dance with me?'

Andy laughs.

How easy she makes it seem.

'Um,' I say.

She pulls a strand of hair away from her mouth. 'You're not one of those cowards who won't get out and dance until the floor's packed, or you're too pissed to know you're dancing, are you?'

'Usually,' I admit.

'But not tonight? You'll dance with me tonight, won't you?'

I look to Andy, unsure what their relationship is. Don't want to get in his way. But then think: what the hell. He's not that close a friend.

He reads my hesitation and deliberately

misinterprets it. 'I don't want to dance with you, Tommo. You're not my type.'

'He dances by himself,' Kate says, raising her eyebrows as if it's some form of self-gratification, like masturbating, that everybody does now and then, but few admit to. 'We're very old friends. Very platonic.' She kicks off her clogs and holds her hand out to me. 'Come on, Tom.'

'I might step on your toes,' I say.

'Then I'll forgive you.'

The dance-floor is a dark, empty expanse. It's early in the evening. She's right: usually I won't dance until the place is heaving and I'm pissed or stoned or both, but tonight — with her — we'll be the first.

I take her hand and she leads me into the music. Sober.

'Hello, Kate,' I say.

'Hello, Tom.'

And we light the place up with a dance that'll last all night and for months to come. For one of many evenings, we'll find the rhythm that draws everyone else to dance. Together, we'll bring in spring and summer.

★ ★ ★

She lives on the other side of the county, in Abetsby, a town I've never visited. Our worlds

77

are separated by the epidemic sprawl of Northampton's suburbs and industrial estates and by the remaining patchwork of villages and fields, hedgerows and fences and spinneys, by the winding of the Nene and its many streams, and by a tired public transport system. She only has a few months before her end-of-school exams and starting university; I've got another year to go. We move in different circles of friends, beyond the forecast of too many freak tides. Yet, she's gripping my hand a week later and smiling.

'There are buses,' she says. 'We got here tonight okay, didn't we? You don't mind catching the bus to see me?'

'No, course not.'

We're inside The Royal Oak, at a table by the door of its crowded bar, amid tobacco and beer fumes, the clatter of a skittles game.

'We can meet midway.'

'Definitely,' I say. 'If that's okay with you.'

'And the telephone. You're on the telephone?'

'Yep.'

'So am I.'

'I know, Kate. I looked your number up.'

'Did you now?' And she slips an arm round my waist. 'Good. I'm glad you did that.'

There's a flurry of people at the door. They're laughing and flushed and bring a cold blast of night air with them. No more seats to be had. Standing room only. From behind the bar comes the sound of a glass breaking and a loud cheer rings through the pub.

'You can always stay over at mine, you know, if there's something on in Northampton and you can't get home,' I tell her. 'There's a camp bed somewhere.'

'There you go, then. No problems. I want to see you again, Tom.'

'Me too.'

'You do?'

'Yeah, I do. Of course I do.'

The door from the street swings open again, someone peers in out of the night, then it slams shut once more. Too loud. The draft slaps us with its icy chill, and the light in the room appears to dull for a moment, but Kate smiles.

I'm a provincial boy hemmed in by short horizons, but Kate the beautiful introduces me to Mozart, Duke Ellington, Artemisia Gentileschi; she recites Leopardi's poems and Alain-Fournier's *Le Grand Meaulnes* to me; makes lasagna, ravioli and minestrone, and I eat it up and hunger for more and more . . . and more than I can give in return. We dance. She pinches me, makes me yawn and stretch beyond my meat and two-veg

79

provincialism, to reach out for something cosmopolitan, to crave other places, other worlds and question my own. We dance. She dazzles me with her brightness, wakes me up with her exuberance, breathes life into me with her vivaciousness.

Breathe in.

Breathe out.

She has long, chestnut brown hair, and the widest eyes of glistening burnt umber that ever smiled. When she kisses me, her lips are fuller and glossier than polished olives, warmer than sun-baked terracotta at the end of day. And when she recites Leopardi's poem to Silvia, I wish I could create such sounds for her.

Silvia, rimembri ancora
Quel tempo della tua vita mortale,
Quando beltà slendea
Negli occhi tuoi ridenti e fuggitivi,
E tu, lieta e pensosa, il limitare
Di gioventù salivi?

On a shelf among other books, next to a tin with two flint points, in a house I call my home, is a copy of Leopardi's poems. (Some memories are impossible to live without, however tormenting they might be to keep alive.) To one side, in a brass frame, is a slightly blurred, black-and-white photo of a man carrying a child on his shoulders. It's my only photo of my father.

★ ★ ★

It's late-afternoon, I've just got home from school, and I'm phoning Kate. Before Mum and Brian get in.

'I'm so angry,' she cries.

'What's the matter?' Maybe there's been trouble at school, or an argument with her parents. Stuff from my world.

'The bloody council. Nothing but vandals. They butchered the trees in my street. Every single one.'

'Chopped them down?'

'Just about. Every year I watch the first buds shoot into leaf, but it won't happen now. They're a bunch of bastards, bureaucratic vandals. I do my homework in the front room so I can see the greenery and listen to the birds singing, and now it's bare. It'll be bare all summer and especially when I'm revising for exams. All I'll see is the bloody factory opposite.'

It's mid-March and a fortnight since the dance. We've met in Northampton to see a film — *Picnic at Hanging Rock* — and at a pub a few days later. Every couple of nights we speak on the phone, even though Brian's getting toey about the bill, and even though I've told him I'll bloody pay for each friggin' call if he wants me to.

'And they've cut them all down?'

'They were just beginning to look like real trees again, after the last time. I was hoping they wouldn't do it again. I guess I'd forgotten. It's a few years back. And now those morons have cut all the branches off, right down to the trunks. Every tree in the street — but especially my tree.'

'Perhaps they've got Dutch Elm disease, Kate. Perhaps that's why. Perhaps they've gotta take them down completely and then they'll replant more.'

'Don't say that. These trees are fine. I don't think they're elms. Limes or planes, I think. They do it every few years. Pollard them. Thinks it makes them look bleeding tidier, but they're more like knobbly poles than trees now. Stumps. Oh, it makes me so angry. It's the Council's fault of course. They're a bunch of knobs. The workmen are only doing what they've been told. I've a good mind to write a letter to the newspaper. I think I will. I'll do it tonight.'

I've little to offer except what an elderly neighbour told me when I'd helped with her garden once. 'If they haven't been chopped back too far, they'll probably sprout again pretty quick. Sometimes, when plants are cut back, they grow even faster. It sort of encourages them.' And instinctively I look out at Dad's almond tree and our spruce.

'Do you think so? You probably think I'm being silly.'

'No. Not at all. Do you want me to come over? We could meet somewhere. Anywhere.'

'Would you? Would you really do that?'

'Of course I will. If you want me to.'

'I'd love you to, Tom, but not tonight. I've got an essay to finish and some reading to do, and I'm gonna write that letter. Saturday though, eh? I'll see you on Saturday?'

'Definitely,' I say, and decide to buy her a plant to keep on her windowsill; something with lots of leaves that won't die in a hurry, like a rubber plant or a spider plant, or maybe a poinsettia.

★ ★ ★

On a night of icy frost, when spring has retreated against winter's return, Kate teaches me the nature of my sex. On this brittle night, when the dark sky seems so bitten by cold it might snap in half and leave darkness floating across the world forever, she leads me through the rites of my first clumsy coupling on the wooden floor of a gazebo in someone's back garden. One of her friends has turned eighteen, been allowed to throw a party; the house is crowded, but Kate finds a space for just the two of us.

I work Saturdays behind a fruit and veg stall on Market Square, and am moved to prepare for this consummation by the way her eyes beckoned the last time we met, the way she embraced me, the way she planted her hands in my pockets when we danced at the end of that evening. During my lunch break, I set out to buy condoms, and sidle up and down the aisles of three pharmacies, hoping to pluck up courage, but turn heel each time a shop assistant approaches.

'Just browsing,' I mumble and scuttle off.

It's a fruitless effort and I spend the afternoon weighing potatoes, onions, Brussels sprouts and rhubarb, cursing my cowardice.

Jumping off the bus in Abetsby that evening, onto a pavement of black ice, I know what I've got to do.

I march into the backyard of The Duke of York, past the stacks of empty kegs and crates, and into the Gents toilets — a weakly-lit bunker of cracked tiles, damp cement, a leaking cistern and a stained, stainless steel urinal. Shovelling a fistful of coins into the condom vending machine, I grapple with the handle, pocket the packets and march out again.

The stench of mildew, naphthalene, urine and bad drains stays with me, so I spit into the gutter and take a deep breath of icy night. There's stuff-all romantic about these preparations, nothing uplifting — I feel shrivelled by the process — and, to cap it all, the crappy bus service has made me late.

Kate'll wonder where the hell I am, whether I've got lost or if I've stood her up. Too much can happen at a party in thirty minutes, and I've seen the way blokes look at her. So I clutch her scribbled map and run twenty paces, walk twenty, run twenty, walk twenty, until the stitch in my side makes me stop.

What really pisses me off is not that Abetsby's bigger than I thought it was, but that there are so many new housing estates beyond the town centre it's a bloody labyrinth. Street after street of identical suburban boxes, accommodating all-too-familiar ingredients: the same old beginnings and endings of never-never dreams and recriminations, TV programmes, mortgage statements, the burden of nine-to-five jobs, the stale defeat of drained love, the prospect of a holiday to Costa Brava in a year's time and a retirement plan in ten or twenty or thirty — the cloned lives of Mum and Brian

. . . from all of which I'm feeling remote because Kate's begun to breathe a different sort of life into me. As long as I don't get lost, as long as I don't lose her.

And then there's the house. I hear the pounding of a bass rhythm from the end of the road, and notice the garish pulsing of yellow, blue and red lights through the drawn curtains of a front room. I knock at the door, but there's no answer, so go to a window and bang on the glass.

'I was worried you'd missed the bus,' she says, skipping into my arms, her arms outstretched.

'It was late. Couldn't find the house. Thought it was closer to the centre of town.'

'You're here now, though.'

I touch the inside pocket of my jacket and nod.

'Yeah,' I say.

She leans closer, embraces me, pushes her hands into the back pockets of my jeans, speaks soft words next to my ear: 'Tonight's a good night, Major Tom.'

But I'm still wearing remnants of winter. 'What for?'

'To fly me to the moon,' she laughs and plants a brief kiss on my neck.

It's hard to thaw from the day's anxieties and the long dash through the maze of this unfamiliar town, and my fingers are numb. 'Pardon?' I say.

She lets go, stands back and smiles. 'Perhaps later,' she suggests. 'When you've warmed up.'

Clutching a plastic beaker of beer, I mumble silly jokes and know she'll ditch me. Of course she will. I watch the other blokes mill around, sometimes laughing with her, and wonder who'll make the first move.

'I suppose you know everyone?' I ask.

'Almost everyone,' she says, embracing me, her mouth close to my ear. 'Only Em, Sue and Andy are close friends though, and you know Andy. Most of the guys are brain-dead pot-heads and acid-droppers, and you know what I think about that.'

'Hmm.'

Still I can't get warm.

Eventually she hushes me, takes the cracked beaker and puts it down, makes me dance, embraces me again, takes my hand and leads me along the passage to the kitchen, through to the garage, to the frosty garden and the gazebo.

'Let's go for a walk,' she says.

'Now?'

'Yes. I want to show you something.'

Unable to speak, I slide a hand towards my jacket pocket.

'It's alright,' she says, 'I'm on the pill. But thanks, Tom.'

In the darkness, we make the gazebo warmer than the house. For us. She thaws me. Somehow we avoid splinters, escape frostbite. Winter is defeated from this nest; it's vanquished by the smell of two lovers, of patchouli oil and musk, by our rag-tag of garments half-off, by the singing of our giggling and panting in the dark and by the taste of Kate on my lips, the warmth of her thighs and the tenderness of her gently guiding hand, the deliciousness of being planted inside her, soft and moist . . . and her generous delight in that first clumsy fuck.

★ ★ ★

Before long she spends the weekend at Nenford. (Annette and Andrew are on school camp, so she'll have a proper bed and there'll be space to listen to records and be alone.) I meet her at the bus station in Northampton, but before heading home and introducing her to Mum and Brian we walk along the banks of the Nene, through Midsummer Meadow. It's early April, and windy and cold — the month that arrives like a lion and leaves like a lamb. The trees are entering bud, the river's swollen and muddy, and the sky's pretty much the same as the river: a sepia brown sky reflecting the churned-up day. To keep her to myself, I'd walk forever if we could, hand-in-hand, arms swinging, our eyes smarting in the wind, following the river all the way to the coast. I don't want to share her with anyone.

But she's been studying Dario Fo on the bus — *Morte Accidentale di un Anarchico* — revising for an exam, and her mood is muddied too. She lights a cigarette, takes two long, deep drags, exhales and then pinches out the tip, before dropping it in a bin.

'What's the matter?' I say.

'Nothing,' she says, walking ahead of me. Then she stops, turns, forces a smile. 'No, that's not true, Tom. I'm sorry. It's just that there's too many thoughts beating about in my head. I've got so much revision to do, I'm not sure I can afford to take time off this weekend. I'm sorry; I shouldn't have come.' She pauses, glances across the river and then at me. 'I nearly phoned and called it off.'

'No,' I say. She's come all the way from Abetsby to tell me it's over and that I'll be going home without her. 'No, Kate.'

'Not us. Just the weekend.'

'Oh. I thought you meant . . .'

'Yeah.' She hesitates. 'But I've been

thinking about that too. At times. It's fair you should know.'

'What? Why? Don't do that.'

'Listen, Tom, I'd already decided to avoid any relationships for the next few months, to concentrate on schoolwork. I've worked too hard to throw it away. University means too much to me — '

'And how much do you think you mean to me?'

' — but then you came along and, well, you've turned everything upside down. I'm not sure about anything anymore.' She kicks at a twig, but it snaps. 'No one's had this effect . . . ' She shrugs. 'I've had two pretty serious relationships in the past, but not like this. I felt I had some sort of control over things before.'

That shuts me up and I catch sight of myself in a different light, and I know I mustn't lose her.

'Why can't you have both, Kate: a relationship and the time to study? Who knows, maybe you'll do better in the exams because of us being together.'

'How? I've got to win a scholarship. I don't have a choice. I can't afford uni otherwise. My parents do what they can, but they're not that well off.'

We're still standing apart and she's rubbing

her hands together against the cold.

'Balance. Happiness. A person works better when they're happy. Besides, I can help you with your revision. I'll read with you, test you on those superlaxative adverbs, even help with Biology. I'll help you, Kate. I will.'

'Superlative adverbs, you dill,' she says and the sky brightens.

'Whatever. Besides, not only am I a whiz in French, but my Italian's getting there too.' And, in the worst Italian accent ever, I recite to Kate, to the river and to a crow sitting on a fence post: 'Silvia, Silvia, alla luna. Alla luna, mama mia, questo spaghetti, macaroni! Pasta, pura, pasta.' A string of words knotted together with starch and nonsense, which forces her to laugh and grip my hand, and we start walking again.

'You don't mind helping me revise this weekend?'

'I'd love to.'

'Really?'

'As long as I'm with you I don't care what we're doing.'

'You're the best,' she says, and the crow opens its beak wide and agrees with her.

'So everything's okay again?' I say.

'It's better.'

'Better than okay?'

On the footpath on the other side of the

river, a white swan stands sentry. Two boys with a dog are walking towards it, until it rears up, wings outspread, and begins hissing. The boys pull the dog back and give it a wide berth.

'Angry swan.'

'Might've been pestered by a dog in the past, or lost its mate to a dog attack,' Kate observes. 'They mate for life, you know, and they'll fight to the death to protect their partner and their young. I love that in them. And so graceful.'

'If you got hit with that wing, it'd break your leg,' I say.

'Isn't it beautiful, magnificent? Even when it's angry.'

She's glowing again. It's never buried too deep. The sight of a swan brings it out.

The river, which is flowing faster than I've seen it flow before, carries a branch past us, towards the bridge. It's a large, forked branch, and snagged between its two arms is a white, plastic carrier bag, a lollipop stick, a few leaves. Caught in the current, it quickly overtakes our casual pace, and I'm about to point it out to Kate when I realise I've dreamt the scene before. Every bit of it. It leaves me uneasy.

'*Déjà vu*,' I announce.

'What is?'

'That,' I say, nodding at the branch. 'This whole moment. Even me saying '*déjà vu*'.'

If I concentrate hard enough, maybe I can work out everything that's going to happen next . . . and know that it'll be okay, and stop anything that won't be. If only. I look back and half-expect the boys to be lighting smoke bombs, but a pain shoots down my leg and I flinch.

'What's the matter?' Kate says. 'Are you alright?'

I've stopped to rub my leg, and the branch — the whole moment — is carried from view.

'A muscle spasm,' I say.

'Cramp,' she suggests.

'Yeah.'

★ ★ ★

Some memories are bones that should be buried and forgotten. Other memories are the sweetest of fruit, which are tasty in small measure but can leave you bloated and a mess of useless sentimentality if plucked and gorged upon too often. And some memories are like photos — snapshots — that hang in neat frames at the back of the mind. Sometimes they shake at night and rattle a train of images into our dreams.

And some dreams are so potent they haunt

93

our waking and grow into memories . . . like slightly blurred photos, or very sweet fruit, or rotten bones.

★ ★ ★

The first time I visit Kate's house, she's waiting at the Abetsby bus stop for me. On one side of her street is a long, brick wall of an empty shoe factory — the name *KETCHELL SHOES* in faded white lettering taking up half the length — while on the other side, flanked by the row of pollarded trees lining the pavement, are the red-brick terraced houses built by Mr Ketchell for his workers. Between the pavement and entrance porch of each house is little more than a yard of fenced garden.

Knowing her parents are waiting to check me out, I count the houses and grip her hand too tight.

'You're hurting,' she says and laughs. 'Relax.'

I nod. I've been to other girls' houses before, to call for them, but this is different.

'They'll like you,' she tells me. 'They do already. Mum loves the plant you gave me. She's made a cake for you. She doesn't often bake cakes. It'll be alright.'

'Yeah.'

'Tom.'

I take a deep breath.

She strokes my hand and whispers, 'Just don't let on you've shagged me silly.'

'No.'

There's about eighteen houses in the street, and above each porch a corbel stone with a motif created in relief. On the first is a sheaf of corn, above the second a fish, then a bird flying, a torch with a flame, a flower, a dolphin . . . until we come to Kate's house and what I take to be an image of a smiling sun.

She leans closer to my ear: 'Thought I'd tell them later how much we enjoy fucking one another.'

'Okay.'

'Tom, relax! You look like you're going to your own funeral.'

Mr and Mrs Hainley are nervous too, and we do the small-talk thing, which is okay: what I'm studying, what my interests are, my part-time job. We sip mugs of tea, bite into slabs of cherry cake, chew our way through the weather, the garden and beer-making, Kate's university applications, until we're nodding and laughing and leaning back in our chairs.

'I like the stone carvings on the front of the houses,' I say. 'That sun — '

'The corbel stones?' her dad says. He's got a soft Liverpudlian accent and I wonder that Kate hasn't picked up the same inflections. 'They're a nice detail, aren't they? All the houses Mr Ketchell built have individual touches like that. They're not always obvious, but they're there for sure.'

'Except it's not the sun on ours, Tom,' Mrs Hainley adds. 'They're not sunrays coming out of its face, although most people swear black and blue they are.' She winks at Kate. 'Go and have another look, love. Take him, Kate. You two don't want to spend your afternoon sitting with us.'

Kate leads me outside and throws her arms around me. 'See, you survived.'

'You've got cool parents. I like them.'

She looks back at the house. 'They're not bad. We usually get on okay. They like you. I can tell.'

I peer up at the corbel stone. 'Still looks like the sun to me.'

'Look closer. Stand on the wall if you want.'

Instead of sunrays, the round face has streams of leaves radiating from it. There are even leaves growing from its mouth and eyes.

'What is it? What's it supposed to be?'

'We call him George. Leafy George. He's

the odd one out in some ways. He's the Green Man.'

And then her mum calls us to go to the shops. And that night, Kate makes gnocchi with tomato and mushroom sauce, and her dad tries his home-brew on me.

★　★　★

On the weekend when Kate's parents visit relatives, we fix it that I'll only work the morning on the market stall. Keeping to the back of the house, so neighbours won't see me if they call round, we wallow in an afternoon and night of forbidden delights; we play 'at home' for eighteen precious hours. We, we, we. We're two parts of a whole.

Supper on the table is followed by love on the rug.

'So I'm *your light, your life, your everything*, am I?' she says, remembering the words I've written in a card to her. A card to accompany the bonsai sycamore I got for a song from the market.

'It's not very original, I know, but — well, yep, that's about the sum of it.'

Astride me on the floor, she unbuckles the belt of my jeans with a flourish.

She tickles me, I tickle her; our wrestling leads deliberately to this moment. And always will. She fumbles with the button to my jeans while I pull at the t-shirt tucked into her skirt. Mauve cotton scented with patchouli oil; black cheesecloth, flashes of gold, tassels and beads.

'Sounds a bit romantic to me,' she scoffs.

'Romantic's okay, isn't it?' I unclip her bra strap the way she's taught me; she pushes back her shoulders to assist.

'Up to a point,' she says, leaning forward, pinching one of my nipples softly between her teeth, leaving a smile of saliva. Then she pauses and slowly licks the smile clean. 'Keep me real though, eh, Tom. Don't romanticise me into someone I'm not. It's too much to live up to. I'm just Kate Hainley, who cops good and bad days like everyone else. I don't want to be perched on some bloody impossible pedestal. It's too far to fall. Okay?'

'Okay.' But I only half-hear as I fumble with the button on her skirt and tug at the zip.

Glory, glory, alleluia!

By the light of a flaring gas fire, we become explorers, mapping a route through jungles we're becoming familiar with. Come and come again. No need for hotwater bottles tonight.

'Mound of Venus,' she whispers. '*Mons veneris. Labia.*' Guiding my hand. 'Gently.'

'Petals,' I say, tracing a passage. I'm

reminded of a crimson pæony unfurling at my fingertips; a moist, expectant darkness of pollen, charged and trembling at each touch.

'My clitoris,' she says, catching her breath. An overdue introduction.

She can give the names of things, summoning words and placing them where they belong. I'm in awe of that, know I have a library to learn, will have to browse the encyclopædia tomorrow.

'We've met,' I say.

'Careful,' she winces. 'It's sensitive there. Not so rough.'

'One clear *It* or *Is of life*,' I murmur, stroking. A rainbow in the making.

'I like that,' she sighs. 'And you. You too.'

Stumped for words and blushing, I whisper, 'John Thomas,' and would shrug my shoulders if I could. 'Say hello to John Thomas.'

She grins and greets me continental-style. 'Bonjour, monsieur.'

Later, we share a bath and soap one another down, giggling over spilt suds. I place a dollop of bath foam on each of her loganberry nipples; she places the raspberry welt of a love bite on my shoulder — tutti-frutti nakedness. We play those games people play when one says, 'If you could be absolutely anything you wanted, what would you be?' and, 'If you ruled the world, what's the first new law you'd pass?' We talk of a life we might share together; we argue, we agree, we explore one another's views in depth and leave no tone unturned.

'Will you still love me when I'm middle-aged and fat?' she asks.

'I'll have grown old and fat too,' I tell her. I'll go anywhere with Kate. For Kate. I will. I'll go to the ends of the earth and back for her. She'll always be beautiful to me.

'It's different for men.'

'You'll always be you and that's who I love,' I say. 'Always. I'd need a lobotomy to stop loving you, and I'd deserve one if I did. You'll always be beautiful to me.'

'Easy to say now, Tom. Some men lust after younger women when they're middle-aged.' She pauses a moment, dabbles with the foam. 'I wasn't gonna tell you this — thought you'd start getting all anxious again — but there was this guy on the bus the other day . . . '

She stops. I sit up. Water splashes onto the floor.

'And?'

'And . . . well, he just about told me his life story. But then he asked me out. He wanted to take me to some nightclub in London. Honestly, he must have been thirty-seven, thirty-eight — something like that.'

100

'He asked you out? Wanted to take you clubbing? That's sick. Did you tell him to piss off?'

'He was harmless really. Probably just lonely. A bit sad, if anything. I told him thanks but I have a boyfriend.'

'He probably had a wife and kids at home. Sick bastard.'

'Told me he was impotent.'

'He didn't?'

She nods.

'The bastard. He was probably hoping you'd offer to prove he wasn't.'

'You see what I mean though?'

'What a creep. Some blokes are like that. Not all. You're the one for me, Kate. Always and always. For better or for worse.'

'Sometimes people fall out of love, Tom.'

'I know that. But not us. Not me anyway. I'm hooked on you, Kate.'

'Yeah. Me too — with you. Weird, isn't it?'

In the night I wake because it's light outside. Brighter than moon-glow, it's the whiteness of snow bleaching the dark and saturating the drawn curtains. Sliding out of bed to stand at the window, I blink, wipe a patch of condensation off the glass and blink again. Kate's backyard is filled with pairs of white swans. All silent, all looking up at her window.

'Kate,' I say. 'Kate.' But she's not in bed. She's gone. And I know this vision is because of her.

I hear a door shut downstairs and footsteps on the stairs.

'Kate,' I say, and meet her in the doorway.

'You've got nothing on. You'll catch your death of cold. Come back to bed.'

'Did you go outside?'

'I went for a pee.'

'Look outside,' I say, pulling the curtains back.

'Beautiful,' she says, and draws a smiley face on the glass with the tip of her finger.

There's thick fog and the swans have gone.

'Beautiful,' I say, and hold her tight as we snuggle into sleep again.

She leads me out of darkness into a new land and hands me an apple. No mean apple, the juice runs down my chin and creates an ocean at our feet. Kate loves me and therefore I exist. One day, when we've both left home, we'll plant the core of our love and let it grow. We need never be alone again. There'll be no maggot wriggling to eat its way out. What more could we want?

'Wake up, Tom,' she whispers. 'Wake up.'

At six the next morning, she wraps the eiderdown around her naked body and goes downstairs to make me a mug of steaming coffee and a cheese sandwich. I tug the blanket over my eyes and slip into the warmth she's left behind.

'Wake up, Tom.'

Sleep. Let me sleep.

I don't want to wake up. I want to stay here forever with Kate. Under the blanket with Kate, lapping against one another.

Drifting.

But to avoid the prying eyes, the busy tongues, I untuck myself from her bed; I drag myself out the house and slide into the current of a mist-filled street. And am awake again.

Quickly, quickly.

I wink at Leafy George.

'Ssh, quietly, Major Tom.'

I keep my coat collar high, my head down, my footsteps soft. Happiness, though, has the clatter of a child playing a new drum and I can't help but kick up a beat that resounds through the old town as I pass one terraced house after another. I wake the starlings roosting on the telephone wires, make dogs growl in their sleep and disturb the dreams of married couples cuddling bum-to-lap in one bed after another after another.

Who cares that it's bitter cold and the bus is forty minutes late? I'm drawn tight against the chill, knowing Kate's only a few hundred

103

yards away huddled in our shared bed, and I'm full to bursting with the memory of our day together and with the life that lies ahead.

★   ★   ★

In Kate's company I watch the months come and go, the seasons turn. The days grow longer, the nights shorter. The trees in her street bud into leaf, miraculously, and masses of fresh shoots sprout out the pollarded trunks in tufts, but at least they're trees again.

On May Day, which falls shortly before the first of her exams, we take her books and have a picnic in the park. There are maypole dancers and morris dancers and a mummers play: *St George and the Dragon*. We spread out on a tartan blanket, as if the earth's our house-without-walls and the cloudless sky our roof. We study, we talk, we discuss our future together, we map out a holiday we'll take as soon as her exams are over and I've finished school.

A short distance from where we lay, St George fights Slasher the Saracen again, while Beelzebub waits to one side.

'This stuff's timeless,' I say. 'Don't you love it? We've been fighting the devil with these rhymes for centuries. Some things never change. I was in a mummers play when I was at primary school, you know. I can still remember the lines.'

She lets her Biology text fall shut. 'Who were you? Not the bleeding-hearted St George, I hope? I always want the dragon to win. The self-righteous bastard deserves to be eaten.'

'No, the Doctor. I had an old Gladstone bag with a saw, a mallet and a drill, jars of medicine and such. I brought the Saracen back to life.'

'You like that old stuff, don't you?'

'It's who we are. It's where we come from.'

St George stands next to his newly-won bride and the Fool enters the arena.

She rolls onto her side to face me. 'Yeah, it's good, but sometimes I reckon this country's so wrapped up in its past — *Land of Hope and Glory*, the old school tie and all that elitist crap — that nothing fresh or new or different can ever properly thrive. One shouldn't be at the expense of the other. It suits the rich bastards, the politicians, the industrialists, the bankers, to keep things the way they've always been.'

I sit up. 'Yeah, like how they go on about the 'Westminster System' and how it's so frigging democratic simply because it's been around a few hundred years. How democratic is it having a House of Lords? Aristocratic

105

inbreds making or breaking laws simply on the basis of birthright, for fuck's sake! You know, some of them only turn up once a year so they can claim their allowance. Nothing a guillotine couldn't put right!'

We laugh, she touches my arm and I reach for her hand. Even so, there's something else I want to say, although I don't know how to express myself properly.

I see the mummers play as being about something beyond History. Like my two flint points. They represent more than a simple measurement of the passing of years and the advancement of ideas, culture and technology. They represent a spiritual connection with the past and the land and with a life determined by the rhythms of nature — by the elements. And there's something constant and nurturing about these rhythms, like waves breaking on the beach, which also reinforces the significance of our relationship, its credibility, its naturalness, its inevitability. And I want to tell Kate this is the reason I enjoy History and why I'll always love her, but the thoughts aren't fully developed yet and the words I might use elude me.

'I guess we're ready to barricade the streets and fire up the revolution,' she says.

'Too right.' And I give up looking for the right words, for the moment anyway.

We join the applause for the mummers. Minutes later, the maypole dancers begin skipping to the scratchy tune of an old tape recording; their steps weaving a dozen coloured ribbons into a pattern, symbolising the end of one season and the beginning of another. The white maypole becomes a tree budding into leaf, then shedding its leaves, then forming another canopy of leaves, and so on. Dance, dance, dance. Turn, turn, turn.

★   ★   ★

Parties crop up every weekend as Kate's friends turn eighteen. One after another; dance after dance; too many to go to.

On summer solstice, a few days after the last of her exams, there's an eighteenth at some fancy golf club, but the function room's too crowded and the music's tacky. We're crammed near a wall of picture windows, beyond which juts the timber deck of a verandah, beyond which a grassy area stretches down to a lake, across which the reflection of a full moon drifts.

'Do you wanna go outside?' I shout across the music. 'Let's take our drinks and go to the lake.'

But she points to the dance-floor, nods her head and shouts: 'Dance!'

I try, but keep treading on some poor girl's foot, who scowls and swaps places with her boyfriend.

'I'm gonna get some fresh air,' I tell Kate at the end of the song, imagining she'll follow me out to the verandah, but she's laughing with friends and, when a new song begins, she starts dancing again.

Two blokes squeeze onto the dance-floor and try dancing with her, imitating her steps to make her dance part of their own. Through the windows, I see what they're up to, the moves they're pulling, and I wait for Kate to move away, or tell them to piss off, but she kicks off her espadrilles, fans her fingers in front of her face, sways her hips and laughs.

I turn to face the lake and beat a slow rhythm out on the balustrade, but when the song changes and she still doesn't join me, I look back and can't see her anywhere. One of the blokes is dancing and one is . . . I can't see him either.

Stuff it. I'm about to go and find her, but know she'll see through me tonight. The miserable thing about happiness is the fear of losing it.

Following the steps down from the verandah, I cross the grass to the edge of the lake, next to the sedge, close to the reeds. Picking up a couple of pebbles, I'm about to throw them into the water to upset the reflection of the moon, but think better of it. The whole fucking bubble might burst. It'd shimmer and shatter; a mother-sized bauble of broken glass raining down. Instead I rattle them inside a loose fist, kick at the spikes of sedge, feel the waves of music pushing down from the hall.

'What's the matter, Tom? I thought you were desperate to party tonight.'

'You came down. I didn't hear you come down,' I say.

'What's up? You've barely smiled since we got here.'

I click the stones from one hand to the other.

'Don't know,' I say.

'Is it me? Have you had enough of me? Are you tired of us?'

'No. Not that. The opposite.' I grind the stones together and then stop. 'I wish we could live together now; not have to wait. And then there's the year you'll be at uni and . . . I don't know how . . . Shit, Kate, I don't have a fuckin' clue what it's gonna be like without you.'

She takes my hand, kisses it, then lets go. 'Jesus, Tom, stop worrying about that stuff, will you. It's Sue's birthday and I've finished my exams, and I need to enjoy tonight. I need to. Life's for living. Come and dance. There's a couple of joints floating around somewhere if you need that crap.' She looks at her watch. 'We've got just over an hour.' And then the moon slides behind a cloud.

I drop the two pebbles by my feet and press them into the ground with the heel of my shoe. 'Come on, then,' I say, painting a smile. 'I'll dance you off your feet.' And we run back to the music.

Later, as she waits with me for the last Northampton bus to arrive, she embraces me and says: 'You shouldn't fret about the future. I love you. I'll always love you, no matter what. I promise. Nothing can ever take that away. No one can. Don't ever forget that. Besides, we have all summer together and our holiday in Yorkshire.'

'And when you go to London, what then? I'll have 'A' levels to study for and you'll be wrapped up with university.' Across the road, the ground-floor windows of a sandstone Georgian house reveal an illuminated room in warm colours and suggest the cosy life we could enjoy if only . . . if only she'd see things the way I see them. 'I could leave school, get a part-time job and finish my 'A' levels in London, you know. At night school. I'd argue it out with Brian and Mum. We could share a flat. It'd be easier on a wage. We're ready for that, Kate. Surely if I got a job . . . '

She puts a finger to my lips, holds my head and kisses me with an olive. The headlights of the passing traffic throw shadows of the bus shelter along the pavement in front of us, to and fro, to and fro.

'What we have is bigger than that, Tom. Much bigger. Trust it. I love you. Trust that. I'll always love you. I'm gonna go through life loving you, you bastard.'

Like all lovers we resort to clichés because these worn-in phrases bind the edges of our over-lapped worlds together, prevent fraying, clamp the whole caboodle together.

'You mean that?' I say. 'Really?'

'I do.'

'Till death us do part, eh?'

'Forever and ever,' she says.

'Amen,' I laugh.

'So be it.'

'I can't imagine life without you anymore, Kate. It'd be too empty — too dark. Like dying.'

'Don't,' she says. 'Please don't. There's no need.'

We wait in silence until the bus pulls in.

'Well, if it ain't love's young dream,' the bus conductor calls to us. 'Come on you two, all aboard the Dream Bus.' He's wearing his cap at an absurd angle, and when I step onto the platform he grins wolfishly at Kate. 'Aren't you joining us tonight then, darling?'

She smiles and shakes her head, he pings the button three times, and the bus lurches forward.

'Phone me tomorrow,' she calls. 'Promise you will. Please.'

'Give me your number then, darling,' he shouts back. Then he nudges me in the arm with his elbow, and the bastard's still grinning. He's got BO and his breath reeks of sulphur or something. 'So where'd you think you're going, sunshine?'

★ ★ ★

Two pings and a ribbon of clicks.

Elspeth is dying. But it can't be. It must be someone else, like Dad or Brian or Mum or . . . someone else.

Two pings and a ribbon of clicks.

5

The front windows of a bluestone Georgian cottage reveal a room in warm colours with Elin reaching up to return a book to its shelf. I'm looking in. She turns and waves and moves to open the front door for me.

Several months after landing in Australia, we find ourselves in Dungarvan, a small fishing town thirty kilometres from Beach Haven, where I'm the new Education and Projects Manager at the city's Shipwreck and Whaling Museum. It's a town with Norfolk pines lining wide, grass-verged streets, and there's a yellow hazard sign, depicting a glorious whale, sticking out of the water as the river enters the bay. There's usually several squid, crayfish and abalone boats moored alongside the wharf and, further down, a clique of sleek yachts. To one side of the river mouth is Rabbit Island and on Rabbit Island the lighthouse: two white flashes every ten seconds — off and on, on and off. But beyond this there's no limit to the sea, the Southern Ocean, all the way to the Antarctic. And the world feels bigger than it has in years.

It's all still new to us when Annette phones. I've just got in from work and the phone rings as I'm walking past.

'Hello, Thomas. Thomas? Dad's had a heart attack,' she says.

'What?' I say. 'Brian? When?'

'Last night. About ten o'clock. Mum called from the hospital. I've just brought her home. We're both beat, but I thought I should phone.'

'Hold on. Slow down, Annette.' I take a breath. 'A heart attack? Brian?'

'Yes. Dad.'

'He's gonna be okay though?'

'It was a close call. The doctors are running tests.' She pauses. 'I phoned Andrew. He's coming down from Scotland.'

'That's good of him.'

Another pause. 'It'd be nice if you came too. I think you should come.'

Switching the phone to the other ear, I stretch its cord until I'm looking out of the window into the back garden, where Elspeth and a new friend are playing. Though our cottage sits on a large block, there's not a single tree or shrub on it — not yet — just fence-to-fence couch grass. We'd hoped to give the kids trees to climb, fruit to pick, jungles to roam, but there's bugger-all in the way of dark corners here, no untamed

114

shadows. The previous owners must've hated the untidiness of plants, but even this gives us the chance to start over and create a wilderness of our own. And before long, we'll plant, plant, plant: coastal wattle, tea tree, grevillea, banksia, a lemon tree and even a couple of almonds; hollyhocks, honeysuckle, nasturtiums and clusters of pæonies. With a pond and a sandpit too, the kids'll always remember their childhood as paradise, and their dad will always be there for them.

'Sorry, Annette; what did you say?'

'I said it'd be nice if you could get here too. Thomas? Can you hear me? It's a bad line.'

'I can't just fly from Australia, Annette. You know that. We haven't got that sort of money. I've not been in this job long enough to ask for a holiday. And we're up to our necks in loans.'

There's a delay at the other end. 'He was in a bad way, Thomas. Mum thought she'd lost him at one point. She's pretty shaken up.'

Daniel's watching a programme about earthquakes and volcanoes, Elin's now in the kitchen, but I don't know where Tamsin is.

'I'll phone her. Tell her I'll phone at ten tonight, your time.'

'That's hardly the same.'

'And I hardly live round the corner.'

'That's your choice.'

I take a deep breath. 'Yes. It is.'

'Sometimes I wonder . . . ' she begins, but lets the sentence trail into silence.

'We don't have a couple of thousand dollars spare, Annette, and I'm not gonna make the kids do without necessities so I can hand-deliver a few grapes to Brian.'

Annette's voice adopts the exaggerated pronunciation of someone trying to shout and whisper at the same time, and I guess Mum knows nothing about this call.

'You're a heartless bastard at times.'

'And you need to know the world's a bit bigger than your fifteen minute car trip from Northampton to Nenford.'

'I'm sorry I phoned,' she spits.

'I'm not, Annette. I appreciate you letting me know, but it doesn't alter anything. I'll phone Mum at ten your time.'

'Sorry to bother you,' she says, and hangs up before I can say goodbye.

Still holding the phone, I follow Elspeth and her friend's motions as they squat in the shade of the fence and tear a sheet of paper into narrow strips.

Later that evening, I'm standing on the beach as the high tide turns. There's a piece of driftwood — a forked branch, one arm broken off — which I pick up to toss into the water, wondering where it might wash up next, and a few minutes later four pelicans fly along the shoreline. Lumbering and graceful at the same time, they fly in a line, one behind the other behind the other behind the other.

'Look,' I want to say, but Elin's at home putting Elspeth to bed.

★　★　★

Two pings and a ribbon of clicks. An ECG and pulse oximeter and an IV drip pump and an oxygen mask, and she has more leads and tubes plugged into her than any parent could cope with.

I'm in my office, costing a new display, when Elin phones.

'Elspeth's ill,' she says. 'I'm at Beach Haven hospital. You'd best come. Can you come straightaway?'

'What's happened? Course I'll come. What's the matter?'

'They're not sure. I think she may have been bitten by something — a spider or a snake or something. But I didn't see anything. We were in the garden — I was hanging out washing and she was playing — and then she started screaming. Her breathing went funny. I thought she'd just got herself into a paddy, at first. The way she does. You know.'

'Yes.'

'Can you come straightaway?'

Running from the car to Casualty, the automatic doors limp open to reveal the hustle-bustle I've dreaded finding: Elin's jacket and handbag bundled on a chair, Elin leaning over a trolley, a posse of doctors and nurses consulting over monitors, passing clipboards, surrounding my daughter, who's more unconscious than anything else. And I walk out again.

'You alright? Don't let her see you like this,' Elin says. 'You'll panic her.'

'That's why I came out. What's the drip for?'

'Adrenaline, I think; I'm not sure. They're very good. They keep telling me what they're doing, why they're doing it, but I can't take it in. They're talking about flying her to the Royal Children's in Melbourne if she doesn't improve soon.'

She fights tears off with a gulp, leaving only a glaze to her eyes.

'There's a plane on standby. One of us will have to go with her; one of us will have to stay with Daniel and Tamsin.'

'Of course,' I say. 'Yes.'

'They're giving her half-an-hour on the drip, to see how she responds. They injected her with something.'

And it becomes a day of waiting and watching.

When they wheel her into Intensive Care and the prospect of Melbourne recedes, Elin and I both close our eyes and sigh. We stand every time she's restless, comment on every flicker of her darkened eyelids, and are too exhausted to be anything but tearful when her breathing comes easier and unconsciousness melts back into sleep. With every half-hour she doesn't deteriorate, we sit further back from the edge of our chairs, and every time the equipment that's plugged into her pings or clicks, we look from her to the monitor to the nurse's station, before relaxing and gazing out the window for a moment.

Clouds move in and it rains, and Elin comments on the washing left in the basket by the washing line. The rain abates and the clouds give way to blue sky and sunshine, but it leaves me with a sourness that makes me want sweet coffee. Only hurricanes will do on such a day.

When Elin returns from making a phone call, I take fifteen minutes to grab a hot drink and some fresh air, but make the coffee sickly sweet and nag myself that the windowless cafeteria is too far away. Anything can happen. Too much can happen. It's too easy to lose the people that matter. In the space of these few hours, I've made all manner of promises to myself and the universe about what I'll do if only Elspeth can remain safe and healthy. Healthy and happy. Elspeth, Tamsin and Dan. I'd sacrifice anything rather than have to cope with losing one of them; which, by some peculiar obversion, gives me a new understanding of my dad.

And why he hanged himself.

She comes round in the middle of the afternoon, puzzled by the leads that tangle her movements and the bandage that holds her drip in place. She opens her eyes, then licks her lips and smiles.

'I'm thirsty,' she croaks, 'can I have a drink please?' and begins lifting herself in the cot.

'Sip this, lovely,' says Elin, holding a glass with a straw for her. 'Take it slowly.'

'Hello, beautiful,' I say. 'What have you been doing to yourself?'

She pauses in her drinking and blinks her big, moon eyes at me; she manages a half-smile above the straw.

'You know, you've got so many leads and tubes plugged into you that when I first saw you I thought you were a bowl of spaghetti. I nearly gobbled you up!'

'Hello, Daddy,' she rasps and takes another sip. Her eyes try to giggle, but the voice and the breathing don't carry it over. Part of her is still lost.

By evening, when I bring Daniel and Tamsin to see their sister, and a nightdress and toothbrush for Elin, Elspeth's gone. In her bed is an old man.

'Where's Elspeth?' I snap at a nurse. 'Where's my daughter?'

'You're hurting my hand,' Tamsin tells me.

'She's fine,' the nurse says. 'She's been taken up to Children's. It's on the fifth floor.'

And that's where we find her. She's almost whole again. The voice is still a whisper, but her movements have their sparkle back. The hollowness is mainly memory, receding into a darkness of its own.

Later, we're sitting in front of a silent television — Daniel, Tamsin and I — a muddle of toys and dirty breakfast dishes littered about the family room, still hungry after our drive-through dinner, and wondering whether Elin and Elspeth will be home tomorrow.

'As long as she doesn't get ill overnight,' I say. 'I'm sure she'll be fine. We'll look on the bright side, eh?'

'Could I catch it?' asks Tamsin.

'Course you couldn't,' Daniel says, almost causing the last quarrel for the day, except the phone rings.

'Bet that's Mum,' Tamsin squeals and runs to answer it. There's a pause and then she says: 'He's here. I'll get him.' Then to me: 'It's Uncle Andrew.'

'I'm phoning from Nenford,' he says. 'It's Dad.'

'Another heart attack?'

'Yes. A big one. He died an hour ago.'

There should be something less predictable to say. 'I'm sorry, Andrew. I really am. Are you okay?'

'We'd been expecting it, not that it makes it any easier. Will you come for the funeral?'

'Elspeth's in hospital. She was rushed in this morning. The doctors thought they'd have to fly her to Melbourne. I can't, Andrew. I'm sorry.'

'Okay,' he says, but he doesn't ask about her.

The following day it's raining again, but that no longer matters. What matters is that we're a family once more. I want to carry Elspeth from the car to the house, but she thinks that's soft. Once inside, she's quick to tease her brother and to exert the rights of a convalescent over her sister, demanding all the space on the couch and every last grape in the bowl.

Standing in the kitchen, with an ear to all this, Elin shrugs and smiles.

'Back to normal, thank goodness,' she says.

'I've got bad news about Brian, my love,' I begin.

Two weeks later, I walk to the river, then along to the beach. The sky's grey, but it'll be summer before long. Elin stays home because Daniel's got gastro, but I need to taste the sea in the November air, and to find my bearings again after the spring gales and the king tides.

From the car park above the dunes, the beach looks different and I can't fathom it at first; not until I follow the path down and find that a metre of sand's been washed away. Rocks appear to have grown where none stood before, and the angle of the beach is different. Turning and looking back, the dunes have been scooped into, eaten out to a point higher than I am tall. The timber posts and handrail to a disused pathway have been revealed, along with old bottles and long-buried driftwood.

Yet even as I watch the sea ebb and am then drawn by the crumbling and collapsing of a dune's overhang, the wind dries the sand and lifts it and carries it back to the base of the dunes. When the tide turns the sea will deposit even more sand, and the beach will rise again, the dunes will grow back, burying whatever's in their way.

The elements play in curious harmony.

Always. Moon after moon after moon. There'll always be a balance in the whole.

★ ★ ★

Despite the turning of seasons, the passing of years, there are times when I drift awake in the depths of a night and can't remember where or when I am. What I'll hear is the drone of motorway traffic — of tyres on a wet road — and then I'll picture the endless rush of cars and trucks cutting through the night, carving up the orange-tinted darkness, hurtling from one exit point to another, and I'll be back in Britain, in the house where Daniel, Tamsin and Elspeth began their lives, with the motorway only four-hundred stinking yards from the back fence. And I'll sit up in a cold sweat.

The first time this happens, Elin, woken by my panic, lays a hand on my leg and murmurs: 'Not traffic. It's the sea.'

There's no night traffic in Dungarvan, she reminds me, no continuous rush. The rolling and crashing of waves kneading the beach just a few hundred metres away creates this bizarre imitation, and the front verandah of our house is like a giant shell — an ear — pulsing with the life of the sea during the cloudlessness of night; swallowing it, reverberating with it.

'Hush,' she says. 'Cuddle up,' she says.

And she's right about the surf, although it's hard to tell the difference even when I listen for it across the years. And I'll learn to listen for it. Whenever I wake in the middle of the night after a bad dream, I'll tune in to the sound of the waves — the rhythms of low tides, high tides, king tides — and drift towards sleep again in the cave of a giant shell.

Comforted like a baby at a nipple, I'll match my breathing to the rhythm of the surf and sleep.

And dream.

And sometimes I dream of Kate.

I'm one of a dozen mourners shuffling through a churchyard in England. Though the place is familiar, I can't recall where it's supposed to be. Maybe it's based on several memories — places I've visited in the past or seen on TV — or maybe it's the generic churchyard of my dreams, where I attempt to bury all my ghosts.

The sun is bright, but low and muted, like the filtered brilliance that occurs sometimes in the eye of a fierce storm, and the churchyard is surrounded by a wall of tall, dense yew trees. The church is a sandstone

125

building, with long, narrow, stained-glass windows, a square belfry and a slate roof; twelfth or thirteenth-century. That the sandstone is the warm, dark orange found in the thatched-cottage villages of my childhood tells me I mightn't be too far from Nenford; in another county perhaps, but bordering Northamptonshire at least.

The grass is dry, knee-high and sprouting seed — suggesting early autumn — and laps against a cluttered sea of sinking headstones. Most of the gravestones are ancient, weathered and covered in lichen, and their inscriptions have been redrafted by the seasons. Some are sinking dangerously from the upright, like the wreckage of abandoned ships, and though I sense this place is a long way from the ocean, something tells me I might comfortably drown here.

We're treading a worn path, the other mourners and I, through the graveyard, towards the lych-gate. The interment has taken place already and the day will now be spent over sandwiches, whisky and tea, mourning our loss, trying to celebrate a life — except I don't know whose funeral it is. My dream has thrown me into the middle of events.

It's only when I stop and allow the others to walk past, so I can peer beyond their

126

sombre suits, their smothered silence, the shuffle and scuffing of their polished shoes, and try to find someone I recognise, that I notice Kate's parents at my side. Mr and Mrs Hainley.

Kate. She can't be dead. How the fuck has this happened?

It's time to speak. It's time to try and change the subject of the place. It'd be a happier story if it was my father I was laying to rest, or Brian. Not Kate.

'She can't be dead,' I try saying. 'It's not possible.' But my voice finds no sound and I know why I might let myself drown here, out of all depth. I might've learnt to live without her, always believing that one day, however much later, I might see her again, but I've never counted on having to live in the knowledge that she no longer exists and that she's absolutely gone from my life for all time. It's a notion of death and loss that still scares me shitless. It's the worst kind of eternity; a void stretching through infinity.

Kate's mum turns to hug me and her dad overcomes his weariness to nod in the direction of the church vestibule. It's the most generous of gestures.

Somehow they've told me that if I leave this procession of mourners and walk alone into the dark shadows of the vestibule, I'll find Kate waiting. If I find her, then I might persuade her that this funeral isn't for her and she'll be alive again. It'll become someone else's funeral instead, such as her mum's or dad's or someone's, but that's okay because it's too painful to outlive your children and no parent should be put through that.

'Thank you,' I try saying, and they limp towards the cortège of cars.

The vestibule is cold, damp and so dark it might have become night in the second it's taken me to arrive there, and I can't see anyone. All the same, just as I'm worrying I've missed her, a figure in black separates itself from the thickness of the dark and slides next to me. With the movement comes a shift in the cold dampness, so that it stirs around me before settling.

Kate.

Though cloaked and hooded in mourning, and even though her face is paler than it's ever been, I know this is Kate. I reach to hold her hand, to lead her out into the afternoon light, but she won't or can't.

'What's the matter, Kate?' I begin, but she flickers and fades at each word I speak, and I have to stop. How can I persuade her to stay without losing her completely?

128

I try again: 'Why — ?' But daren't utter another syllable.

Reaching out to touch her and to stop her looking beyond me, she dissolves into the darkness swamping the vestibule and I lose her all over again.

Again.

The swell of grief that swamps this dream washes me awake and I struggle to untangle a sheet from my face. Elin stirs, turns and stretches an arm across my chest, and I try enjoying her closeness, hoping it might buoy me up, but it pins me down instead.

'Too hot,' I say and move away.

It's then I listen for the sounds that might be the rushing of traffic on a motorway or the rolling of endless train carriages along a track, but which will really be the crash of waves on the beach, resonating across the front verandah outside our bedroom window. I hear nothing. Not a murmur.

The curtains hang limp at the open window.

Sliding out of bed, I stand in my boxers and peel back one curtain. The night-street is suspended in a milky sea-mist and there's not a whisper of a breeze; only the ghostly silhouettes of trees, shrubs, the picket fence, a car parked in a neighbour's driveway . . . until I see a black swan standing in our front

129

garden, by the gate.

Wiping the glass clear where I've fogged it, I hold my breath and try not to blink, and wait for some movement.

'Elin,' I begin, but then remember how, after pruning the wattle and grevillea last weekend, she dumped a pile of weeds in that very spot.

I look away, then back. No swan, just a mound of twigs.

* * *

In the morning, the sea-mist lays drawn across Dungarvan like the finest of drift nets, capturing the day and holding it still. The streets, the dunes, the beaches, the river, the outlying paddocks and farms — all will be blanketed in its filaments for an hour or two of suspension, until the sun rises higher, bolder, and its warmth generates a current to stretch the mist out and dissipate it.

'You're up early,' Elin says, entering the kitchen and making for the kettle. She lifts it, testing it fulness, then switches it on. 'And you look like shit,' she laughs.

'Thanks. You too.' There's a half-empty bowl of cereal in front of me and I'm dragging the spoon through the milk in figures of eight, steering a course between raisins and almond flakes.

'Couldn't you sleep?'

'No. Bad dream. It woke me. Couldn't get back to sleep. Thought I might as well get up and steal a march on the day.'

'And have you?'

'What?'

'Stolen a march on the day. It doesn't look like it. You look wrecked.'

'Another cup of tea might help.'

She sluices the stale tea slops down the sink and rinses the pot with hot water.

'What was it about, your dream? You could've woken me.'

My dreams of Kate are always vivid. Twenty years on. And often share common elements: I've found her after a long search, she's hurt but I can't help her, she's speaking a language I don't understand, when I talk to her she disappears, but this is the third dream on this theme in as many weeks.

'I forget,' I say. 'Death, I guess. Loss, perhaps.' And, to stop the conversation there, I ask: 'Are the kids awake? Maybe I should get them up.'

'Or we could enjoy five more minutes of peace.'

Holding my spoon, I return to the thoughts I've woken with: how can I find out where Kate now lives, and how can I make sure she's okay? She won't necessarily need to know about it of course. Maybe I'll get lucky by 'Googling' her on the internet, but what if there's nothing there?

The water in the kettle boils and Elin pours it over fresh tealeaves. The steam billows and rolls from the kettle, from the teapot, up to the window and across the glass, fogging it over.

The mist rises and dissipates, but the sea remains mirror-flat all day and so invitingly clear it tempts us into bracing ourselves for the first swim of the season; to plant our footprints in the sand and splash out towards the reef.

★   ★   ★

Elin makes room on the garden table for a plate of uncooked sausages, a plate of burgers. She slides the salad bowl across and rearranges the tray of skewered vegetables, then pushes the bag of pulpy white sandwich loaf until it hunches over the salad. One of the beer bottles teeters against the pile of cutlery, then balances again neck-to-neck with another. As the gas flares, I pour oil onto the cast iron plates and spread it with a spatula.

'We need a bigger table,' she says.

'You always make too much food. The size of the table's got nothing to do with it.'

'Better too much than too little.' She hands me a beer. 'Can you open this?'

'I guess the kids are hungry. All that swimming.' I wave my hand close to the surface of the flat-plate to test the heat, then turn down two burners.

'First swim of summer,' she says, and takes a gulp of beer. 'That's good.' She combs fingers through her damp hair, straightening the knots — always a dirtier blonde during winter and spring, and the dampness brings that out, but by the end of summer it'll be bleached a lighter tone of corn altogether. There's sand on her feet, salt on her lips. 'The kids are ravenous. They'll eat the lot.'

And with that, from their bedroom at the other end of the house, comes the first bleating appeal in an argument.

'Mum,' Elspeth calls, 'tell her she's got to take her wet towel out. Not leave it on the carpet.'

Elin raises her eyebrows, mouths the word 'hungry' and heads indoors.

Ten minutes later, we're all hankered round a table crammed with plates and glasses, bottles and food, and the sun's still high and grinning with heat. After the first blustery week of December, summer's arrived in style. Snorkels, masks, fins and two wetsuits hang from hooks at one end of the back verandah, still dripping. In several days, the school year ends and the kids'll have five weeks of summer freedom, to snorkel and surf, sleep late in the mornings, stay up at night, see friends, be outside, and with Christmas thrown in too.

'Heaven,' Elin observes, then licks a speck of sauce from the corner of her mouth.

'Bliss,' I agree, reaching for my beer. 'It's been a beautiful day, but so still.'

'Not in my classroom,' she says.

'We had to do a test,' Tamsin begins, but from across the paddock and dunes, less than a kilometre away, we hear the sudden change in tide.

Often when it happens like this, it's like someone switches a machine on or turns the volume up. For hours on end it's so quiet you become oblivious to it and you might be anywhere, but then it announces its presence again and you know there's this awesome, pristine, untamed other world just a walk away — just a dive and a splash away.

One wave roars, crashes, marking an abrupt shift of rhythm, and the symphony of the surf begins again. With it comes the faintest suggestion of a breeze, to which the wetsuits twist on their coat-hangers in a light dance, and the snorkels and masks spin. Except for Daniel, we pause in our eating to listen, then smile as the new rhythm establishes itself, and the girls giggle.

'What?' Daniel says as he looks up from his plate and reaches for another slice of bread, another sausage, a dollop of sauce.

And then the phone rings.

Elspeth runs to answer, leaving a clatter of chair legs and the slamming of the screen door in her wake.

'Careful,' Elin calls.

Within the minute, Elspeth shouts back: 'Dad, it's Annette.'

It's not even seven in the morning in Britain, and bitterly cold and dark for another hour. She rarely phones — we rarely talk — except on birthdays, and Elin and I both frown.

The phone line is poor and for a moment I hear a gale blowing, but it's just the hollow crackle and echo of a bad connection.

'Mum's ill,' she says. 'Very ill. The doctor's really worried about her. Andrew and I both are.'

'What? What's happened? What's the matter with her?'

She attempts to muffle the phone and I hear the muted sound of her blowing her nose.

135

'Are you okay?'

'It hasn't been easy. But Andrew's been good. Very supportive.'

'What's the matter with her, Annette? What's happened? When did this happen?'

Leaning in the doorway, Elin whispers, 'Your mum? Is she alright? Ask if there's anything we can do.'

'She was a bit poorly for a few days,' Annette replies. 'I thought it was a cold, but then she got worse. The doctor thought it was pneumonia to start with, but they're testing for Legionella or something now. The thing is, they're worried about her kidneys.'

'When? When was she admitted?'

'Yesterday morning.'

She could've phoned sooner — much sooner — but I know why she hasn't.

'Her breathing's not good,' she continues. 'But it's more than that. She's let herself get old very quickly.'

'Old? She's only sixty-something, Annette.'

'I know. But it's like she doesn't want to get better. Not yesterday anyway.'

'And they're worried she won't make it?' I ask. 'That she won't survive? Really?'

'Don't say that.'

'Isn't that what you just said? I'm asking you.'

'It's the way you say things, Thomas. Like

you don't care. They don't know everything.'

When I fail to bite back, she says, 'I don't want to argue. I'm tired. I've been up most of the night worrying about her. You don't have any of this.'

'Okay,' I say. I put one hand on the kitchen bench and take a breath, then I pull a face at Elin, who stands opposite me frowning. 'She may well get through it, Annette. She's always been a fighter and tough as old boots.'

'I'd like you to be right, but I'm not sure. She wasn't coping well yesterday. The doctors and nurses were worried. I've never seen her like this before. She's always been so strong and . . . you know.'

'Cantankerous,' I suggest.

'Spirited,' she says. 'Anyway, Andrew and me thought we should let you know, so that you can come if you want, before . . . before . . . '

Again, I hear the emotion in her voice, the muffled sob.

'Thanks. I appreciate that. I do. Can you hold a second? I need to speak with Elin.' Placing a hand across the mouthpiece, I explain: 'Mum's sick. Very sick by the sound of it. Annette's in panic-mode. She and Andrew say I should go over there to see her. The doctors — '

And wonderful Elin, without hesitation,

137

says, 'Go. Say you'll be there as soon as you can.'

'How?'

'Compassionate leave, unpaid leave — it doesn't matter. There'll be a way. The museum can cope without you.'

Rubbing the tip of my thumb and index finger together, to indicate the need for money, I shrug. It's a big question mark. For too many years we've struggled to be clear of debt and out of the strangulating grip of the bastard banks.

Again, without hesitation, Elin says, 'That's what our savings are for, Tom. Use them. We'll have to hold on a bit longer to replace the car.'

'The car's a dream. We don't have that much saved. Not enough to buy a ticket.'

'Then flash the credit card. We'll manage.'

Compassionate first, practical second. There's never been any confusion between the two for her. It's a beautiful quality, but frustrating at times.

Taking my hand off the mouthpiece, I say to Annette: 'Of course I'll come. I'll start making arrangements straightaway. I won't be able to speak to my manager until the morning though.'

'Really?' she says.

'Of course.'

On the evening of the following day, after tea has been eaten and with the dishes waiting to be dried, I'm kneeling on the carpet in Daniel's room, surrounded by an open suitcase, a flight bag and a money belt, when Elin pushes open the door. In front of me is a bundle of about fifteen green envelopes, tied together by a piece of red cord. At the sound of her footsteps, I fold the letter I've been reading and push it back into its envelope.

'Do you fancy a walk soon?' she says. 'I need sea air.' She props one hand against the door frame and massages the other into the small of her back; then moves her head in a slow, deliberate motion from side-to-side, easing some of the tension in her neck, her shoulders.

'You look the way I feel,' I tell her. 'A walk? Yeah, that'd be good.'

It's been crazy trying to arrange such a trip at short notice, but I'm set to fly from Melbourne in two days.

'What have you got there?' she says.

'Nothing. Not much.' I slide the envelope into the bundle of other envelopes. 'The past.'

'Love letters?' she suggests and laughs, squinting to recognise the writing.

'Yes.'

'From me? Did I write that many? I don't remember.'

'From you and Kate.'

'Do I profess my undying love for you?'

'Possibly.'

'Can I read one?'

'One of the ones you wrote?'

'Yes.'

Reaching into the suitcase, I take out a second, smaller bundle of letters. These are held together by a length of gold ribbon. The top one, which I draw out, is in a white envelope and still scented.

She takes the letter and sniffs it, but doesn't read it. Nodding at the other bundle, she says, 'Were all those from Kate?'

'Yep. I found the whole lot stashed here. Plus all this stuff.' I pull out a bag of badges, a couple of old wallets, a collection of pre-decimal coins, a collection of postcards and the corn dolly.

'The corn dolly — I remember that. We used to have it hanging up.' She draws a hand across her forehead, pulls back a stray wave of hair. 'Memory lane, eh?'

'Pure nostalgia. It's a trap. Are you going to read that?'

She's still holding the letter.

'Did I ask you whether you fancied walking down to the beach?'

'Give me ten minutes. I'll put back the stuff I don't need.'

She hands back, unread, the letter she wrote eighteen or nineteen years ago and continues massaging her back. 'I've done the lunches,' she says, and heads down the hallway.

I pick out the corn dolly and put it with the flight bag and money belt, then shove everything else from the suitcase onto the topmost shelf of the wardrobe.

6

I know this beach, with its rock-pools, pebbles and driftwood. It's close to Elin's parents' home in Cornwall and she brought me here from London that first autumn together. Sure enough, when I look over, a young Elin walks to the side of me, kicking sand, tossing pebbles; she's twenty or twenty-one maybe. The sea is the colour of granite and the sky is rusty-veined quartz, and between them they're grinding the day smooth, clean, polished.

'Lustrous' is the word I want to shout to the sea and the sky and Elin, but the wind whips down and, with the playfulness of a kite, steals both syllables.

Elin places a hand on my arm and laughs, and is about to say something too until I hold a finger to my lips.

All the same, she shouts a string of three words into the day and I cover my ears.

'Don't!' I shout back. 'You mustn't! Everything vanishes!' But the wind whips down and snatches, and Elin carries on laughing and is laughing as she strides from rock to rock.

This is her home. She glows by the sea. It's her belonging-place. Her skin shines, her eyes sparkle, she lives with a smile. For her, it's the antithesis of London, and I learn from that.

She crouches and picks up a shell; she strokes its contours with one finger, turns it over and drops it in her coat pocket. She's wearing her dad's old herringbone coat, which blends with the colour of the clouds and the crashing of the waves. And it's cold. The air's so cold.

A pair of oystercatchers wheel through the morning ahead of us, stabbing at rock-pools, flying on when we get too close, and I stumble and scramble over each slab of rock to keep up with them, but it's not an easy task. There's something wrong with my balance; a middle ear thing, perhaps. The rocks appear a tad further away than they really are and the shadows more substantial than they should be, so I'm teetering like a drunk, afraid that if I fall and take my eyes off the beach for an instant, it'll shimmer and vanish, and Elin'll vanish too. Forever.

Noticing something caught on the rocks, she points and calls me over, except there's still no sound to the words. Snagged in a crevice is a bundle of black, sodden fabric, and I imagine it must be a blanket or a dress, or a dead seal or seabird or something.

143

'Don't,' I try warning her, and reach for her arm to stop her, but miss and she tugs it out and unravels it until she finds its shape. After all, she knows this beach.

Heavy and dripping, she turns it and holds it up by its shoulders for me to see. It's a full-length Abercrombie overcoat; the sort with a black felt half-collar, which someone with a bowler hat might wear. What makes me shrink from this bloody coat I don't know, and I wonder if there's something I should know, something that's in the pocket or close by. All the same, I guess it's a good find and, as Elin holds it against the sky, I turn to look for the missing hat, and lose my footing, slip and am sucked backwards into darkness.

It's only as I'm falling, to the alarmed cry of the oystercatchers, that sound breaks properly into this world. Bigger than any rock-pool, the darkness is cavernous, and the birds' calls are echoed, amplified, distorted, until they fade into a persistent and chirruping ring.

'Phone,' I say, pushing a blanket down, reaching out wildly for the phone sitting on our bedside cabinet, only to find a larger piece of furniture in the way by crunching my knuckles against its sharp edge. 'Fuck!'

I'm bound in seaweed — wide belts of

dried kelp — and the phone scares the oystercatchers away, and then my mother's answering machine cuts in.

Unwrapping the sheet from my shoulders, I make another grab for the sound and press the Talk button several times before she shuts up.

'Yeah, hello,' I say.

'Tom? Is that you, Tom?'

'Hello, Elin. It's me.'

'Are you alright? You sound like you've just woken up.'

'What time is it?'

'Well, it's seven in the evening here. It'll be eight in the morning with you.'

'Shit. I keep sleeping. And — '

'What?'

'I keep falling asleep.'

'It's jetlag,' she says. 'We thought you'd ring when you got there, but figured you were out for the count. How was the flight? How's your mum?'

'Everything's fine, I guess. I think.' Leaning over, I tug at one of the closed curtains with a hand that's still half-asleep. 'It's so dark here. I thought it was night. It feels like night. And cold. Bitter cold.'

'But you're alright? You are alright?'

'Yeah. Of course.'

'You sound distant.'

'Well, I am.'

'And half-asleep.'

'That too. I was gonna phone yesterday evening, but . . . can't remember going to bed.' (I'd intended phoning Kate's parents again too, and not hanging up this time.)

There's a slight pause and I hear Elin saying something to Daniel; then Tamsin and Elspeth shouting in the background: 'Hi, Dad.'

'You can speak to him in a minute,' Elin tells them, and returns to me. 'Did you get to see her yet?'

'Who?'

'Your mum of course.'

'Oh, yeah.'

'How was she?'

For a moment, I've forgotten. It's completely gone. Then it comes back, like retrieving a distant memory, even though it was only yesterday. 'She seemed okay; older perhaps, a little frail, but as sharp as usual and ready to shred. Annette took me straight from the train to the hospital.'

'What was that? There's an echo on the line.'

'I think she's having problems breathing at times, but isn't half as bad as I expected.'

'But she's not uncomfortable?'

'They're waiting on results, but apparently

146

she was better than the day before. She's keen to get home.'

'Really? That's good.'

'Yep. And she'll give the nurses a hard time until they let her out, poor buggers.'

'She hasn't changed then?'

'No — still the cutting tongue. Some people never do.'

'And Annette's okay?'

'The same. Although I don't know why she doesn't tell Mum where to go at times. She cops a bit of flak, just for Mum's amusement.'

'She'll appreciate that you've travelled so far to see her.'

'Maybe.'

'She will, even if she doesn't tell you.'

'I guess.'

'Elspeth wants to talk. They've got some news for you, but Elspeth wants to tell you first.'

There's a quick shuffle at the other end, and I imagine my family gathered in the lounge or on the verandah at the end of a bright summer's day. The smell of ozone will be drifting in on a south-westerly breeze, taking the edge off the heat, and the shrill lorikeets will be flying in and out the gum trees, dangling upside-down from the slenderest of growth, feeding on the nectar of red and yellow flowers — a raucous cacophony of high-pitched calls punctuated by the angry growls of the resident wattle birds trying to chase them out.

'We saw two whales today, Dad. Me and Tamsin.'

'Whales? Where? It's the wrong time of year.'

'At the end of the jetty.'

'Are you sure they weren't dolphins.'

'They were whales, silly. Lots of people saw them. They were massive and we got sprayed when they spouted water out their heads.'

'You were that close?'

'They were almost next to the jetty. We could hear all their snorting noises and see the barnacles growing on them. They were ugly, Dad, but sort of beautiful too.'

'Wow. I wish I'd seen them. That would've been magic.'

'Mum's taking me down in the morning to see if they come back.'

'I miss you,' I say. 'I miss all of you.' But the truth is more that I feel they're my anchor and I'm cut adrift.

Daniel is given the phone next. He's late for a game of cricket with some friends, he tells me, but has been made to wait until after Elspeth, his youngest sister, has said her piece.

'You're a good brother,' I tell him. 'Who

are you playing with?'

But he doesn't want to talk about this it seems. 'Will you be back for Christmas?' he asks.

'I'm not sure. It's only ten days away, Dan. Everything depends — '

'That's crap,' he says. 'Won't we get a proper Christmas this year then?'

'We spoke about this before I left, matey. You'll have a great — '

'I don't see why you have to stay so long. You don't even like it there.'

'That's not the point, Dan.'

'Isn't it?'

'No.'

There's a moment's pause, then he switches into a different tone altogether. 'Anyway, I've got to go now. I'll speak to you next time. See you. Here's Tamsin.'

'Hi, Dad.'

'Hi, Tamsy. How are you?'

'Good. How are you?'

'Stuffed. Jetlagged, I think. I don't like sitting on planes for twenty-three hours at a time. So you saw two whales, did you?'

'Yeah, it was great. They were so close — much closer than that other time. Their spray reached where we were standing, they were that close. There were some Wildlife and Fisheries officers talking to us, and one said they were probably a mating couple. It was brilliant. You'd have loved it.'

When the call ends, I'm surprised to find that I'm still in an English winter with the curtains closed. For a moment I was back in Dungarvan, and Britain a distant memory. I could've easily slipped from one place to the other.

★ ★ ★

At the village bus stop, it's half-an-hour or so before the bus arrives and the number of people waiting grows from four to nine. An icy wind cuts round the shelter, and we're crowding to one end to avoid a patch of pavement where a dog has crapped. If it weren't so cold it'd be pissing with rain, and the sky is only propped up by telegraph poles and cement-tiled shop roofs.

I try to catch someone's eye to say 'G'day' and pass the time, but everyone makes a point of staring away from one another — at the crap on the ground, at the sky or across the road. Not only does no one talk, except for the hushed tones of a mother and daughter, but even the elderly married couple have nothing to say to one another.

The real problem, though, is that things

aren't much different between Mum and me. We exhaust a few superficial pleasantries within five minutes, and the ensuing silence confirms that, even on her sickbed, she isn't going to let me past the barrier she's spent a lifetime constructing. There'll be no sharing of intimacies or confidences here, thank you very much, no talk of regrets or missed opportunities, no discussions of dreams, hopes, aspirations. The past is dead and gone, the future a predictable routine, and the present a vacuum.

'I'm tired,' she says. 'I hope you don't feel you have to come and sit with me. It's going to get tedious if you do, and I can do without it.'

'You can read your magazine or watch TV if you want. I'm just here if you need me.' And I wish she'd begin gasping again, so I might at least pass her the oxygen mask.

'I can't think why Annette asked you to come. She's always made big dramas out of everything, even as a little girl.'

'Well, I'm here now,' I say, 'and I'm sure she meant well. I might as well sit with you here as sit in a chair in Nenford.'

'Aren't there places you'd like to visit, people to catch up with?'

'Yeah, I'll do a bit of that, perhaps. But it's the wrong time of year to play the tourist. I'm

151

here to keep you company and see if you need anything.'

'I don't. Just peace and quiet.'

'Fair enough.'

'As long as you don't think I'm gonna be curling up my toes any time soon.'

'I don't.'

'Then you've had a wasted journey.'

'Not at all.'

'How can I rest with you sitting there like a blooming vulture?'

'Then I'll read your magazine and you close your eyes.'

'I will. Didn't get much sleep last night. This place is too noisy. You don't mind if I close my eyes?'

'Be my guest.'

'I'm somebody's guest,' she says, 'but I don't think I'm yours.'

Behind where I sit is a window, and beyond the window, in the foreground, a skeletal tree. The view wouldn't be bad in spring, summer or autumn, when the tree is dressed in blossom or leaves, but at the moment there's only the hospital car park to look at, and a busy intersection with traffic lights.

Annette arrives for ten minutes during her lunch break. She sees Mum asleep and has a whispered conversation with me.

'You're here with her,' she says.

'Yeah.'

'That's good.'

I smile.

'Thought you would be, so I didn't take time off today.'

'You don't need to. She's fine. Just tired.'

'But I'll come in after work, after they've served tea.'

'If you want.'

'Then she'll have someone with her most of the time.'

'She wants to be left alone.'

'She only says that. You don't know what she's really like.'

'That's true.'

On seeing the magazine in my lap, she nods at the bedside cabinet. 'I bought that edition for her the other day and she's read it from cover-to-cover; even did the crossword.'

Glancing across at the cabinet, I notice a stack of magazines and one with the same cover as mine sitting on top.

'Buy her this month's *Home & Garden*, if you want to get something she hasn't read. And tell her I called.'

'I will.'

By two-thirty she's awake and by quarter-past-three I'm on the bus back to Nenford. I don't care if she'd rather be by herself. Not really. There's little she can say these days

— or fail to say — that'll hurt. It's all been said before, or failed to be said. I'll go and see her tomorrow, and the day after, and the day after that, until they release her or she releases herself, because she's my mother and that's mainly why I'm here.

★   ★   ★

Moving through the house from room to room, I turn the lights on against the dying of the day and try sweeping the corners clear of shadows. In Mum's bedroom, I drag open her wardrobe doors and drawers, but there's nothing to find except twin sets, dresses, skirts, blouses, five pairs of clean shoes, underwear, a jewellery box . . . Every cupboard, shelf and drawer in the house is too bloody ordered too, and a quick glance in the attic tells me it's been cleared for years. Even Brian's ready-decorated, miniature, plastic Christmas tree no longer awaits its annual unwrapping. In fact, apart from his recorded presence in the three photo albums, there's almost as little trace of Brian here, to confirm he ever existed and was part of her life, as there is of Dad, and I almost feel sorry for the poor bastard.

Even now, as an adult, I can't accept that

154

Dad wouldn't have left behind the briefest note before he took his life, or that she'd have destroyed it. It'd only take a phrase or two to please me: 'Let Tommo know I always loved him, and that I'm sorry.'

But there are no boxes stacked with diaries or old love letters, no mementoes in the way of Mother's Day gifts we'd made at school or bought with precious pocket money; no concessions to nostalgia or sentimentality. Even the photo albums are a bland and edited selection of memories that give little away except changing fashions and hairstyles in various holiday locations. What's she done with the negatives and unwanted photos? Burnt them? We're so different to one another, my mother and I.

By the time I've finished searching, it's dark outside. My father left nothing — except a wristwatch and a few memories. The process leaves me empty, purged and strangely at ease. In this respect, I've done everything I can expect of myself. The house is an empty shell, just a husk.

Standing at the French windows, I peer out at the bare and treeless winter garden until my breath mists the glass, and I begin drawing a smiley face, but then rub it out again. Already the grass is white with frost and there's an almost-full moon rising above the roofline of the houses. A coldness is seeping into me, numbing me, so I close the curtains and set about making the heater work harder. Tonight, the sparrows and finches will freeze and drop from a brittle sky.

★ ★ ★

At six o'clock, with my address book open and several rehearsed dialogues running through my head, I pick up the phone and dial Kate's parents' number again.

After five rings, there's no answer. I'll give it ten rings, hang up, and never do another thing about finding her. On the twelfth ring, Kate's dad answers. I recognise his voice straightaway.

'Hello,' he says. 'Happy Christmas to you.' The first unconditionally friendly voice I've heard since arriving in England.

Silence.

'Hello,' he repeats.

'Hello, Mr Hainley. My name's Tom Passmore. I'm an old friend of Kate's — a very old friend. I don't know whether you remember, but you and Mrs Hainley met me several times, years ago.'

'Tom? Tom Passmore?'

'Yes. Tom Passmore. An old friend of Kate's.'

'Just wait a minute, will you, while I turn down the radio.'

I hear footsteps, a door shutting; no radio.

'I think I remember you, Tom. It was a long while ago.'

'The reason I'm phoning,' I continue, 'is that . . . well, I moved to Australia a few years ago and never had a chance to keep in touch with Kate, and — '

'You phoning from Australia, Tom?'

'No. I'm in the country — back in Nenford actually. That's why I'm phoning. My mother's sick, so I've come over for a couple of weeks to be with her. She's in hospital.'

'I'm sorry to hear that. Remember us to her. We met her once, didn't we?'

Did they? I don't remember, but I say: 'Yes. I'd forgotten that. Thanks.'

This is going better than I'd hoped.

'But it was a long while ago,' he says.

'About twenty years,' I admit.

There's a pronounced silence at the other end.

'The reason I'm phoning,' I hurry on, 'is because I was hoping to get in touch with a few old friends again while I'm here. For old time's sake. While I'm in the country. And I wondered if you could give me Kate's address or a telephone number or something.'

'You want me to give you Kate's address?'

'Yes please. So I can drop her a line. Or a telephone number, so I can ring her. That'd do.'

There's a few seconds hesitation and then he says, 'Look, I'm sorry. It's not . . . Well, over the phone, you see, I'm not — '

And I know what he's struggling to say. He can't be sure who I am. I could be anyone on the phone claiming to be Tom Passmore, so I interrupt him. 'No, you're quite right, Mr Hainley. That's okay. I hadn't thought about it like that. Well, look, I was hoping to travel around and play the tourist and to definitely get across to Abetsby at some point, so perhaps I might call round and explain instead, if that's okay?'

The pause is too long.

'You want to call round?'

'If it's okay. Just to explain.' And as I'm repeating this, I have no idea what it is I'll explain. I can't fully explain it to myself, let alone to anyone else.

'I see.'

'Would that be okay?'

'When?'

'How about Thursday morning?'

Too quickly he says: 'Sorry, we'll be out all day.'

'Friday then. Or Saturday. I don't mind. Whenever suits you best.'

'Won't your mother miss you?'

I laugh. 'Not at all. She's feeling crowded already. She's not one for too much attention.'

'I see.' There's a pause. 'Hold on a minute.'

I hear him put the phone down, and I'm even less sure why I need to do any of this. Not for the sake of a twenty-year-old promise, nor even for what that promise represents, surely? It's like I'm following somebody else's script, or that, like a sleepwalker, I've become detached from my own sense of self. I'd put the phone down if I could, but I can't, and a couple of minutes later I hear footsteps and the sound of him clearing his throat.

'Tom?'

'Yes.'

'You best come on Friday then, at eleven. We have to go out at twelve though; my wife's got a doctor's appointment.'

'That's fine,' I say, and take a breath. 'Thanks. I'll look forward to seeing you then.'

The last time I saw her parents was just before Kate and I went on holiday together, to Yorkshire.

'Goodbye then,' he says.

'Goodbye, Mr Hainley, and happy Christmas to you too.'

At the dining room windows, I lift a curtain

and note that every house has Christmas lights blinking into the night; winking and blinking; punctuating the long evening with coloured beacons. In this country most people would rather stare at dog crap in a bus shelter than pass the time of day, but they dress their front windows and illuminate the winter for one another — everyone except my mother.

7

There's a spattering of eight squat buildings in a valley of moorland, with a river cutting the village in half and a road-bridge over the river. There's a shop, a pub, a red phone booth and half-a-dozen stone cottages (thick-walls, small-paned windows, slate roofs), and it's more a hamlet than a village; compact enough to be captured picturesquely, in its entirety, within the frame of a picture postcard.

Wightdale, Yorkshire.

We choose the renovated, ex-farm labourer's cottage from a holiday brochure. We can't afford the rent by ourselves, so Kate asks her friend, Anita, if she and her boyfriend want to share it with us, and we don't care that we'll have to catch trains, buses or hitchhike to get anywhere; only that we'll spend a whole week together. And afterwards — well, we'll have the remaining summer together too. I've got my job on the market and Kate's hoping to find temporary work wherever she can; she's asked around and given her name to every shop, café and pub in Abetsby.

Several days before our holiday, though,

she phones earlier in the evening than usual. It's a warm day and the windows are thrown wide open. If I listen hard enough, I'll probably hear a song thrush singing on the fence.

'It's for you, lover-boy,' Brian says, holding up the phone, his hand over the mouthpiece. 'Don't be long, I'm expecting a call.'

'You'll never guess what?' she begins, and her voice is a couple of excited notes higher than usual.

I know it must be something fantastic, but not her exam results because they're not due yet. Perhaps she's discovered the rental for the cottage covers two weeks instead of one; perhaps she's found a way we can live in London together; perhaps she's decided to defer uni for a year.

'What? What's happened?'

'My French teacher phoned today. Angie Taylor. My old French teacher from school. She's found me a job in France. As an *au pair*. With a Parisian family. Imagine, three months in France. I can't believe it. Paris. An apartment over-looking the Seine. Isn't it great?'

'Across the summer?'

'Yes. As soon as we get back from Yorkshire.'

'Oh.'

'I know there's things we have to talk about,' she says. 'But isn't it wonderful all the same? Say you're pleased for me.'

Silence. I let it hang there, drifting down the telephone like thick fog.

'Tom?'

'I'm still here.'

'Please. Say you're glad for me.'

'How can I? I won't see you. I thought we'd have summer together. That at least.'

'You could visit for a few days. I'll show you Paris in my time off. We'll have a brilliant time. We'll hitch to Brittany or down south — whatever you want — or be lazy in a Paris hotel room. Visit galleries in the morning, make love in the afternoon, sit out at pavement cafes. Imagine what a time we'll have! I'll show you the Georges Pompidou Centre, Montmartre, Notre Dame, or take you to Le Mont Sainte Michel. There's so much we can do.'

'Three months?'

'It's a great opportunity. And it's not as if I've been offered any other work. You know I need the money for uni, Tom. I can't sponge off my parents. You know that. They can't afford it. Say you're pleased for me. I have to know that. Please. Don't spoil it by being upset.'

Brian comes back into the room and points

at the phone, then starts flicking through the TV guide, pretending not to listen. The fuck-wit.

'Yeah, I am pleased. Really. It's great for you.' I lower my voice to a whisper. 'I'm just being . . . well, you know. But it's because — '

'I know. Me too. I feel torn in half. I'll miss you more than you can imagine. But at least if we're both earning, we'll be that much closer to affording what we want in a year's time. We'll have money for a bond on a flat perhaps — to live together.'

'Yeah,' I say. 'That's right.'

★ ★ ★

The scent of warm, cut grass after light rain; blackbirds rustling through the shadows of shrubs; the gossiping of crows in the crown of a spinney . . . There's something idyllic about our first evening in Wightdale, even though we're stuffed after the day's journey. Once we've unpacked and eaten, we leave Anita and Mike watching TV and follow the steep, narrow path that leads from our low front door down to the road, the shop, the telephone booth, the pub, and a couple of beers before bed.

Halfway down the path is a thick slab of slate, which straddles a brook that feeds into the river. We pause here, watching the water twisting and gurgling, listening to sheep bleat on the hill above, breathing air that's clearer than back home.

'This is great,' Kate observes.

'You like it?'

'Yeah, don't you?'

'Definitely.' And I can't help but try imagining what it'd be like living here, just the two of us, with nothing else to worry about. *Happy Families*. 'I wish we could stay,' I say.

'We've only just got here.'

'Stay longer, I mean. You could probably do with a couple of week's holiday. Not just one.'

'That's true,' she says.

★ ★ ★

The following day starts brightly enough.

We're keen to be up and doing, so we run down to the shop to buy milk, bread, eggs, a newspaper. And laugh all the way back, swinging our arms together, hungry for this new day.

Mike and Anita are still in bed, so we've got the kitchen to ourselves to pretend we're on our own. Kate's flicking through the Sunday magazine, sipping coffee, and I'm flicking back through the news, from the world news to the national stuff, heading towards the front page.

It's on page four.

A shadow strokes thin, icy fingers across my neck.

'Shit,' I say. I feel the colour drain from my face.

She looks up from the magazine. 'What?'

Pushing the newspaper across, I point to the column.

TEENAGER DIES IN STOLEN CAR.

Gary Fletcher, 17, died in Northampton last night, after the stolen car he was driving left the road and smashed into a tree. Two teenage passengers were cut free from the wreckage and taken to Northampton General Hospital in a critical condition. Police, who pursued the vehicle at speeds of up to 70 mph through the town centre, called off the chase two minutes before the accident happened. It's believed the driver lost control of the car on a tight bend. No other vehicle was involved. The death comes in the wake of the Barrow Report, which criticised police procedure in maintaining high-speed car pursuits through residential areas. Police spokesperson . . .

★ ★ ★

'Someone you know?' she asks.

'We went to primary school together; were best friends for a while; a year or two. Gazza.'

She reaches a hand across the table, then moves round to sit on my lap.

'That's terrible,' she says. 'You must feel terrible.'

Do I?

The last time I saw Gazza he pushed past me in a pub and ignored me. Not even a nod, the ignorant bastard. That was a year ago. Today it's bright outside and I've got Kate. Already my surprise over his death is fading. It's more disappointment than surprise. And I don't feel terrible.

'No. I don't think I do.'

'It probably hasn't sunk in yet. That sort of news is a shock. When did you last see him?'

And I tell her a story or two. 'Gazza and I broke into a building site when we were ten,' and I tell her about the flint he found and the making of the doughnuts and about the smoke bombs, his light fingers, and how we went our separate ways. I end up by saying: 'I'm not really surprised he's dead. It was bound to happen.'

'Will you be okay?' she asks again. 'Will it spoil the holiday for you?'

'No way,' I say, and am probably too enthusiastic.

167

'You must feel something though. It's okay to be upset, you know. You can cry if you want. It's alright. Don't give me any of that macho bullshit.'

I laugh. 'No bullshit. I don't want to. Why would I? It'd be hypocritical to say I'm upset if I'm not. I haven't properly spoken to him in a few years, and well — stolen cars, burglary — that was the way his life was going.'

She regards me for a moment and I drag the paper back across the table.

Kate then says, 'Poor bloke. What a waste.'

'He was always heading for that tree, Kate. Even as a kid. If it hadn't been yesterday, it would've been next year. If not then, some other time. It's probably lucky no one else was killed.'

She stands up, moves to the kitchen window. 'That sounds callous. A little cruel.'

Maybe I *am* upset. Maybe my childhood knowledge of loss makes me shut some emotions down, treat other emotions carelessly. Maybe Kate is such a strong antidote to the worst of the past, I won't think about any of that stuff when I'm with her; I don't need to. Should I tell her that death frightens me shitless, especially when I try contemplating the vast permanence of it — that infinity of nothingness? Instead, I shake my head. 'Life's cruel,' I say.

She turns then. 'You don't have to be,' she tells me, and walks out.

There's a small garden surrounding the cottage, edged by the moors, separated by a low brick wall. A quince grows along one side of the house and a straggly dog rose by the wall; there's a stone patio in front of French windows, a couple of stunted shrubs, but the garden's mainly cropped grass and heather, like the rest of the landscape. I join her out there, staring at the hills.

'What's the matter?' I say, putting my arms round her waist from behind, breathing in the smell of her hair, the sensuality of her neck.

'Do you want to go to the funeral?' she asks.

'I don't know. I don't think so.' I feel her stiffen. 'I'm only being honest, Kate. I'm not sure what the point of it'd be, what good it'd do. We haven't spoken in years.'

'His parents might appreciate it. After losing their son, their child, and so young . . . It might mean something to them, even if it doesn't to you.'

'His mum probably wouldn't remember who I was.'

'Why does that matter? It's not just about you.'

There's no way I'll let anything break apart our week, but I tell her: 'I'll find out when the funeral is. If it's after we've returned I'll try and get there.'

'Good.'

'Is that better?'

'It's not about me either, Tom. Don't go for my sake.'

What remains of breakfast is sour and indigestible. Abandoning the newspaper and avoiding one another, it takes us the morning to move beyond it.

In the afternoon we're standing at the road-bridge, Kate and I, peering at the river below, hypnotised and comforted by the incessant rush and rumble. It's only a foot or two deep, but fast-flowing — the sort of river I expect to see fat trout lazing in, jumping for flies — and there's no shopping trolleys dumped in it, no plastic bags snagged against the bank, just a couple of bottles and a faded Coke can basking among the polished rocks. Running alongside one bank is a narrow, dirt track, worn enough to suggest it's a popular walk; so we begin following it up-river to see if we can discover, somewhere at the valley's end, the water's source. Maybe there'll be a spring or a waterfall.

We're among the damp shade of trees before long, and the track becomes a mat of rotted leaves and bark. In a couple of places it's straddled by a fallen tree and, in other

170

steeper places, has been eaten away by landslides of soil and scree. Ambling along, we chat about the clearness of the water, the colours of the stones, the nuisance flies, the tones of the landscape — safe subjects. In and out of the shade. Then we find ourselves at a set of small rapids and, because our feet are hot and because there's no hurry to do anything whatsoever, we tug off one another's shoes and socks, sit and dabble our feet in the icy water.

After a long silence, she says: 'Is it because of your dad?'

I know what she's talking about and wish we'd never bought the bloody newspaper.

'What?' I say.

'The thing with your friend — your old friend. I can't believe I'm more upset about it than you are. I *don't* believe it. I think you're just not showing it, either deliberately or without realising it. It's not you. It's not the you I know.'

She might have added: 'It's not the you I want to know'.

She stops kicking at the water and remains still, hands pressed flat against the slab of rock we're sitting on. 'Is it because you lost your dad that you're not showing it? And the fact your mum lied about it? It must have affected her terribly.'

'That was more than ten years ago. I can't remember it.'

She looks at me and says nothing, then looks back at the water and says, 'Bollocks.'

'What is?'

'You can be a real plonker at times.'

'Why?'

'You remember it well enough to describe the way the policeman leant his bike into your hedge, how he got off the bike before it properly stopped, how . . . You remember it well enough. Don't bullshit me, Tom. We mustn't bullshit one another — not ever. Okay?'

I bite my lip and nod. 'What I mean is that I'm over it.'

She reaches forward and plucks a pebble out the water. It's grey and smooth and quickly dries in her hand. 'Some things take an age to get over.'

'I was seven. It was more than half a lifetime ago.'

'I believe there are things which people never fully get over.'

'I'm over it,' I say. 'I'm a resilient bastard.'

'Would you get over me that quick?'

'Don't, Kate.'

She drops the pebble back into the water. Her silence has the same effect on our conversation. The ripples come back at me.

172

'It's not the same. It was Dad's decision. He chose to end his life. There's no arguing with that.' I have to move her away from this topic, before she completely reassesses what she thinks of me and whether we fit together.

'And you've never found out why he did it? You've never been told?'

'Mum won't talk about it,' I say, 'not even to Brian. It's not as if I haven't asked enough times — and got my head bitten off.' There's a thin, flat pebble, which I pick up. I turn and try skimming across the water to make it skip, but the angle's wrong and it sinks straight-away. I wipe a drop of water off my watchstrap and it leaves a dark spot there; it's no longer the same brown leather strap of course, but I always think of it as his. 'He left a letter, I think, but she destroyed it — burnt it. I'm not sure whether I was told that or whether I've dreamt it at some point. I've imagined all sorts of reasons why he did it: maybe he discovered he had some incurable cancer, maybe my mother was about to leave him, maybe he was depressed. She only ever said that he was weak, but I think he was probably sick.'

'Do you get angry with him?'

'Why? What for?'

'For leaving you.'

'I don't think so. With Mum perhaps. I

wonder if she might have stopped it. I don't know what I think about him anymore. It's easier to imagine he died in a car crash. I try and do that sometimes, to see how it feels. But even so . . . '

'What?'

I say: 'It's not knowing the truth, that's the worst bit; wanting to know and feeling it'd make a difference.' And I almost tell her that, to me, it seems that death is always just a fragment of a larger loss, but the phrase sounds phoney and so I keep it to myself. Even so, I believe that when we grieve, we grieve for ourselves more than the person who's died; we grieve for our lost opportunities and our sense of being less complete, and for the reinforcement of our own mortality. Grief is natural, but it isn't selfless, and it certainly doesn't do the dead any good. But if I said this, the words would come out wrong and I'd sound even more callous.

Kate says: 'Maybe you should ask her again. Choose your moment. Tell her why you have to know. Try and get her to see it from your point-of-view.'

'Easier said than done.'

She shrugs.

'I will one day,' I say.

Kate finds another pebble. Once more she wipes it dry, holds it against her cheek, then

174

drops it into the water.

'Splash!' she says.

She lies back on the rock and closes her eyes, and the day clouds over. It's hot in the sun, cool in the shade. There's a bank of clouds moving in, but just a small one in front of the sun. We've conjured up a couple of ghosts and I can feel them standing behind us, looking down, but I think I've learnt how to ignore ghosts and don't want to dwell on death, not now I'm with her — she's a stronger presence. What matters most is that it's the second day of our holiday, and that in just over a week's time she'll be leaving for almost three months in France; I might only see her once in that time, and then she'll go to London, and I might only see her once again between the end of September and Christmas. It leaves me anxious with wondering what we should be doing to make the most of every second. All I know is that she shouldn't be finding fault with me and I shouldn't be letting her down.

Leaning over her, I blow on her face, kissing her. She opens her eyes and the sun comes out again.

'How did you do that?' I say.

'What?'

'Work the sun. When you closed your eyes

you made the sun go in. Do it again.'

And so she does, but it doesn't.

'My batteries are low,' she says.

'I'll recharge them for you later.'

'Promises, promises.'

But even our banter sounds tired, preoccupied, as if we're trying too hard not to think of some other thing — a dangerous thing to think about — which might trip us up again on one pretext or another.

In the evening, we go to bed early, planning to make love for hours on end, but it doesn't happen. When we get there, we talk, I yawn a couple of times and she grows cross. I feel drained and she seems impatient, so that when we try playing after that it's clumsy and forced and we can't find the fun in it, and so go to sleep irritable and more anxious than before.

★   ★   ★

Two days later, we're sitting in The Hare and Hounds beer garden having a drink for lunch. After a night of drizzle, the plastic chairs have dried in the sun, but the lawn's still damp. With the village huddled into the crease of the valley, surrounded and overlooked by untamed moorland, there's a sense of equilibrium between the natural environment and the imposition of humanity. The balance seems right.

I place a hand on Kate's hand. 'I like it here. Do you?'

'Love it,' she says. 'Although I'd prefer the cottage to ourselves. Mike left the bathroom in a pig of a mess this morning. Again.'

I nod. 'We couldn't afford it without them.'

'I know that.' She's wearing a headscarf today, Romany-style, and frees her hand to retie it. 'It's great leaving suburbia behind. I love breathing clean air.'

One of her gold earrings is hanging awry and I lean across to straighten it. 'I could live somewhere like this,' I say. 'A cosy cottage, a kitchen garden, few other houses in sight ... It'd be heaven, don't you reckon?' I'm thinking of Nenford and what's been lost — of the imbalance.

'No.'

'No?'

'How would you earn a wage? How would you live?'

'I'd commute, or work from home — my own hours — or, with a couple of acres, we'd be self-sufficient. With a small orchard, we could grow our own fruit, make apple and blackcurrant pies; run a cottage industry.'

'We? Count me out. I've had enough of the small-town mentality in Abetsby. How

177

narrow-minded would somewhere like this be? I want to see something of the world, Tom; to visit other places, other cultures, meet other people and new ideas. Don't you? I thought you did.'

'We could do both,' I say. 'Have a cottage in the country, you know, and an apartment in Rome. It wouldn't have to be Britain.'

She stares into her pot of beer before speaking. 'You're joking, right?'

I shrug. 'Why?'

'Your view of the world. It's too romantic. Romantic at best, naïve at worst. A holiday's one thing, but you've been soaking up too much Hollywood crap, Tom. The real world isn't like that.'

'I wasn't meaning it like that. I meant I'd be happy whatever we were doing, as long as — '

'Life's about more than just being with someone.' She reaches up to her hair, undoes her scarf and shoves it into her bag.

'Yeah,' I say. 'Of course.' But I don't really believe it.

We drink our beer, follow the road out the village, and then leave it to trek a zig-zag route to the top of the moor. Halfway up, we've both worked up a sweat, despite the wind singing through the heather and pushing at our backs. Close to the highest point, we follow sheep tracks on soil that's peaty black, dry and spongy, like the softest carpet, and then we plant stones on the cairn, in the manner of a hundred walkers before us.

We have to raise our voices to cut above the pounding of the wind.

'Heaven!' I cry.

'I'm beat!' she returns, and drops to a crouch against the heap of stones. 'Out of condition. Couldn't manage another step.' Pointing to the horizon and three giant golf balls perched on a plateau of distant moorland, she says: 'What the hell's that?'

'Fylingdales, I guess. Shit, I never thought they'd be that big.' And I squat beside her.

'Some sort of observatory?'

'Radar. An early warning system. Gives the politicians and royals four minutes' notice in case the Soviets decide to nuke us — enough time for the Yanks to retaliate, for the world to blow itself to smithereens. Welcome aboard the USS Great Britain.'

'The fifty-first state.'

'Yeah.'

'Very comforting.'

I squint to try and see beyond Fylingdales. 'I wonder if you can see the sea from here.'

It's possible to trace the shape of the moors and a few valleys, but we can't see the sea and

179

we can't even see Wightdale, which clings lower down one side of the hill. After ten minutes we walk on, brushing through dry bracken and over mounds of heather, our backs to the giant baubles.

'No people!' she shouts. 'Just us!'

And less than two steps in front of us, a hare breaks cover. It leaps from where it's been basking into a manic zig-zag dance across the heath. A few seconds of explosive energy and then gone again. We're frozen still, startled by the sudden burst and the frenzy of its dance.

'Bloody fantastic.'

Dropping lower, round the hill, we find ourselves on the lee-side, heading towards a sharp, wooded tributary of the valley. Protected from the wind, we feel the smack of the sun on our skin and know we'll burn.

Sitting down to admire the view, Kate undoes her shoes and peels off her socks and wiggles her toes in the coarse stubble of cropped grass. She lies back, eyes closed.

'It's good to stop, finish exams, be lazy for a while. I need this holiday.'

A skylark starts belting out its song: rising and falling, climbing and hovering, then dropping again. And then, without any rumble of warning, two Air Force jets scream through the sky, bursting along the valley and over the moors like bullets. Kate sits up, shields her eyes to see them strip away the distance — two red blades cleaving the sky in half, cleaving the day.

'Well!' she says, then lies back again, throwing her arms out wide to embrace the sky.

'So much for paradise,' I say and lie down beside her.

After a couple of minutes, and without changing her position, as if speaking to the sky, she says: 'There's danger in being too much of a romantic idealist, Tom. If you expect too much you'll always be disappointed. It worries me what you might expect of me sometimes, in case you think I'm someone I'm not. One day you might wake up and realise I'm not the dream you thought I was. Nowhere's perfect, no one's perfect, and it makes life bloody impossible if you expect them to be.'

I say nothing, hoping she might think I'm asleep.

'Tom?'

'I know,' I say. 'I don't.'

We stir at the end of the afternoon, stiff and sunburnt, and trudge in silence back to the cottage, both nursing the beginnings of a headache. Sore, tetchy and quiet.

★ ★ ★

The air's heavy the following morning and it's difficult to shrug sleep off. In the kitchen, Kate's got a book open at the table, which she appears to be reading as she picks at her toast. Mike and Anita are laughing in their bedroom and I know what they're up to. To drown out their happiness, our silence, I clear the table, run water into the sink, wash the dishes. The day's been sucked dry before it's even started.

As I stack the last of the dishes on the draining board, Kate stands and drops the remnants of toast into the bin. She's barely eaten. She picks up a tea towel, but then folds it in half and folds it again.

'Let's do something,' she says. 'I can't stand this anymore.'

'What?'

'We need to get away. You and me. Be properly on our own. Something isn't working for us here.'

'Where can we go?'

'Anywhere. We don't have to stay here. Why don't we hitch to the coast? What about Whitby? If we like it we could find a small hotel and stay overnight. Treat ourselves.'

'Do you reckon we can afford it?' I know she's not wanted to draw heavily on her savings.

'I don't think we can afford not to,' she

says. 'Besides, now I've got a summer job I don't mind blowing a little cash.' And she chucks the towel at me to dry my hands. 'Come on, we'll shove a few clothes in a backpack. I'll leave a note for Anita. They can have the place to themselves for a night.'

And so we do. The air's humid, we're sore with sunburn and it takes three rides and a couple of hours to reach Whitby, but we sit up at our first view of the sea.

The lorry driver who delivers us to the town centre says little once he's asked us where we're heading, whether we're on holiday together and what Kate's name is. He asks her because she's sitting in the middle, next to him, and she has to shout because of the racket of the engine, but he keeps grinning at her. After a few minutes she slides closer to me and places a hand on my knee, but he laughs and says something about the gear stick, which neither of us properly hears.

'How old are you then?' he asks out of the blue.

'Sixteen,' she lies, and I place an arm round her shoulder.

When we climb down from the cab and he drives away, she shakes her head. 'I wonder what he's got on his mind,' she says.

And I almost tell her how it is that most

blokes look at her like that, but then change my mind.

We paddle in the sea and push the sleazy bastard out of our day; we write postcards in a tea shop and wander the streets during the afternoon, looking in shop windows and at craft stalls, and I start imagining how it'd be if we lived somewhere like this.

We like Whitby well enough to book a room in The Anchor, an ancient inn close to the quay, and feel that, despite the mugginess, we've taken control of our world again. We might be back in a town, but with the North Sea lapping at the trawlers — with the tide slowly rising — it doesn't seem much tamer or less natural than being in the middle of the moors.

It's a tiny attic room, swamped by a queen bed and a large, mahogany wardrobe, and a sloping floor. A pocket of thick, hot, stale air is trapped there, but we push open the casement window in the gable wall and a pivoting window set into the pitch of the roof, and the air shifts a little.

Sitting on a bench overlooking the harbour, we fill our faces with cod and chips, soak up the smell of brine and old fish that drifts towards us, lick the salt and vinegar from our fingers. Even with the sun starting to dip, it's still clammy, but the air's so still that any movement seems to generate static. We share a bottle of lemonade, drop the occasional chip for the squabbling seagulls and smile at their edgy raucousness. We're sweaty and smelly, but who cares?

'This is good,' I say. 'I'm glad we're doing this.'

'Sometimes you've gotta grab life by the short and curlies,' she says, 'otherwise it'll pass you by while you're waiting for something to happen.' I nod, toss another chip.

'I felt like something was going wrong back there — in Wightdale,' she adds. 'It's a nice place, but was making me uptight.'

I look at her, then back at the seagulls. 'Perhaps because we're having to share the house.'

'Perhaps. Well, they're welcome to it.'

Shortly after nine, the sky darkens prematurely and the first peal of thunder grumbles over the sea, rumbling across the distance. We're sitting out at the front of the inn, finishing pints of cider, and night swallows day in one mouthful. It feels like we've been outside forever, so we climb the stairs to our room, stand at the window and watch the gathering storm, waiting for rain.

Within minutes, sheet and forked lightning begin pounding the sky into turmoil, whip-cracking it to shreds; volley after volley. No rain, just electricity. Lightning and thunder bounce around the town, the delicious row of it growing beyond all reckoning, so that we hold our ears at one point and laugh. Then, with the loudest crack of all, the lights of Whitby die — every single house light and streetlight.

It's beautiful.

Finding her hand, we lean against one another and count the bristling seconds between lightning and thunder. It begins raining then, throwing large gobbets so hard we reluctantly pull the windows almost shut, although it's cooler now and the humidity has dissolved. And it isn't long, with the rain beating against the roof and the air so much fresher, before we turn to face each other and, helping one another with buttons and zips and belts, step out of our clothes and move towards the bed. When we make love, it seems as though it's the first time in an age.

★　★　★

The following morning we hitch to Scarborough. Reluctant to return too soon, we stretch the day as far as it'll go. A lorry takes us from Whitby to Scarborough, and then we thumb a ride to Pickering where we climb to the castle, buy more postcards, before catching the Moors Railway steam train back to Grosmont, where we hitch another lift to Wightdale.

It's early evening when we cross the slate bridge and arrive at the low front door, and Anita and Mike are arguing over whose turn it is to wash the dishes, and I'm delighted. Kate and I are glowing; I can see it in her, can sense it in myself. It feels as if we've been travelling for a week, and have shaken whatever jinx was trying to trip us up.

On Friday, the last full day of our holiday, we're sitting on the lounge carpet with the Ordnance Survey map spread out and a stream of sunlight motes angling across the room. We're gonna take the map, a compass and a packed lunch and cut across the moors for two or three hours. It'll be a challenge and an adventure to bind us, to see how far we'll get, to see where it'll take us. And I think we might find a bed of cropped grass or soft peat to lie on a while.

'When we're walking we'll talk about France,' I promise, 'and plan what to do when I come out and visit you.'

'You want to talk about it?'

'Yes. And London too. We can plan some of the things we'll do when I come down to see you.'

'One thing at a time, eh? I can only cope with thinking about France at the moment. I don't want to think about London yet.'

'Okay.'

'We'll be alright,' she says. 'You and I. You know that, don't you? We — '

She's about to say something else, but a bird smashes into one of the French windows. Kate screams and I duck.

Seeing a reflection of the summer world it's just flown through, the song thrush's line of flight is broken by an invisible wall. It lies crumpled on the patio outside the windows, a feathery bag of bits and bones, its head at an obtuse angle, a dribble of red stickiness beside its beak: viscous, smooth and syrupy — too dark to be nothing. It hasn't even left a crack in the glass.

'See if it's okay, Tom,' she cries, still crouching on the floor.

'It's not,' I mutter, standing by the window. I close my eyes, but when I open them it's still lying there, not even twitching. 'Hit the glass like a rock.'

'Go and check. Please. It might just be stunned.'

'There's blood by its beak, or something. Look at the way its head is. That's not natural.'

'Just check. Please. We might be able to do something.'

In truth, I'm as afraid of the bird being badly injured as I am of confronting its death, and don't know what I'll do if it starts twisting in demented circles on the paving slab or if it blinks at me. I couldn't club it with a lump of wood to end its misery.

'I'll put the kettle on,' she says, escaping the room as I unbolt the doors.

A breeze ruffles its feathers and I shiver. I don't need to touch it to know it's dead. I'm only going through the motions to show Kate I care. I'll have to find a spade or something to pick it up and bury it, even though every instinct tells me to leave the broken bundle by its trickle and wait for a cat or a hawk to fetch it. I know she might despise me if it's still there when she comes back; both of us too superstitious of what it might represent.

8

The early train rattles my dreams apart and rattles the bedroom window too, even though it's thrown open against a warm night. Swansea to Paddington: a blur of sound, zipping through the dank cutting that lies beyond the back fence. Elin's got the sheet pulled taut across her face, shielding her last scraps of sleep from an intense sunshine that makes the curtains glow and saturates the room with light. Through a gap in our curtains, I watch a sparrow land on the window-ledge, preen itself, crap and fly away.

Fly, birdie, fly.

Morning glory. I follow the rhythm of Elin's breathing, and then slide out of bed, drag on some clothes and step into the day.

It's Sunday morning and, except for the newsagent and milkman, the world's deserted. It's too early for church bells to be tugged awake, thank God, and the chapel doors remain bible-bolted against the carnal delights of Saturday night. In Main Street, I step over a limp condom, discarded in the gutter, pass empty beer cans and greasy fish and chip wrappings that litter shop porches and municipal flower beds, and imagine living some place with fewer people, fewer tensions, a slower pace.

Our Sunday morning ritual involves buying a newspaper and returning to bed for breakfast, to browse or read and, sometimes, to play a while, but today's different. Pausing to sit on the low wall that surrounds the locked public gardens, I flick through the headlines: *UDA CLAIMS BELFAST KILLINGS, THATCHER CONDEMNS WET TORIES, UNIONS VOW TO FIGHT CAR PLANT CLOSURE, NUCLEAR FAILSAFE FAILS SAFETY TEST, KIKI THE PANDA SEEKS MATE.* It's all too depressing and too familiar, so I head back to our flat above the toyshop.

Pausing at the bedroom door, a floorboard yawns and Elin stirs.

'What time is it?' she drawls, eyes screwed tight.

I lean against the door jamb. 'Seven o'clock, just gone.'

'It's too early. Where've you been?'

'For a walk. To get the newspaper.'

'Already?'

'There's hardly anyone about. It's very peaceful.'

Elin turns and pulls the pillow against her eyes. 'The sane ones are still in bed.'

'It's a beautiful morning.'

'Come back to bed, Tom. I don't want to wake up yet.'

Sunlight sets the whole room aglow, but, in discovering a gap between the curtains, it paints a slice of the bed and the wall above with a sharper brilliance. It illuminates the corn dolly I've hung there — above where I sleep — and, above where Elin sleeps, the framed icon of a Madonna and child that she bought in Greece a couple of years before meeting me. She knows the history of the Whitby corn dolly and, perhaps, why I keep it, but seems content to let it hang there. The polished timber of the bed-head is a honey russet in this light, although the ribbon of dust along the topmost edge is obvious too, and Elin's hair is blonder and finer than I know it to be.

Two hours later, she stands at an open window breathing the morning in. 'It's now or never, I think. What d'ya reckon?'

'It's perfect. Idyllic.'

It's twelve months since we completed our degrees and left London behind, and we've both got jobs. Our one-bedroom flat in the Wiltshire market town of Great Shentonbury is small and often makes us impatient to be outside, but is paradise compared to any bedsit we'd pay three times the rent for in the capital. We've decked the place with the greenery of pot plants, seedlings and cuttings: spider plants, poinsettias, geraniums, herbs of every description, African violets, primroses, succulents, the first shoots from several Norway spruce seeds — anything that'll grow. They stand in saucers, margarine containers, old chamber pots we've bought from jumble sales, along the window ledges, on the toilet cistern, on book shelves, on the fridge — anywhere there's space and light. But we need space and light too, so for several weeks we've talked about a three-day walk along the ancient Ridgeway.

* * *

It's a day purring with heat, the intermittent silence of crickets, the three-dimensional dancing of dragonflies. We'll walk about eighteen miles all told, setting a pace that finds its rhythm in the lazy sighing of the grasses.

'Burderop Down,' announces Elin, waving her left hand vaguely at the countryside about us, as if she's a tour guide. 'There's a field system over there, according to the map. Doesn't say whether it's Middle Age, Iron Age, or what. And then, beyond, there's Smeathe's Ridge and another track leading to Ogbourne St George. We could've started

193

from there, I suppose.'

'I like this well enough.'

'Me too. The downs are riddled with tracks.'

It takes an hour or so to reach Barbary Castle and, after walking the embankments of this Iron Age fort, we unplug a flask of water and drink to the day. If it's possible to find it anywhere in modern Britain, with the soul-destroying stink of its motorways and ring-roads and housing estates and nuclear reactors, and to claim any sense of aboriginality, here's the pulse of that primordial past and here's the link. Only in places like this can we recognise our connection with a past rooted in the land, the elements, the seasons: birth, life, death, decay, birth. The roots are stretched thin, but this is where they're tapped into; this and the occasional discovery of a point or scraper at the bottom of your garden or a builder's trench.

The flask keeps the water cold.

'Cheers,' I say.

'Here's to us,' and she holds the flask up and laughs.

We follow the track above Uffcott Down until reaching the White Horse figure carved across Hackpen Hill. But it's early evening by the time we stroke the raw cut of chalk and wipe our hands on the grass, so we backtrack a few hundred yards and pitch our tent in the lee of a spinney.

After eating and sitting a while, we zip our sleeping bags together and stare at the night through the insect gauze of the tent. A crescent moon cuts an arc across the sky and, in the middle distance, a vixen's scream rips a small hole in the stillness; it's more the sound of an animal being torn apart than a mating call. Elin unzips the tent and sits our enamel mugs outside: the clink of metal on metal, the drone of a car a mile or two distant, the whine of a trapped insect. It's enough to wallow in the stillness of night, soaking it up. And we're silent so long I think she's fallen asleep, and begin moving my arm from across her, but she sighs at that.

'You're awake,' I say.

'Mmm.'

'What are you thinking about? A penny for your thoughts.'

'Kids.' And she turns to face me. 'About having a family, being parents — you know.'

I say nothing.

'It's not something I want to leave too long.'

'I know. You keep saying.' Brian's revelation of why Dad took his life is uncomfortably new, even though a year's passed. 'Doesn't seem fair to bring kids into this world,' I say.

'Britain's over-crowded and too much has been fucked up.'

'Then we'll never have kids by that reckoning, and nothing'll ever change. Or we can bring up our kids to care enough to make things different. Besides, I don't want to be one of those older mothers; I want to still feel young for our kids. It's important to me.'

'I'm not sure I've got patience enough to be a parent. I've learnt nothing from Mum or Brian I'd want to repeat, and even less from my dad, except how to vanish when the shit hits the fan.'

'You'd make a good dad,' she says.

'You reckon? Based on what?'

'Based on the fact that you worry whether you'd make a good dad or not. I don't suppose everyone worries. They just have kids and sort it out as they go along — or not.'

'I don't know.'

'If we keep talking about it, it'll never be the right time. Sometimes you've just gotta live life, Tom.'

'Grab it by the short and curlies?'

'These things shouldn't be too coldly planned.'

She sits up and pulls off her T-shirt, slides out of her knickers. The sleeping bag rustles, the zip comes undone a little. It's hot in the tent and I suck a breath of cool air through the insect gauze.

'As long as we can give them what they need,' I say. There's so many things to consider, like where we'll live, whether we'll ever save enough for a deposit on a house, whether the mortgage rates will sky-rocket or drop, whether we'll get by on one wage . . . the economic rationale.

'I don't want my kids — our kids — to be second to a career, Tom. I can always go back to teaching later.' She places a hand on my chest. 'Come on. You'll enjoy it.'

I begin dragging off my t-shirt and pants, willing the uncertainties to vanish. I lean closer to her, draw my hand across her stomach to stroke one of her breasts, bite the soft lobe of her ear.

'And if at first we don't succeed . . . ' she whispers.

★   ★   ★

The morning light wakes us, but by the time we're on our way the sun's climbed bright and hot in a sky that's a high, cerulean blue, and the downs stretch into an ocean of too many greens to name. The dew underfoot dries rapidly and each sea of grasses we wade through has a rich, sweet scent. Mushrooms

197

and toadstools have sprung into existence overnight and the number of darting dragonflies has multiplied.

By mid-morning, we're at the sarsen stones on Overton Down. These are the Grey Wethers. We explore a couple of other tracks and try finding a field system on Fyfield Down, before dumping our rucksacks and boiling water for coffee. We sit and sip, and drink in the landscape.

Elin squints at the fine print of the OS map. 'According to this, one arm of stones leads towards Fyfield and another points towards Devil's Den, whatever that might be.'

'You wanna take a look?'

'It's about four miles, there and back. Might not leave much time for Avebury. Think I'd rather pick a few mushrooms for a fry-up tonight.'

So we stroll back to the track across Avebury Down, which leads us to the gigantic stone circle at Avebury and the accompanying crowds of sightseers.

Each stone is a massive exclamation, and the imposition of their collective pattern on the landscape is an exclamation beyond awesome. And yet, the closer we get to the hordes of camera-wielding album-fillers, posing against each megalithic sarsen — leaning on them, pretending to hold them upright

— the more diminished each stone seems to become. As if they can be reduced by such profane inconsequentiality.

Elin and I walk in silence past these chattering people with barely a sideways glance, and look to The Red Lion. Today, we belong to two separate worlds, them and us. While we know they can't see us, their noise and synthetic colours and frenetic movements are unnervingly amplified. A pub lunch is one thing, but I doubt it's worth the price.

The Red Lion is at the centre of all activity. Usually, I'd admire its thatch roof and exposed timber-framed walls — seventeenth-century oak, perhaps — but today it seems ill-placed. And the bar's too dark and crowded.

Elin finds seats out front, but we're edged against the road and a constant stream of traffic changing gears to negotiate a sharp bend.

'Crazy,' I say, having inched between the packed benches and a crowd of standing bikies without spilling more than the head off our beers. 'Couldn't you find a cleaner table?'

'Where?' she says, and motions at the crowd.

'It's too packed.'

'Holiday season.'

'This is crazy.' I bite a slab of cheese,

scrunch half a pickled onion, gulp a quarter pint of ale. 'I'd trade all this crap for a desert island any day,' I say. Buttering a chunk of bread, I stretch my neck and try easing the tightness forming there. 'No more swarming people. Why would anyone wanna get rescued?'

'Robinson Crusoe?'

'Yeah.'

'You'd go mad,' she says.

'I don't mean just me. I mean the two us. Somewhere warm, exotic.'

She shakes her head. 'Scavenging for food, shelter; no medicine when you're sick — no comforts. It might be fun for a couple of days . . . '

A group of people squeeze by and one knocks Elin's back. She looks up, but the guy doesn't notice.

'An island with palm trees,' I say, conjuring the picture for her. 'Dates, coconuts. Clear blue skies. There'd be fish in the sea — warm tropical waters to bathe in — beaches without a single footprint except our own.'

'And sharks, mosquitoes, malaria, typhoons. Count me out.'

I slurp my beer and chew on her dismissal. Her words have a ring to them, as if we've had this discussion before, and she utters them with a finality that stings.

The silence grows between us. We're swamped by the din of raucous people at tables that are set too close.

'It's a great lunch,' she says, mopping chutney off her plate with the last piece of crust.

'It's alright,' I say. 'The bread's a bit dry.' It isn't, but I no longer want to agree with her. I'm sitting with an empty plate and pot in front of me, wishing she'd down the last of her beer.

Picking up her glass, she looks at the contents, swirls the liquid round a couple of times, and then sits it back on the table.

'Come on, Robinson Crusoe,' she says, reaching for her rucksack. 'I've had enough.'

Half-heartedly, we stroke our hands across a few mammoth stones and begin tracing a segment of their pattern across the landscape, but when I see a woman using the edge of a sarsen to scrape sheep shit off her shoe it's time to get away from the place. Avebury will have to wait for another day. We plod along Stone Avenue among a herd of Friesians, then turn to Silbury Hill, where we sit before heading back through West Kennett towards Overton Hill, eager to find some solitude on the Ridgeway again.

In this manner, we walk without saying much through the heat of the afternoon. We pass The Sanctuary, cross the river and amble through East Kennett, but it's only as we leave the bitumen behind and find a track that takes us past a long barrow that our mood becomes easier to carry once more.

We walk through blue milkwort and yellow horseshoe vetch and there's the smell of wild chive or onion and, then, what might be the scent of thyme, except it's too faint to be sure. Along one stretch of track, as we near Grennard Hill, we come across honeysuckle tangling along fence wires, and, round the next bend, quite absurdly (given the lateness of the season and the cultivated nature of the plant) a clump of pæonies.

They're long past their best and wilting for a drink. One crimson flower is still in bloom — just — but the remaining flowers have dropped their petals.

'This is weird. They don't grow in the wild,' I say, removing my backpack. 'And they've usually flowered by now.'

'It was a late spring,' Elin remarks. 'Maybe that put them back. Maybe a bird carried them and a vole buried them,' she says.

I laugh.

She lowers her pack and massages her shoulders, then reaches into a side-pocket for her water. 'I remember reading an article,' she tells me, 'about a woman in India who, whenever she travelled by train, would take packets of seed with her. She'd lean out the window and scatter the seed as they went along. Apparently there are heaps of flowers along some stretches of track now.'

'Really?'

'Yeah.'

'When I was a kid, about eleven-years-old,' I tell her, 'I stole two packets of seed and scattered them across a demolition site. Nasturtiums came up for a couple of years until they built the new bus station there.'

'Northampton bus station?'

'Yeah.'

She puts the stopper back in the flask. 'You stole them?'

'I didn't mean to. Some mates went shoplifting and I got caught up in it.'

'You took two packets of seed? Not sweets or toys?'

* * *

On Grennard Hill, with evening pulling tight around us, we find another spinney and pitch the tent close by. The sun drops low and becomes a yolk of bright orange in a salmon pink sky, and the day's shadows lengthen and begin stalking us. It's set to become an evening of fire and shadows on a day of stones. Stones, trees and earth.

As I push the tent pegs into the ground on one side of the groundsheet, while Elin works the other side, it feels as though we're not alone in this place and that someone might be standing in the spinney spying on us. I look over my shoulder, but see only shadows.

'What's the matter?' she says.

'Nothing.' But once we've spread the flysheet over the tent and tightened the guy-lines, I say: 'I'm just gonna stroll over to the trees and take a pee.'

'Be my guest. I'll unroll our sleeping bags. Wouldn't mind closing my eyes for a few minutes.' She pushes the hair back from her face and she's squinting with tiredness. 'Might have a catnap before we start cooking. Ten minutes'll do. I'm beat.'

There's no one in the spinney. Only trees. I look up into the foliage as I splash the ground at my feet, and think I see someone looking down, but it's just a face of leaves — an optical illusion that reminds me of Kate's Leafy George. Sculpted from the shadows of leaves, I see a face, a nose, an open mouth and a mane of hair that grows out and out until I'm looking at the crown of the tree, and then the face slips away from me.

If the sense of being watched remains though, even as I return to the tent and find

Elin sleeping, there's nothing malevolent about it, and so I lie down too. For what seems like an age, I dream of open spaces and sunlight and oceans of sky; of stones and shadows and trees and earth, and of yesterday and today and . . .

Tomorrow we'll climb Furze Hill and cross Wansdyke. We might follow its route a while, but then we'll carry on to the White Horse hill figure on Milk Hill, the Neolithic camp on Knap Hill and Adam's Grave long barrow on Walkers Hill. This'll bring us to our last mile into Alton Priors, where we'll reluctantly drive away from the footsteps we've followed and return to the uncertainties of our present.

I stir first. My mouth's dry, my throat rasping. Sleep is the easiest sea to drown in. The lapping of dreams against dreams. I struggle awake against the flow, knowing we have to eat, but drowsy with the warmth of the evening, the whispering of the grasses, the comfort of these waters. We're in the proximity of long barrows and sacred circles, magic lines and the echoes of long-forgotten truths. Shivering, I try casting it off.

'Wake up, Elin,' I say, shaking her slightly.

'What time is it, Robinson Crusoe?' she groans.

'Time to wake up. It's almost dark.'

'It's not morning?'

'No.'

'Thought it was.'

'We fell asleep; longer than we meant.'

'Nice though,' she croons. 'Put water on to boil, eh. You make a brew and I'll cook tea.'

'Okay, sleepyhead, it's a deal.'

'Mmm.'

In the last of the day's light, I find dry wood scattered among the trees and start building a real fire; a fire to sit over and feed against the dark uncertainty of night.

Crouching on haunches, with the billy swinging in its own nest of heat, the flames erupt into a beacon of spear-jabbing, dancing brightness and molten darkness, and I glance over my shoulder at the woodland.

Darkness has its own form of shadow. There are shadows among the trees that grow like ivy and mistletoe. Each standing stone is pitted where shadows attach themselves daily, season after season, age after age, creating footholds for lichen. If I stay here forever, I'll be robed in a cloak of shadows too. And yet the fire's brightness creates new folds of darkness, beyond which I'm blind.

Am I a part of this world or apart from it? Familiar or at odds?

But the warmth of the night and the whispering of the grasses and the singing of the fire comfort me into stillness. The night is at bay and I won't be a stranger to it.

'I think I've caught the sun,' I say, as we sit on a log I've rolled into position.

Elin cracks a second egg into the pan and scrapes shell away from several rashers of bacon and the heap of fresh mushrooms. The mushrooms hiss and bubble in their own juices, which trickle into the spitting egg white, turning everything grey-brown.

'You should've worn a hat like I suggested,' and she'd wag a finger if she wasn't busy. 'My, you're a stubborn bugger at times.'

'Yes, Mother. It's mainly my neck and arms. I can still feel the heat there. A hat wouldn't have helped.'

'Like a mule.'

After we've eaten supper, we feed the fire until it swells and its crackling laughter natters with the night, then we stand and dance a few brazen, clumsy steps among the shadows, letting ourselves know there's nothing to fear. And because it's still and we feel strangely euphoric, and because there's few opportunities in a lifetime to do such things, we undress one another as we dance, until we step out of our clothes and dance naked across the dark.

As we dance, my gut tightens into a knot. I ignore it for a few steps but it rises to a lump in my throat, and then, as quickly, transforms into a lightness which spins through my head, disorientating the moment and startling consciousness. I stumble.

A swan's trumpet call and the slow beat of wings. The trees shift and the earth spreads wide and moist.

The grass is wet with evening dew and cold against my back and bum. She lies next to me and I turn, turn, turn to kneel between her legs.

'Yuk,' she says, 'it's wet.'

I roll with her until we've changed position and I'm on my back again, gazing across at a forked tree, which stands sentry in front of the spinney. She's above me, wearing the galaxy like a shell. The moisture is refreshing and welcome now. Now that I'm burning.

She presses up and peers down.

'Are you alright? Your forehead's sweaty.'

'Never better. Just hot, that's all.' Then, remembering, I laugh until I'm giddy and can't hold the silence any longer: 'Babies!' I shout. 'COMING UP!'

'Ssh,' she laughs.

Lying prone, arms spread, I'm a swimmer doing backstroke. These limbs stretch wide across this cool ocean of grass, clawing deep. Splashing out and ripping handfuls of grass with each stroke, I rub them down Elin's back, roll the grass against her thighs, push the bruised wad into the hair where our pubic mounds meet.

'*Mons veneris*,' I say. 'Mound of Venus.'

'What?'

'Nothing.'

She's salty with the sweat from two days walking. Our bodies are earthy, peaty; her hair tastes of wood smoke.

Crying out, she scratches me and, knowing I can't, I groan, 'Hold on!' Looking across at the tree, in one swimmingly long instant I notice everything I've failed to notice before:

In the altar of the shadows, braced wide against his own proportions, stands a phallic tree god: Phallus dei. This god has a penis almost as tall, erect and solid as himself, and he leans back to maintain balance, and leers at us from the corner of one eye. He is timber and stone and fifteen-feet tall. He owns a wooden grin and his teeth are sharpened flint points; he has knots for eyes and a crown of leaves for hair. He is anchored to the earth, who is his mother, but he lusts after the sun and the moon, day and night. His penis is a maypole for the seasons to dance by . . . and there's a figure standing close to him, watching us.

The figure of a woman.

Hold tight to Elin. Mustn't lose myself.

*She's little more than a silhouette, but I
can tell who she is by her stature and the way
she sways her hips slowly to a music only she
can hear, arching her arms above her head
and making a fan of her fingers. She'll have
long chestnut hair and pale skin, and eyes of
glistening burnt umber; her lips will be as full
and glossy as a polished olive, warmer than
sun-baked terracotta at the end of day and
. . . I'll know every inch of her, from her
smile and her sadness to her loganberry
nipples, all the way to her one clear it or is of
life — as she knows me.*

We're still connected.

I almost say her name, but bite on my lip.

*And corn-blonde Elin is wearing a shell,
and Phallus dei stands sentinel, close by, and
gawps and laughs and is rooted to the spot.
And Elin smiles and I come and strangest of
all, don't lose my erection.*

Evening glory.

'Don't go,' I say.

'What?' she says. 'Where?'

The shadows change shape and I lose sight
of Kate, but Elin's closer than ever. She's
deliciously close, straddling the altar she's
turned me into. I'm about to retch, but
breathe deep, until the scent of torn grass fills
my lungs, and then it's alright again.

'Tom, are you alright?'

210

'Never better. Just hot — so hot. Never better.'

'Tell me.'

'What?'

And I fall out of one world into another.

There's a gash in the landscape, out of which I spin. Her womb is moulded from clay and rain, hollowed by the seasons, lined by leaves, baked by the sun; her eyes are the wind singing. Phallus dei sprouts a long tongue, like a white snake, from his flint-toothed grin, and then becomes a tree again.

'Lie still,' a voice says.

I twist beneath her — Elin — and spew into the grass.

'Take a deep breath.'

When the sky stops accelerating and the gash vanishes, Elin's kneeling over me and a fire flickers at the edge of my vision; semen trickles down my thigh and a string of vomit dribbles from my mouth.

' — something you ate,' she's saying. 'Perhaps one of those mushrooms. Or heatstroke. You passed out — fainted. Twice.'

'Think I'm going to be sick again.' And am.

When the craziness has passed, she steers me back to the tent and zips me into a sleeping bag. All I'm left with is a sore head and a pain-wracked stomach and a nervousness about sleeping; little of which stops me from drifting into a sleep which is deep enough to be dream-free, but not immediate enough to purge my memory of events.

In the morning, the headache and stomach pain will be gone, replaced by a huge thirst, but the visions will linger and live on in a peripheral world.

As we pack the tent away, I'll say: 'This is a beautiful spot. I might come out here again sometime and plant a couple of our spruce saplings down in that spinney. It'd be a good spot for them.'

'You can't do that.'

'Why not? We'll never afford a place with a garden big enough to take them. They need to grow somewhere.'

'It is a beautiful spot,' she'll agree.

'I'd like to stay here forever. It's unspoiled.'

'And live off berries and nuts and mushrooms?' she'll tease. 'All tainted by years and years of insecticides, pesticides and herbicides.'

'I'd make an enclosure for animals — goats, poultry, sheep perhaps — and sow a few crops.'

'And reinvent the wheel, then the car, then the motorway?'

'Even so,' I might add.

'Poor Robinson Crusoe. I'll think of you

from afar, and especially during winter. If you're lucky I'll send you a letter or two — by pigeon post, of course — to see how you are, and if you're ready to escape the past.'

'Even so.'

★　★　★

Martin Reynolds is a sneaky shit, but in Class Six we have to do a group project on a foreign country and he teams with Gazza and me. We draw China out of the hat and begin making a plasticine banquet of Chinese food, we copy heaps of notes from two books, make a poster about the Chinese calendar and zodiac (drawing a picture of each year's emblem), and I get the brainwave of making a ceremonial dragon mask using papier mâché.

'Walters has got gold paint in his desk,' Gazza says. 'We'll paint the face gold and red, and have ping-pong balls for eyes.'

'And red crêpe paper coming out the mouth like flames,' I add.

As we work on our pictures representing the Year of the Rat, the Year of the Monkey, the Year of the Rabbit, the scale of our dragon grows bigger.

'We've got an old bedspread in the garage,' Martin Reynolds says. 'We could use that for the body. It's got tassels on it.'

Me: 'We could get some more of those smoke pellets and have clouds of smoke shooting out its nose.'

Martin: 'What smoke pellets?'

Gazza looks at me and I concentrate on tracing the outline of a rat from the encyclopædia.

'Nothing,' I say.

He may be a sneaky shit, but he ain't stupid.

'What are you talking about? Have you got smoke bombs? Tell me.'

'It's nothing,' Gazza says. 'It was something we were talking about, that's all.'

'You did something. I can tell. What did you do?'

'It's a secret,' Gazza says.

'I can keep a secret. We're working on this project together, aren't we?'

It isn't the same. We say nothing.

Then he puts his hand up and calls across the classroom: 'Mr Walters.'

'You say anything and I'll flatten you,' Gazza snarls. He's the shortest of the three of us, but height has sweet nothing to do with the will to scrap and the will to hurt.

'I can keep a secret.'

'You better.'

When Walters gets to our table, he says, 'What's the matter, Martin?'

'Can we make a Chinese dragon and do a parade in front of the class, Sir?'

'That sounds like a bright idea. Who thought that one up?'

He hesitates. 'Gary did, Sir.'

I hope Gazza'll flatten the creep, but Gazza beams and Walters smiles at him the same way he did when he brought the flint side-scraper to school.

'And would we be allowed to make it breathe out smoke, Sir?'

'Not with fireworks, I hope.'

'No, Sir. Gary knows a way of doing it.'

Walters looks at him and raises his eyebrows, the way teachers do. 'Well?'

Gazza pauses, considers, then says: 'Greenhouse fumigators. My uncle's got some.'

'Interesting,' Mr Walters says. 'Make the dragon first and we'll see about the smoke. We'll have to do it in the playground, if we do it at all.'

'Yes, Sir.'

The following Saturday afternoon, we're standing with our backs to a market stall selling cheap china, furtively glancing across at Thorby's Hardware & Garden Supplies. It's like we're planning to rob a bank and I don't want any part of it, but it's my big gob that got us here. At least Martin Reynolds isn't looking so cocky now.

'Tommo, you wait by the seed stand, like you did before, and, Martin, you stand outside.'

'Forget it. I'm not staying outside. I'm coming in with you two.'

'It'll look too obvious if we all go in,' Gazza explains. 'It's not half as busy as it was last time.'

Me: 'I'll stay outside. Someone's gotta.'

Gazza: 'Nah, you're my watch-out, Tommo.'

Martin: 'I can do that.'

Gazza: 'No. Tommo knows what to do. He's done it before.'

And I feel a moment's pride, even if he's only saying it because he doesn't trust Martin Reynolds, who he eventually agrees to let come in with him.

By the time we get into the shop there's just five other customers. Gazza and Martin walk to the back and make a show of looking at lawnmowers, while I stand by one of the seed carousels and pick out a couple of packets. I pretend to read the instruction, as if I'm some pint-sized professional gardener researching the growing techniques for prize nasturtiums.

As Gazza and Martin edge towards the fertilisers and begin studying the insecticides on the shelves above the fumigators, there's something wrong. One of the shopkeepers

216

stops tidying the hose nozzles to watch them. The shop's too empty, too quiet. Maybe the police have been tipped off and there's a whole squad waiting to rush in and arrest us. Should I stroll over to Gazza and tell him, or shout and run?

Gazza and Martin huddle closer and Martin reaches out and slips something into his jacket. The shopkeeper stands upright and begins marching towards them. He puts his hands out to grab them by the collar and I croak: 'Gazza!'

Gazza turns, sees what's happening, ducks the man's arm and runs the length of the shop in two seconds flat. I've never seen him move so fast. Martin Reynolds stands there gawping with his gob wide open, held tight, and so I follow Gazza.

We run down the same side-alley we used before and dash across the car park. Gazza doesn't slow down for me to catch up, so he must be scared big-time, but when he finally stops and, like me, bends double to ease the stitch in his side, I can tell he isn't scared but pissed off. We're back at that same demolition site we found our way to before.

'We made it,' I say, panting for breath, trying to stand upright.

Instead of thanking me for warning him, he snarls, 'Are you bleeding thick or something?'

'What? Why?'

'You called my bloody name out.'

'Oh,' and I crease over again. 'I had to.'

'They got Martin.'

'He was too slow,' I say.

Gazza pauses, takes a deep breath, and his tone changes. 'Yeah, he messed everything up. Talk about bloody obvious. What an amateur. I bet you he gives them our names.'

'You think so?'

'I know so. He'll squeal like a stuck pig. The moment they get a cop there he'll pooh himself.'

'But you didn't take anything.'

'Doesn't matter. I been in trouble too many times.' Gazza bends down, picks up a brick and throws it across the site. 'He'll blab how we took the smoke pellets last time, if only to make us seem like the real trouble-makers. We're in trouble whether we like it or not.'

'Just because he put those pellets in his jacket doesn't mean he was gonna steal them,' I point out. 'Don't they have to wait until you're out the shop before they can nab you? He might have been going to the counter to pay for them. Who's to tell?'

'He will. He'll spill his guts. You're right, they nabbed him too early, but he won't think of that.' Then he looks at me and grins. 'But

218

they didn't get you, did they?'

In my hand are the two packets of seed I was holding when Gazza did his dash.

'Shit,' I say. 'Bloody hell.'

'What are they?'

I read the label on each packet. 'Nasturtiums and tomatoes. These ones are called *Money Maker*.'

And he begins laughing.

'Should we take them back?' I say.

And he laughs louder. We cack ourselves laughing.

'Nasturtiums,' I say.

'Tomatoes!'

When we stop laughing, the packets are still in my hand and nothing's changed.

'What'll I do with them?'

'Get rid of them,' Gazza says.

There's so much rubble and rubbish around, it'd be easy to lose two packets of seed, and I'm about to post them into the cavity between several broken bricks and chunks of concrete, when I have a better idea. Tearing the packets open, I empty all the seed into the palm of my hand, and share this out with Gazza.

'Here,' I say, and begin running round the site like a mad bastard, leaping over broken tiles and bin bags, sprinkling tiny amounts of seed as I go.

'You're crazy,' Gazza shouts, then starts jumping around too.

When I get home, Martin Reynolds' dad has already been on the phone, and Mum and Brian are waiting.

It's easier to play innocent than I'd thought.

'I don't steal,' I shout back. 'I never have done. It was Martin Reynolds who wanted to go into that shop today. Gary and me didn't want to.'

'What about last time?' Brian demands. 'It was just you and Gary Fletcher then.'

'I didn't take anything then either. I've never stolen anything. That's stupid.'

'You stay away from Gary Fletcher,' Mum says. Her voice is thin and sharp, like a knife. 'He's trouble. You're not to play with him, do you hear?'

I stare mutely at an invisible point somewhere between and beyond them. How can they say such a thing? They don't know him.

'Do you hear your mother?' Brian shouts. 'If we hear you're still going around with him, you'll be banned from going out for a month. You'll stay in your room. Do you hear?'

He takes a step in my direction and I sort of nod. But there must be something in my expression he doesn't like, because his voice gets louder and he's all red in the face.

'And if I ever find out you've done something like this again, I'll knock your ruddy block off. I'll knock you from here to Kingdom Come.'

He lifts an arm with the last few words, and I flinch, jump back.

'Mark my words or you'll feel the back of my hand,' he yells.

'You're not my dad,' I say.

My mother reaches me in an instant and side-swipes me across the head, and I go flying, my left ear's ringing.

Brian looks down at me as if I'm dog shit. 'No, I'm not your dad. That's right. And I'm glad of it.'

Which stops everyone mid-breath: me, Mum — even Brian seems surprised by what he's said.

Shouting a string of blubbering abuse at him, at her, at every adult I've ever come across, I run out the room, slamming the door as hard as I can.

The paintings on the wall rattle. The door flies open.

'Come back here,' he shouts. 'This minute.'

'No! I hate you. I hate both of you.'

In my room, I take out the diary bound in black, pretend-leather, which they gave me last Christmas. The novelty of the present inspired me to keep a journal for five days, but then I gave up. It's got a clasp and a small lock for privacy and, though I've lost the key, it isn't hard to pick with one of Annette's hairpins. I grab a pen from my school bag, turn to today's date and write across the page: *BRIAN IS A FUCK-WIT*.

Then I write it on the next page and the next page, and the pages after that: *BRIAN IS A FUCK-WIT*. When I come to the end of the diary, I turn back to the beginning and scrawl it as my entry for 6th January and 7th January and 8th January, filling every page, except for those first five entries. It's a leap year, so I write it three hundred and sixty-one times in total, until I decide to write it twice on the anniversary of my father's death, twice on my birthday, twice on his birthday — until I lose count.

Across the first page of the diary, under the calendar year, I draw some pretend Chinese calligraphy and write: *THE YEAR OF THE FUCK-WIT*. Then I draw a picture of Brian.

★ ★ ★

It's a couple of fuck-wit years later that I'm sitting on the top deck of a bus going to a friend's house and, in passing the demolition site, I see nasturtiums growing over the rubble, across the split bin liners and weeds growing between the broken slabs. Long tendrils of tiny umbrella-like leaves and masses of flowers: yellow, red, orange. Several clumps are dotted across the area. The bus is moving and so I don't get to see if there's tomatoes growing too, but the site's been fenced off so I know no one'll come along and pick them.

A few months after that, the site gets cleared and Northampton's new bus station is built.

Sometimes, as a teenager, when I wait for the Nenford bus to take me home from my Saturday job on the market, or from a party, or a dance, or especially when I'm waiting for Kate's bus from Abetsby, I'll look at the expansion joints in the slabs of concrete and in the mortar lines between the brickwork and half-expect to see a tendril of nasturtiums pushing through or a tomato vine sneaking out.

9

We're making doughnuts and Gazza says: 'When you die your whole life flashes before your eyes.' He talks about the speed of time and about death and dreams.

And so does Kate.

They're regular conversation pieces, are these. Maybe my old man once talked about such things with my mother.

Kate says: 'You know the dream where you're falling off a cliff and, just before you hit the ground, you wake up?'

Morning sunlight floods through her cream curtains, illuminating the yellow wallpaper and its faded pattern of roses, as well as the silhouette of a pot plant or two on her windowsill. At seventeen, the world's brighter and sharper than ever before.

'You had that dream last night?' I say and reach for her hand. She's naked against my skin; her long, chestnut brown hair lies across my white shoulder. To be naked with Kate is a new and delicious nakedness. 'You should've woken me.' Why hadn't she woken me?

'No,' she says. 'I was just thinking about it,

that's all. But you know the one I mean?'

'Yeah.' I relax again, but keep stroking her fingers, tracing the size and shape of each one, remembering how she traced my shape and made me grow to bursting. It's my duty to keep darkness from her door — unless of course I'm that darkness, which is something I won't understand until too much later. I know what she's going to say (about dreams and dying), but I want to hear her say it anyway. I love listening to her speak in English, Italian or French — about her love of Paris, about music, the books she's read, about films she admires, about the sun rising, the moon setting, about anything and everything . . . except why our relationship might be bad news, why a shallow fling would've been better, why it'd be more sane if she never saw me again.

Kate: 'People say that when you dream you're falling off a cliff or whatever, that if you don't wake up before you hit the ground, that's the moment you die.'

Me: 'Yeah.'

Kate: 'Do you believe it?'

Do I believe it? What's the right answer here? Is it a test? Maybe she's had a bad dream after all and the doubts are back, except she's brooding on them instead of letting me know. If I don't say the right thing, she'll know I ain't worthy of her, and then I might lose her forever, which is a bloody long time to be without a Kate, now that we're together, now that I know her, now that I'd know what I've lost. (There are some things in life you never get over losing.) Maybe she's woken to an overwhelming sense of mortality, or maybe this is just trivia we're discussing here and everything's hunky-dory.

'I don't know, Kate,' I say. 'How could anyone prove it? It's just an idea.' These sound like valid comments to me, and she's more logical than me.

'It makes you wonder though.' She isn't frowning, but she isn't smiling either.

I begin feeling clever. What a clever bastard I am these days — she's made me cleverer — and so, so, so, so lucky. Underneath the single sheet and blanket, I have her warm thigh next to mine, her foot stroking mine, the knowledge of her breasts and her loganberry nipples a lick away, the delicious-ness of her neck stretched back for me to kiss and another night of shared sleep between us to make me recklessly, fucking confident.

'It's a philosophical question,' I point out.

She turns and faces me, side on. 'Why? Why's it a philosophical question?'

'Because.'

'Because what? Don't just say *because*. That's lazy.'

'Well, how does anyone know about the nature of death? We imagine what it might be like. We think about it because we're intrigued, but we can't know for sure. We can't, can we, Kate? Not even those people who reckon they've had near-death experiences can really know, can they?'

'We'd be better off asking how we know we're alive?'

'Exactly.'

She blinks, smiles, leans across and kisses me. I don't want the conversation to go much further, because the idea of the vast permanence of death is too scary to comprehend, but I feel we've arrived somewhere new together all the same. She'd hate me to think I have to prove myself to her, but I do, I want to, and in doing that she's made me more alive than ever before. I grow every day I'm with her; I stretch towards her. The world's a big place for us and I know we've got adventures ahead.

Kate reaches for my hand, blows across my fingers and brings them to her lips.

★   ★   ★

Dearest Tom,
    We waved goodbye only ten minutes ago, but I've already started writing this. Is

227

all this too absurd? I want nothing else than to get off at the next station and return to you, but know I mustn't think like this . . .

The Channel crossing was awful and most passengers were hogging the toilets or heaving over the rails. It was vile, but I arrived at Boulogne without disgracing myself . . .

I don't ever want to lose you, Tom. Promise you'll always be there for me. Whatever I do, whatever I say. Promise. How many times have you said you'll love me forever? Whatever happens, please let that be true.

Sorry, I'm being melodramatic — I know I am — but it's because I'm scared of losing you. I wish there was some other way of doing this.

<u>Chez Picault. Evening</u>. I've unpacked and am taking ten minutes to finish this first letter before joining the family for dinner. Monsieur and Madame Picault (Alain and Chantal) have made me very welcome. Obviously, we're all on our best behaviour, but I think I'll be happy here — as happy as I can be. Xavier and Marie-Laure are four and six respectively . . .

★　★　★

Dear Kate,

I'm nothing without you. I'm empty, lost, adrift. Being without you is a death of sorts.

Even though I've just got home from waving you off, I'm counting the days until you return from France. As soon as you let me know when you'll have time off, I'll be counting the days until we meet in Paris, Calais, Boulogne, Vladivostok or Timbuktu if you want — wherever. Let me know as soon as you can.

It rained for a short while after you left; the sky turned black . . .

★ ★ ★

We write every day. Sometimes she can't get to a postbox, so she packs three letters into one envelope, and receiving this makes up for the smothering silence of the days in-between.

It's a summer of endless parties and dances, but I want no pleasure without Kate. And my old friends, bored by my abandonment of them, no longer press me to join them.

I keep the letters in a bundle and read them over and over; a stash of green envelopes tied with a piece of red cord, and almost every letter is written on matching green paper. It's Kate's favourite stationery, which, by way of a farewell gift, I add to before she leaves. The length of red cord comes from the wrapping of a present she hands me at the station: a corn dolly woven into the shape of a figure eight.

'I thought you might like it,' she says, 'because you're into that pre-Christian stuff and because the figure eight symbolises eternity. That's how strong our relationship is.' She's leaning into me, face-to-face, the way lovers sometimes stand in public places to embrace and kiss, in greeting or farewell, and her eyes are red. Her luggage sits to one side. The air is humid. 'You can hang it over your bed and, who knows, you might get lucky and dream me next to you.'

'You got this in Whitby,' I say. We saw them on a craft stall there. 'I didn't see you buy it.'

'I hadn't known what to get until we saw them, and then it seemed perfect. There's an explanation on the label.' She lifts the piece out of its wrappings and twists the card round to show me: 'People believed a corn spirit or goddess lived in the corn and that she made the crop grow each year. At harvest-time she retreated into the uncut corn until only a sheaf was left. So as not to kill her, the harvesters would cut this last sheaf and plait it into a dolly, which would be hung in a sacred place throughout winter. Then, when it was time to plough the ground and sow the first corn in spring, the corn dolly would be ceremoniously ploughed back into the earth so that the spirit could be re-born.'

I tuck it in my pocket, place my hands on her waist. Her magic is stronger than any corn dolly — light and life. 'It's great. I love it. Thanks.'

'It's not much. I wanted to buy you a ring, but couldn't afford it; they're out of my league.'

'A ring? Really?'

'Yeah.'

'This is just as symbolic, Kate.' I hold her left hand out and examine her fingers. 'Would you wear a ring if I bought you one?'

She nods, smiles. 'As long as we both had one. As long as it was an exchange. Would you?'

I nod.

The platform fills and we shift her suitcases and shoulder bag against a pillar to make room for a family heading off on holiday.

'Tell you what, at the end of my first year in London, when you join me and we get a place of our own, we'll bury the corn dolly together somewhere and exchange rings with one another. We'll create our own ceremony.'

231

'It's gonna be a long winter,' I say.

'But we'll see one another every few weeks.'

'And we'll meet up in Paris as soon as you say.'

'I'll write every day,' she says.

'I'll have to study flat-out next year.'

'There's bound to be a good History course.'

'We'll walk to lectures together in the morning, meet for lunch, go to galleries at the weekend, see bands and concerts . . .'

* * *

Dear Kate,

Is everything okay? Haven't heard from you in four days. At night I can't sleep — it's like a choking darkness presses down — and it's because I'm without you . . .

* * *

Dearest Tom,

I'm sorry for the delay in posting this, but I've tried completing this letter several times, and have screwed up each pathetic attempt. I've been sick too, which isn't like me, and I think it's because I've been so worried about how unhappy this will make you.

When I asked Chantal about having a few days off, she was bemused at first, but became almost hysterical when I insisted. She understood, she said, that I'd be with the family (as a member of the family, she emphasised) for the entire three months — every day — and that they'd rented a gîte in Brittany for a fortnight in a week's time. She said she was happy for me to take an occasional half-day, as long as I arranged it with her first, but that the whole idea of having an au pair was to have a full-time companion and carer for the children and to give her a break. Hadn't this been explained to me when I took the position? What was I thinking of? How could I suggest such a thing?

I told her it hadn't been explained that way, Tom, and I tried telling her about our plans, but she was practically shouting at me — the spoilt bitch — and I was getting emotional myself, which meant I couldn't express myself the way I needed to.

I can't tell you how much I've cried over trying to write this letter. If they hadn't been as generous in other ways and if I didn't think it might reflect badly on Angie Taylor, I'd have told Chantal she could shove her job where the sun don't shine! But then, what chance would I have of finding another job now?

Tom, I know how upset you'll be when you read this, but please know that I love you more than ever. I wish I could tell you these three words face-to-face: I love you. The written word is too inadequate, but there's enough between us for you to know how much I mean it. I'd say come to Paris for a half-day, for an hour, and I know you would; however, I can't think of anything worse than seeing you for a short time and then having to say goodbye again . . .

★ ★ ★

My letters to Kate grow bleaker and I foist my darkness upon her. Stupid, stupid, stupid!

★ ★ ★

Dear Tom,

Arrived back in Paris three days ago. Hope you got my postcards. Alain and Chantal have been very kind recently. They thought I was getting tired and bored, so arranged for me to meet people my own age. Jean-Paul (the son of one of Alain's colleagues), Stefan and Sylvie took me to a carnival and a nightclub. I felt guilty going without you, but it was good to let my hair

234

down, even though I drank more than I should, and my conversational French is now probably better than it was. Being with children all the time is exhausting, Tom.

Even if I tried to stop loving you, I wouldn't be able to. I'm not sure how that makes me feel. It's as you said, we seem to be tied together in so many ways that, when we're apart, it's hard not to think about each other almost every minute and feel more incomplete with each day that passes. Is this a healthy thing though? It seems wrong, if not self-defeating, and I want you to promise that you'll still go out, meet up with friends, and not simply 'cross the days off the calendar until we're next together.' I can't stand thinking of you locking yourself away because I'm not there. It's not healthy. Life's for living, remember. I need to do this myself, otherwise I know I'll be sick again (I still have a hacking cough). I can't bear to be so unhappy all the time, nor to suspect that we might be expecting it of one another. So on Saturday I'm going to a party. I'll probably be miserable without you, but I need to do those things again that make me feel I'm actually alive.

Oh, Tom, maybe you're right; maybe we should find a way to stay together this year, no matter what. Life's too short to regret being apart . . .

★ ★ ★

Dear Tom,
    Alain and Chantal have asked me to stay an extra week. This will mean that I won't have time to return to Abetsby before starting uni. It'll be the middle of the week and you'll have started school by then, so my parents are going to meet me in London on my way back from France and bring all the stuff I need down with them; I'll move into Halls of Residence straightaway and begin getting settled. I know you'll hate this idea, but it'll probably be less upsetting than meeting up for the evening only to say goodbye again, and a lot less tiring too . . .

★ ★ ★

Dear Kate,
    No. No, no, no . . .

★ ★ ★

I hear nothing for a fortnight. Write letter after letter, trying to change her mind. Dark letters.

236

Dear Tom,

I agree, we should meet — it's been too long. Unless I hear otherwise from you, meet me in Euston Station next Thursday at 11:00 am by the main entrance.

Kate

★ ★ ★

It's a day towards the end of September when I finally lose Kate. It's early autumn, but autumn's arrived early so it feels like mid-autumn. Winter's breathing down everyone's neck. I skip school to catch the London train, but there's no pleasure in the journey.

Although the carriages are dragged slowly past the new sprawling housing estates between Northampton and Nenford, where the last fields of my childhood are being bulldozed, we rush through the remaining rural vestiges of the Home Counties (halting a minute opposite the fibre glass statues of cows near Milton Keynes) before hitting the sprawl of London at Watford. There's too little left in-between. I know I'm travelling to my own dying, but cling to a stupid belief in the last minute reprieve.

I haven't thought about Old Lofty, that

237

Angel of Death, since I can't remember when. He's the bogey-man of a childhood, which, thanks to Kate, I've moved far beyond. On this day though I realise he'd returned in the guise of the postman who delivered the last of her letters, and I know he's the driver of this train. He's fucking with me in the same way he tries fucking with almost everyone at some time or another. I smell him in the stink of diesel, recognise his reflection in the dirty windows, see his hand in the destruction of every hedgerow; know his bony fingers are pressing around my throat.

Euston is crowded and I almost walk past her.

'You're late,' she says.

'The train was slow,' I say. Why should I apologise? I've travelled seventy miles for this death.

'You didn't recognise me.'

She's ghost-like; pale, thin, gaunt.

'Aren't you well, Kate?'

'We have to talk,' she says. 'Over here.'

We sit outside the station on a concrete bench spattered with pigeon droppings. A few yards away, a slip road leads to a taxi drop-off point and a constant stream of black London cabs drives past us — cab after cab after cab. Across the road, a building site is partitioned off from traffic and pedestrians with plywood panels, scaffolding, tarpaulins and planking; beyond it the hammer of pneumatic drills and generators all but drowns the noise of cranes and concrete mixers. It's the dullest of days, as it has to be — a day of concrete, glass and petrol fumes; polystyrene beakers and plastic bottles discarded in dead flowerbeds. Too difficult to distinguish between sagging clouds and rising smog. And Kate tells me how everything between us is finished because she has no choice but to finish it.

'I can't live the way we have been, these last few months. It's tearing me apart, like living two lives: one for you and one for me, neither of them honest. And struggling to remain true to something that doesn't exist anymore. Not for me, not now. It can't. I'm different — no longer the person you knew. We have to move on — both of us, on our own — begin to live again.'

'It does exist,' I tell her. 'I am alive. I felt alive. Alright? We . . . ' She's vanishing in front of my eyes. She's made herself ill, almost incorporeal, and she's vanishing. There's nothing to clutch to. Her eyes are red-rimmed.

'It has to be this way. There's no choice.'

'Why?'

'You mustn't make this difficult, Tom. It's

hard enough as it is. I'll just walk away if you do.'

'No. Why?'

'And you must see it the way I see it, for both our sakes, Tom. I can't live this way anymore. It's making me ill. It's self-destructive. Look how sick I've been. I've lost weight, I keep running temperatures.'

'But why?'

'We'll remain friends if you make this easy on us. We'll remain friends. We'll keep in touch. That's what I'd like. That's how I hope you'll want it to be.'

There's nothing left. I shake my head.

'Everything has its time, Tom. I thought we'd last forever, but I was wrong. We were both wrong. We've had our time. It's time to move on.'

'But — '

'There's no going back. We can't turn this clock back. It's over.'

'No.'

She stands up, looks down at her feet as if they might know where to go next, and then sits down again. 'I feel — I realise I'm too young — we're too young — '

'Too young? Too young for what?'

'Too young to decide to only be with one person. We've got the rest of our lives in front of us. I want to experience life, not make all my decisions when I'm only eighteen. It's too soon.'

'Well, you're nineteen next week. I've got a present for you.'

'It's too soon.'

'We can experience life together. We said we would. We'll make decisions together — live life together. I love you. You're the one I want to do all that stuff with. What does age matter?'

'I can't explain it any better. It's the way I feel now. It's the person I've become. I've changed. I'm not the person you loved anymore.'

'Of course you are. That's for me to know.'

'We haven't seen each other in — '

'I still feel the same way about you.'

She looks down at the ground. 'Well, that's it, isn't it? I no longer feel the same about you. I'm sorry.'

Then she stands and I stand, and she takes a step away from me.

'Don't make it difficult, Tom. I haven't slept all night. I'll walk away.'

'I don't understand,' I say, only half-hearing. How have I made her afraid of me? I'll do anything for her. Anything. Even this.

'Let me go, Tom.'

I've no idea what I've done. It'll take an age or two, and experience, which'll shift me further and further from her, before I'll begin to understand how I let this happen and what I might've done to prevent it.

'You'll be okay,' she tells me. 'You'll see.'

'Yeah.' She has no idea.

'Do you want to go for a coffee and a bite to eat? You don't look too good either, you know. We've made ourselves sick. I'm going to meet some people I share Halls with. You can join us.'

'Food? A drink? No, I don't think so. Not with other people. I think I need to go. I need to go. Be somewhere else.'

'Yes. Okay. But you won't do anything silly? I'll still worry about you, you know.'

She's thinking about my father. That I'll hang myself from the nearest tree, nail myself to the nearest cross.

I grunt.

'I mean it,' she says. 'Tell me you won't.'

'Do me a favour.'

'Promise me that one thing, Tom. Please.'

Who does she think I am?

★　★　★

We share the same compartment back to Northampton, my Angel of Death and I. His stony smile grips and wrenches my guts as he perches on the edge of the seat opposite,

242

round-shouldered, hunched forwards — the habitual posture of every gargoyle. His eyes are fathomless holes that try penetrating my thoughts; his legs are tightly crossed, the bollocks-less bastard, and his hands are clasped across his knees one moment and are then held up to his jutting jaw in a parody of prayer. I don't need to see him to know he's there, nor to know how sodding pleased he is with his work. We travel in silence.

Staring at the handle of the carriage door and the blur of tracks — a moment's work to exit — I wait for him to say: 'Told you so.' But Old Lofty's smarter than that. What's death without foreplay?

He renews our relationship that day and becomes my closest companion for an age or two. Indeed, there's cold erotic comfort when, in Kate's absence, he wraps his fingers around my throat and presses gently, and when, his tail around my leg, he lies with me at night.

Without Kate, I can't avoid betraying myself.

It's the middle of winter — winter solstice, that is — when I next see her; almost three months since Euston Station and a year since that New Year's Eve party. The bleakest part of the season is yet to inflict itself. I've travelled to this party in Abetsby on the flimsiest of invitations and with the notion that someone here might've kept in touch with Kate; and they'll tell me how she talks about me all the time. Can't stop talking about me.

Clinging to her promise that we'll remain friends, I wrote at the beginning of October, the beginning of November, the beginning of December, but Old Lofty, jealous bastard that he is, steals every letter she's mailed in return. I posted my Christmas cards early in the hope she might choose this occasion to reply and knock on my door again, but nothing's sacred anymore.

It's the shortest day of the year (surrounded by the longest nights) and I've been at the party for an hour, pickling my sorrows instead of drowning them. We meet in the hallway and she's holding the hand of a foreign-looking guy with a short, black beard.

'Hello, Tom.' Her hair is up — formal — and she's wearing an evening dress.

'My God! Kate! Shit. It's you. Sorry. Hello, Kate. It is you, isn't it?'

This is it, the absolute proof. Can't she see our worlds are destined to overlap against every improbability? One syzygy after another.

There's too much I want to say and need to say.

'You're smoking again,' she observes.

'Life's for living,' I remind her and take a deep drag, then laugh. She'll appreciate the wit.

When she introduces the Spaniard and gives him the name — 'Tom, this is my boyfriend, Jesus. He's on an exchange programme from Spain. Jesus, this is Thomas, an old friend of mine' — I laugh again and know I'm done for.

'You here for the millennium?' I ask.

Kate glares, but Jesus offers his hand.

'I study the Biochemistry in Kate's university. London. This is very good place we meet.' His accent is warm, lyrical, enriched by a Mediterranean sun; Moorish delight.

'How nice,' I say, taking his hand, turning it. 'Be careful, Kate, this bloke's an impostor. No stigmata. Never been nailed to a cross in his life. Not the hands of a carpenter, nor a fisherman. Definitely not the real thing.'

'Go easy on the booze, Thomas,' she says, directing Jesus into a room swimming with dancers.

'Can we talk, Kate? Please.'

'You're pissed.'

'He's not the real thing,' I mutter to her back. 'Coke's the real thing. And it's Tom, not Thomas!'

245

Where's the Kate I've known? Where am I? We've both vanished.

Grabbing a bottle, the first couple of swigs inspire a noble idea: I'll apologise and tell her I'm leaving the party so as not to embarrass her or spoil her fun. She can dance to her heart's delight with the Spaniard. She'll appreciate my generosity and find it impossible not to love me again.

When I look for her though, someone tells me she and the Spaniard have already left. Didn't even take their coats off.

'Should have thrown him to the fucking lions,' I mumble, making my way to the bar in the kitchen. 'Crucify the bastard.'

So it's me who stays at the party, determined to drink myself stupid — more stupid — until a half-familiar figure sidles up with an alternative proposition. He offers me a magic tab of acid in exchange for the contents of my wallet.

'Magic?' I say.

'You bet,' he promises, plucking a white rabbit from a tiny plastic bag. 'This is a ticket onto the Magic Bus.'

'Which is heading the fuck where tonight?'

'Wherever you want. The land of your dreams.'

'It'll have to be a fucking long way from this hole.'

I open my mouth and drop the ticket in.

'All aboard the Dream Bus,' he calls, and I sail away.

Standing by a window, I press my head against the glass, but it doesn't take long for the bus to be hijacked and, if I care to focus, I know who I'll find at the wheel.

His timing stinks.

'Not tonight, Lofty, you evil fuck,' I say, but it's probably a drawl or a shout. 'I wanna find Kate.'

'You alright?' someone asks. 'I think you've had enough. I'd lay off the booze if I were you.'

'No more,' I say. 'Enough.'

'Good idea.'

'Rather walk. Don't wanna be on this bus.'

'Whatever you say.'

And they leave me to walk round the house, from room to room to room, hoping she might return and that I might find her.

In one room, in the centre of a lonely expanse of beige wall, hangs a large Bruegel print of a peasant walking, and it seems we've something in common, especially when he starts walking on the spot. 'I know you, don't I?' I say, peering at his sharp, angular features.

He turns his head to smile and I close my eyes, but when I open them blood starts running down the wall from where the

247

picture hook is nailed, and I escape into the kitchen.

I duck my head under the tap and drink; pooling water on the floor.

'Easy,' someone says.

'Easy,' I agree.

But from behind every cabinet edge and every socket and every tile, a line of blood begins seeping — weeping from viscera, a viscous crimson swelling to a trickle. If the glass on the bus wasn't so thick, there'd be screams, and I guess it's time to leave.

With enough loose change in my pocket to snatch a bus ride almost to Northampton, I stumble the last few miles home on foot, shouting at the traffic from the middle of the road. The world is shit and life is shit. There's nothing spectacular about the shooting star dying across the sky, nor the frost patterns spawning across the front of my trench coat; it's a mistake to acknowledge the poetry in life. Stupid.

By the time I clamber into bed, I reckon the trip's over; it's gotta be. What a waste. But the moment I close my eyes several gargoyle faces move in and start pressing down. Snapping my eyes open, I sit up and rub my face. The sound of Andrew breathing a few feet away is a comfort and I wish he was louder.

After a couple of minutes, I try again, but the demons return immediately, waiting to collect. But I'm fucked if I'll deliver.

'Shit.'

I'm stuffed, but there's no way I'm closing my eyes with hell building across the backblocks of my mind.

I try to make out Andrew's sleeping figure in the dark room, and refuse to think about blood spilling from walls, and how this must always be happening but can only be seen at moments of heightened awareness. This is when a gargoyle face drifts in from a corner of the darkness, and then another and another and another. I try opening my eyes wider, but it makes no difference.

'Fuck off,' I say, and Andrew stirs in his sleep. 'Shut up and fuck the hell off.'

I shut my eyes and the faces disappear . . . for a second or two. Snap them open to an empty room, and it stays that way a few seconds . . . until darkness takes shape again and again and again: demons laughing in silence, sneaking closer.

Shut.

Open.

Shut.

Open.

Shutting and opening for ten blinking minutes, until I'm too beat to care about

249

sleeping with demons or not, and scared senseless about not waking again.

Old Lofty comes courting that night. He wants to make amends. I half-wake to find him sitting on the edge of the bed, whispering love words, still wearing the bus driver's cap and the minister's black vest and white collar, smelling of damp stone and mildew.

'I'm here,' he says. 'Let me in.'

'Piss off,' I shout, lashing out with a clenched fist. My hand crumples as it connects with the cold stone of his face, but I pummel at his beak of a nose until I'm sure I've done damage. When I stop, I cry out, because it's not Old Lofty at all, but Kate.

'Kate!'

'It's alright,' she says. 'It wasn't me. He stole you from me. I'm back now though.'

'Forever?'

'Forever and ever. I'll never lose you again. We have to be together. You promised you'd never give up on me, no matter what. You promised.'

'Amen.'

We tumble into making love, and it doesn't matter that Andrew's sleeping a few feet away, nor that Mum and Brian are in the next room. It doesn't even matter when our love-making loses its gentleness and becomes brutal, ferocious, and more to do with martyrdom and possession than love — until I recognise the incongruity of this.

'Kate?' I say, squinting through the dark at my empty pillow, and discover it hasn't been her at all. She's long gone. And the incubus is slinking off too. Bastard!

In the late morning, when I stir, I'm raw from fucking with granite. There's blood on the wall and my knuckles are split open; there's blood on the sheets and my prick stings when I try sitting up. I pull the sheets to my chin, and they smell of damp stone and mildew.

If I could dig my way out of here I would, and so I shut my eyes to dream of sleep.

10

I haven't allowed enough time to get to Abetsby. I know it. Stupid! Drum the steering wheel, ride the clutch. Crappy little hire car — no, the car's fine. Northampton's a snarl though; a snarl of Christmas shoppers, delivery lorries and office workers dragging themselves between mid-morning piss-up parties, and the one-way maze is a trap — a fucking labyrinth of traffic lights, designated lanes, roundabouts . . .

At the roundabout by the hospital, I'm forced to stay in the wrong lane by a taxi and the queue of cars behind. I'll be late if I miss this turn and have to crawl through the town centre all over again, so I indicate right, but the traffic bunches tighter, bumper-to-bumper, and the drivers stare straight ahead, pretending they can't see me. All I can do is inch forward into straddling two lanes and hold this position until the driver of a van hits his horn, waves his arms at me as if I'm the lowest form of life and lets me pull over. The car behind flashes its headlights.

Smiling through gritted teeth, I mouth my

gratitude back at him, windscreen-to-windscreen: 'Fuck you very much!'

Passing the hospital entrance, there's no guilt at not stopping. I'll call on my way back this afternoon.

After a twenty-minute journey across a million tons of concrete and bitumen, through a landscape that's no longer recognisable, I reach Abetsby, but that's almost the end of my story. Turning from a junction, an oncoming coach almost collects me side-on. Spam jam. The driver swerves, hits the horn and sticks a finger up. He slides open his window and shouts, 'Learn to drive, moron!'

Shit, why am I doing this? Is it only to know that Kate's alright? Is it really out of concern for her, or is it all for me? Is there any part I can claim I'm doing for Elin? And what if I'm mixing something up that'll never settle again? Am I dreaming that Kate needs to be saved, simply because I want her to save me yet again? And if so, from what? Mundane middle-age? Ennui? The loss of youth? The absence of something more poetic and lyrical? The acceptance that all love is finite, without even dust and ashes left behind?

Has love aged gracelessly into obsession? Can we honestly say there's ever a distinction between the two? Is this what Kate recognised in me and escaped from all those years ago?

Life's for living, I remind myself, but what does that justify? Anything and everything? Perhaps there's no one answer.

After starting off late, I arrive early. Too early to knock on the door, too awkward to park outside and wait, I drive down the street and leave the car close to the main road, then dawdle towards the house. My feet are silent on the pavement, and I miss the happy clatter they once kicked up along this very street.

The first thing I notice is that the old factory has a vinyl banner hanging along the wall, over where the *KETCHELL SHOES* sign once was. The banner reads: *DISCOUNT FURNITURE WAREHOUSE SALE NOW ON*. The second thing I notice is that the trees, which are leafless, haven't been pollarded in several years; they're full-crowned, which would be sure to make Kate happy. The third thing I notice are the corbel stones above each porch: a sheaf of corn, a fish swimming, a bird flying, a torch . . .

'She's made a cake for you,' Kate said. 'It'll be alright.'

Relax, relax, relax. But I'm still not sure what I'm going to say.

Their front door has an elaborate holly wreath mounted above the letterbox. I haven't seen real holly like this in years. I knock at the door and wait.

And wait.

There's no answer, no sound within.

I knock again and the knock echoes back at me from an empty and hollow house. It's a minute to eleven. Perhaps they've decided not to see me. Perhaps they moved years ago and I've got something wrong in all of this. Then I hear footsteps on the stairs and a shadow approaches the glass of the front door.

'Tom Passmore,' I say to her dad, holding my hand out. 'Thanks for letting me call.'

'Come in,' he says, and directs me down the hall.

'Thanks. Thank you.'

I recognise the smell of the house after all these years, and there's something hopeful in this: the yeasty smell of home brew, the gas fire, a scented laundry powder or fabric conditioner. But how is it these things can still be the same?

'You best give me your coat and sit yourself down,' her dad says. He points to a chair close to the heater.

I give him my coat, but remain standing.

Like the hallway, the living room is festooned with Christmas decorations: ribbons of red and yellow crêpe paper plaited together, twists of tinsel, paper bells and

255

coloured lights. There'll be a Christmas tree in the front room.

Her mum comes through from the kitchen and says: 'Hello, Tom.'

'Hello, Mrs Hainley. It's good to see you again.'

'So you live in Australia now?'

'Yes.'

'And you have a family?'

'That's right. Elin, my wife, teaches at the local primary school. We have a son, Daniel, and two girls, Tamsin and Elspeth.'

'Ah,' she says and smiles. 'And they came with you, did they?'

'No, it was a last minute thing. Everything happened in a rush.'

'I see.'

'You're looking well. You're both looking well.'

'You'd probably like a hot drink. It's bitter outside. I'll put the kettle on. Will you have tea or coffee, Tom?' She places a hand on my arm as she says this, and I remember how she made me realise years ago that not all mothers are the same.

'Whatever you're having,' I say. 'Don't make anything on my account.'

'It's time for our elevenses.'

Mr Hainley returns from hanging my coat somewhere and I wait until he's seated.

'How are you both?'

'We can't complain,' he says.

'Wouldn't be much point,' she adds, standing in the doorway to the kitchen. 'Good health's a blessing, don't you think? To be healthy and happy. We're very lucky. And you, Tom? How are you? Apart from being worried about your mother, of course.'

'Good, but jetlagged. My body clock's all over the place. I keep expecting to look out the window and see a bright summer's day. But apart from that, I'm good.'

'And the flight? How was your flight? It must take a few hours to fly from one side of the world to the other.'

'Twenty-three. But it wasn't too bad. I slept a lot — I think.'

The kettle whistle blows and Kate's dad says, 'That was quick.'

'I boiled it earlier,' she tells him. 'How do you like your coffee, dear?'

'White; one sugar please.'

Mr Hainley leans forward. 'It's been a long while. A very long while.'

The past has been my shadow all my life. I've sought my connection to it without fully realising that it's always been attached and trailing along wherever I've gone. It shapes the way we walk through life.

Why do I realise that now?

Before I can stop myself, I say: 'Twenty years or so since I was here last.'

He nods and sits back.

'Seems like yesterday though,' I add. 'Of course, I met Kate a few times in London, when she was at university.'

'Ah.'

There's the clink of a spoon against a porcelain cup, the rattle of a tin. Close to, the gas fire hisses, and I avoid fully remembering lying in front of it with Kate by counting the Christmas cards on the string above their mantelpiece. Eighteen. Surely one's from her?

'Here you go, Tom,' her mum says. 'Help yourself to a biscuit.'

'Be a devil and take two,' her dad says.

There's a silence that beats two moments too long and sucks me unaccountably forward until I'm spilling all my questions at once: 'How is Kate? Is she okay? I thought I might drop her a line for old times' sake. Where does she live these days? What does she do? Perhaps you could give me her address?' And I'm probably the most surprised of the three of us.

Her dad sighs and her mum puts her cup down.

'Why?' he says.

'Is she well? How's she doing?'

They pause and look at one another and I fear the worst: she died shortly after I last saw her and I've spent years mourning the wrong kind of loss; or she misinterpreted my reason for abandoning her when we'd begun getting close to one another again and has spent her life despising me.

The gas fire hisses. The clock ticks.

'She's fine,' her mum says. 'She'd want us to give you her regards if she knew you were here.'

'Really?' I say. 'Thanks. That's nice.' But it's not enough. Not now I've come this far. Regards aren't big enough to span twenty years and link two people who once touched one another and danced to the same song. The last few days have left me needing more. If I create a silence vacuous enough then maybe they'll fill it.

The clock on the sideboard ticks, the gas fire hisses.

Mr Hainley leans forward in his chair. 'What were you hoping for, Tom?'

'How is she? Is she well? Is she happy? Does she ever . . . ' I look at the clock, I look at the gas fire. 'I mean, does she have a family of her own and what does she do and where does she live? I always imagined she'd end up living abroad somewhere — on the continent.'

Her mum turns her mug. 'No, she doesn't live abroad.'

'Not London? She didn't stay in London? I'd have thought she'd have had enough of London?'

'No, not London. She could never stomach the pace. And so expensive.'

'So, what's she doing with herself these days?'

The coffee cup goes down again and it's her mum's turn to lean forward. 'Don't you think the past is sometimes best left alone, love? Let sleeping dogs lie, eh, for both your sakes.'

'I just want to know she's okay.'

'She is.'

'Will you be speaking with her anytime soon? On the phone perhaps?'

'Why?'

'Will you let her know I was here? Please.' I take a breath. Among the crêpe paper decorations and the balloons, there are garlands of red-berried holly above the doors and a sprig of mistletoe hanging from the ceiling. 'And tell her I asked to see her, if she wants to, just to catch up for old time's sake. I'm not in Britain for long.'

For auld lang syne.

Her father opens his mouth, but then shuts it again. Her mother says: 'How old are your children, Tom? Did you say it's three children you've got? And your wife, is she Australian?'

I lift my cup to drain my coffee, but it's all gone. And I want to see what time my watch says, but I resist.

★ ★ ★

The moment the doors to the ward close behind me, the heat stifles my breath. It's an airless place this hospital, and I'm annoyed no one's considered it might actually be killing its patients.

'You don't look well,' my mother says.

'Thanks,' I say. 'You're looking fine.'

'You can't bury me yet,' she replies, a tad too loud.

The woman in the next bed glares from her one unbandaged eye, as if I'd wished my mother dead . . . which I might have done at times, but not today.

'I can see that.' And I raise my voice too. 'As I said, you're looking a lot better. It's good to see.'

She's got more colour to her face, her hair isn't as limp; there's an edge of mischief to her voice. She's better and I'm worse. The jetlag is dragging me down. And the sense too that I'm trailing something alongside me; something I can't identify and

261

something I can't shake. I'm tired, but far beyond sleep.

'I feel better,' she says.

'Good.'

'Heaven knows why. The way they're treating me, you'd think they're trying to finish me off so they can give the bed to another customer.'

I imagine a nurse being rough with a needle or an auxiliary dropping her into a wheelchair. 'What happened?'

'Today's lunch. I wouldn't feed it to a dog. In fact it probably was dog. Maybe they've got one of those foreign cooks.'

I wince. 'So, you didn't eat lunch?'

'I had lunch. I sent the first tray back though. Disgusting. Even during the war we did better than that. Why they give these people jobs in the first place, I'll never understand. It might be okay in their country, but . . . '

There are ways of not listening to this. I try closing my eyes. The world tilts a little.

'You tired?'

'A little.'

'You don't have to come and sit here, you know.'

'I know.'

She motions for me to close the curtain that separates her from her one-eyed neighbour. 'Makes me feel like I'm on public display,' she pretends to whisper. And then, when I'm seated again, she says: 'I appreciate you coming, Thomas. Really. It must have taken some organising. And so close to Christmas too.'

'That's alright.'

A woman coughs. A telephone rings.

'Things haven't always been easy between us, have they?'

The question stops me. For a moment I hold my breath, then shrug and try smiling, but end up looking at the bump in her bedding where her feet are. It's one thing wanting all your life to have your mother be honest and to clear the air, yet quite another to face it.

'But we were very close once, you and I, Thomas, when you were little,' she adds. 'We used to have a great time together. You were such a funny little boy.'

I nod.

'Do you remember?'

I shake my head. 'No, I don't think I do.'

'I didn't think you did. That's a pity. Sometimes we forget the wrong things.' She closes her eyes, then opens them a few seconds later. 'It's a pity we want to remember the bad things in life rather than the good. That's human nature, I suppose. We all do it, even when we try not to.' She pauses, as if expecting me to agree or disagree, but I say nothing. 'Parents sometimes make their biggest mistakes trying to do what's right for their children.'

'Perhaps. I've always found it's important to listen and be open. Listening and wanting to understand — nothing's worth a damn without that.'

'But we did have good times together, Thomas. You mustn't forget that.'

I want to be generous here. 'I remember when you baked cakes; you'd sometimes get me to help. It was always a treat to lick the bowl.'

'Did I? I thought that was Andrew.'

'It was probably all three of us.'

'Probably. Do you remember the picnics we used to go on, down by the river? Or how you always wanted me to play with those toy animals and soldiers you collected? We built a big farm once under the dining table. You insisted on having dinosaurs among the cows and sheep. It made me laugh. Do you remember?'

'Vaguely.'

'Like I said, you only remember — '

'That was stuff before Dad died. What about after?'

For once she doesn't purse her lips, but she

stares at me and through me. Even though tiredness is weighing me down, I hold her gaze in a way I wouldn't have been able to once. The heaviness in my head makes it easier.

'I was sorry you emigrated to Australia,' she eventually says. 'It would've been nice to see my grandchildren grow up.'

'We never saw one another much when we lived only a hundred miles away.'

'It was always possible though. We could have done. Being on the other side of the world though — '

'We could've done,' I point out, 'but we never did.'

She leans awkwardly to one side and tugs at her pillow, and I move to help her but she waves me off. 'I can manage,' she says. Then, once she's settled again: 'I felt like I lost you when you emigrated.'

I want to say: you already had, years before. Instead I say: 'You could always fly out and visit us. It's not that far. Not really. We'd collect you from the airport.'

'Too far. It felt like I lost you all over again.'

'Then it would've been nice if you'd said something.'

'Would you have changed your mind?'

'No, I doubt it, but it would've made a

difference. It might've helped.'

'It was too late by then. Way too late.'

'It's never too late,' I say.

She huffs. 'That's a lie. It's been too late for too long.'

I shake my head. I don't want any bite of her bitterness. She's welcome to it.

'Things have always been different with Annette and Andrew,' she continues.

'Very likely,' I say.

'Always. When they were born I realised what an odd little fellow you were. Quite the odd one out.' She stops and seems to be thinking of something else. 'But we can't change the past, can we?'

'No.' I shake my head again, but my eyes are too heavy in this heat, and I hear the ocean slapping across the beach, or the traction of tyres on a wet road.

'You're not much company,' I hear her say.

★ ★ ★

Little has changed about the evening news on TV when I find myself sitting down in front of it. It's the usual stuff about unemployment, environmental disasters, car accidents, crime and terrorist threats. When the phone rings, I automatically look at my watch, and the hands are still sticking.

Nine-twenty. It'd have to be about eight o'clock and, although I haven't eaten yet and can't remember the last time I ate — not properly, like a meal rather than fast food shit — I'm not hungry. I think I've forgotten the taste of food. There's a glass of whisky in my hand, but I don't recall pouring it or sipping from it. I move towards the phone, expecting it to be Elin, but then it stops.

A couple of minutes later, it begins ringing again and this time I pick it up.

'Hello,' I say, 'Tom speaking.'

There's nothing at the other end. The line isn't dead, but whoever's there isn't saying anything.

And because it might be one of my mother's cronies ringing, I add: 'Margaret Taylor's phone.'

Still no response.

I wait, and listen hard. Maybe Elspeth's phoned and has muted the microphone by mistake.

'Hello,' I say. 'Elspeth?'

All I hear is the crackle and rustle of a distorted line. It's the flurry of dry leaves or the rolling of distant surf. Then the receiver's returned, ending the call, and the house is emptier because of it.

Perhaps it was Kate. Perhaps her parents

phoned her, let her know I'd visited, and what I'd said. Maybe she'd decided to call, and then lost her nerve.

If it's Elin she'll phone again, but no one does.

11

Someone's let off smoke bombs, the little buggers, and there's a gargoyle standing over me. His eyes are empty pits, his beak cranes forward, his teeth are shards of flint, his breath stinks.

Sleep. Let me sleep. Let me drift with the flow of a rising tide.

★　★　★

School's behind me and I shift to London to study History at uni. I move into Stoneyfields Halls of Residence and Old Lofty tags along as my roommate. He takes up fuck-all space and his presence is as reassuring as a dirty old habit.

In part, I'm in London to paddle after the memory of Kate. I know I am. I'm carried here on the notion that somehow, among seven million bobbing people, I'll drift into her at least once. When that happens, she'll haul me in and give me the kiss of life again, and I'll be able to give Lofty the flick. She'll save me from the worst of myself. She'll realise then, for all time, how such love conquers all things — *amor vincit omnia*. The vague hope that this might happen becomes my buoy, enabling me to bob up and down too, scanning the horizon, drifting further and further out.

'This place seems alright,' Mum says outside Stoneyfields — a maze of pathways and small lawns between brown brick buildings, each house containing twelve rooms in glorious breezeblock grey.

'It's fine,' I reply. Two cases and a couple of boxes sit in the middle of my room, along with the keys to this new beginning.

Andrew and Annette are back in the car and Brian's standing at the open driver's door, his hand on the steering wheel.

'You don't mind if we head home then? Leave you to get on with it?'

I shake my head. 'There's nothing else you can do. I'll unpack, have a look around, get to know a few people.'

'Sounds like you'll have fun,' she says.

'We'll ring when we get home,' Brian calls and turns the ignition.

'I'm gonna shift your bed over,' Andrew shouts. 'Mum said I could. It's my room now.'

'It's all yours. You can have it.' Then I lean through the open back window and whisper: 'It's haunted anyway.'

But the ghosts are of my own making and I've brought them with me. We're a circus, my ghosts and I, and the ringmaster lives at my side.

★ ★ ★

All the same, I'm almost right about Kate and it's not long before I come close to finding her again.

In the week before Christmas, I catch the train into the city to spend an afternoon searching for affordable trinkets — a simple matter of stretching a thin overdraft until it snaps — and, having wandered up Oxford Street and Tottenham Court Road (garlanded with bright and wonderfully gaudy decorations), I begin drifting down side streets, letting the current take me where it will. The billboards outside newsagents read: *IRA CLAIMS PADDINGTON LOCKER BOMB* and *UNEMPLOYMENT RISES.* It's festive stuff and has been defining this world for as long as I remember. Too foot-sore to walk anymore, I decide to catch a tube and head back to Stoneyfields, until I realise I'm opposite Kate's university.

Her place.

Whatever it was that first pulled us together now draws me to this spot, as it always will, and any moment Kate'll walk round the corner and everything'll be hunky-dory.

She'll be here somewhere, walking towards me. Somewhere close by. Ready to reach out if I can catch sight of her.

In fact there's someone who's just passed. I turn, but notice another girl across the road who might also be her. Twisting to look behind, in case she's part of another group walking by, then spinning round to peer ahead . . . and round again, like a dog chasing its tail. But what style of clothes might she wear these days, and what if she's cut her hair? And, even if she does pass by, will she recognise me? Would she want to?

I stop, close my eyes and stand still. Why am I really looking for her? Is it actually Kate I'm after or a replay of what we shared? Is this about keeping blind faith or am I looking for the person she helped me become?

This is stupid. Worse than stupid.

All the same, I cross the road to be closer to the university buildings, then wander down another side street because the name's familiar — her faculty site or her first year Halls address, perhaps — and come up against a tall, brick building, five storeys high. This must be it. I examine each row of windows for any sign whatsoever (a candle, an arrow, a beacon, a face, a wave), but find nothing . . . until a set of doors swings open and out steps the bearded Spaniard wearing a white lab coat.

Jesus! Alleluia. Amen.

This is it. A sign.

It *is* the bearded Spaniard, and then it isn't — I can't be sure. I head towards him, until another bearded Spaniard steps out behind him, and then another two. The doors clatter open again and remain open as a flood of bearded Spaniards in white lab coats wash out and down the street in one direction.

Any number from forty to five-thousand.

And Old Lofty squats on the kerb between two parked cars and cacks himself laughing. He slaps his bony hands across his knees and shakes, and I spit at him and turn on my heels and stalk away. Stuff the rest of the presents; I'll get myself a bottle of cheap whisky instead. I'll sell some books for a tab or two of the good stuff.

'Wait up!' he shouts.

'Fuck you!' I snarl.

★   ★   ★

The following June, at the end of first year, I tell Maureen Bonnard, my History tutor, I'm quitting the course. Maureen asks me into her office, offers me a seat, a mug of coffee and a biscuit, and tries talking me out of it, but it'd be a lie to continue studying when I can't see any point in it. The only thing it's taught me is how much I hate unanswered questions — why Dad killed himself, how I mightn't have lost Kate, what purpose there is to life — and that I need absolute truths. Studying History is all too wanky and academic.

'It's your decision,' she eventually tells me, as if I mightn't be sure, 'and the faculty will respect that.' She clasps her hands round her cup of Maxwell Gold Blend, leans forward in her swivel chair. There's a framed print on the wall of Bosch's *The Garden of Earthly Delights*. 'However, what I'd like you to do, if only to humour me, is to postpone Part Two rather than totally pulling the plug. Don't give up the course completely. Ask for a deferment, Tom.'

So much bullshit. She's okay, but this is bullshit. Where's the sense in always worrying whether you've got a safety line or not? Life's a slow drowning anyway. I'm sick of compromises and soft options — essay choices, negotiated extensions, interminable discussions and interpretations — and of justifying myself.

'I'll think about it,' I say. 'I'll decide tomorrow.'

'Are you sure everything's alright, Tom? Would you like a referral to the counsellor? Someone you can talk things through with?'

'No, it's nothing like that. Everything's fine. Everything's hunky-dory.'

The phrase brings a smile to my lips, and she smiles back.

★ ★ ★

To begin, there's short-term casual work in a plastic foodware factory, and a squalid bedsit in Whittington, north London. And it's a release to focus solely on the present: eight-to-five with nothing either side, and the notion that this grittier existence is, if nothing else, honest. Boring and meaningless, but honest.

Then, when summer and seasonal work ends, I sign on the dole. Nothing else is available. There's no other choice. No choice at all, thank God. The cheque goes no further than paying the rent, buying a few groceries, the odd bottle of whisky, but it's still honest.

Summer. Autumn. Winter.

As seasons pass, I coil tighter. Spend months pulling the world in on myself. Become my own black hole, sucking the bright energy out of my most colourful dreams, spitting out nothing. Old Lofty's good disciple. And even the memory and hope of Kate begins to fade, which is the kindest loss of all, until (absurdly) she writes and I start coughing the world up again. Like a dog with a fur ball.

A cold, dirty, February drizzle has been smothering this unremarkable day, from the first scratches of a vague light through to the first itchings of darkness again. All that's survived is a grey, lingering twilight. The day was stillborn, and night's arriving prematurely. I'm trudging back from cashing my dole cheque, buying a few provisions, and the air tastes rank, of wet newspapers, while the parade of lost-hope shops and the houses and roads are shabbier than ever.

'We deserve this shit,' I mutter. 'What else is there?'

Nothing, replies the silent voice of an invisible figure limping at my side, grinning with pride.

'Too right. Nothing.'

Nothing.

'Fuck all.'

I've discovered a world without real dialogue. Just one long soliloquy punctuated by silences and the occasional banalities of the supermarket, the Unemployment Office.

Turning from the main road into my street, I can't help but sneer: 'Home, sweet home.'

The street might be called Albenry Park, but there's no tree or shrub in sight; only a few spindly weeds breaking through cracks in the concrete and clinging to the broken-backed channels of roof guttering. It's a long street of four-storey terraces set on a hill, but the houses stand derelict at the bottom of the hill, with sheets of corrugated iron nailed over doors and low windows. The iron is loose in places, where squatters and truanting children have broken through, and sometimes claps forlornly in the wind, applauding nothing. Almost every pane of glass in the upper windows is smashed, and out of one dangles a ragged curtain. Plastic bin bags and soggy, split, cardboard boxes, overflowing with empty cat food tins, ketchup bottles, cigarette ends and greasy hair trimmings, spill up from the basements. It's a rising tide, flowing up and spewing over. The beginning of a great flood.

'Dying world,' I mutter against the collar of my coat, the edge of my scarf, then remember the newsagent's billboards two hundred yards back: *BARCELONA BOMB HORROR* and *INFLATION RISES*.

Not a world worth keeping. Not worth keeping in the world for.

Is this why Dad hanged himself? Perhaps he discovered a world he couldn't live in. And maybe Gazza aimed himself at that tree, unbuckled his seatbelt and planted his foot on the accelerator, for the same reason.

Cold. So cold.

I imagine a pregnant woman pushing a pram onto a railway platform in Barcelona on a day of pressing heat and gun-clutching Guardia Civil. (Why bring children into this world?) She's a tanned figure among a mid-morning crowd, rocking her pram to and fro, to and fro. Madonna and child. The air shimmers like a sheet of molten glass. To one side of where she waits, the metal petals of an ornate rubbish bin unfurl in beautiful slow motion, blossoming into flower for only a second before sprouting a flurry of nails, bolts, shards of metal. Seeds spurting; exploding like a dandelion head. Only then comes the noise of explosion and the screams of a terror to tear the morning apart in that small slice of the world and stop the trains a while; to stop the Guardia Civil from slouching for a day or two. To make ears ring deaf and eyes vomit blind shadows. Not a politician or corporate executive in sight, but a headline or two for their newspapers. Nothing left of the pram or the child. The crumpled Madonna a headless mess of meat and sodden fabric. A bag of blood and bone. *BARCELONA BOMB HORROR*.

I wince, shrug, refuse to falter in my walking.

Pavement flagstones rock uneasily underfoot. Muddy water oozes out of others. My boots leak, my socks are saturated.

A church clock, two roads away, chimes nine. It's got to be somewhere between three and four o'clock. On the last chime, Old Lofty appears at my side, limping and half-striding along beside me, knees clicking, hunched shoulders scooping forward a bucketful of washed-out day with each stride. Stride, scoop, stride, scoop. And even through the cold, I can smell the stale sweat of his clothes, the spunky sweetness of damp stone, the acrid funk of his black powder breath.

He says nothing, but grins as he walks. Then he takes on the exaggerated gestures of a mime artist and pulls an invisible rope from the sleeve of his robe. Poking his tongue out one corner of his mouth in concentration, he takes an end of rope and fashions an invisible knot to make a noose. He slips it over his head, settles it around his neck, holds one arm aloft and pretends to hang himself. His head droops, his eyes bulge and he wets himself laughing.

'Now you,' he says, showing me one end of the rope. 'It's your turn.'

'Piss off,' I say, and grin. 'Fuck the hell out of here.'

And, after a moment's pause, he does.

The drizzle grows heavier and a sharp wind cuts through the streets and round the corners with the cold, keen edge of a skinhead's flick-knife. The sky is cast from granite — rock heavy, too low — almost grinding the houses into the ground. But I refuse to hurry up the steps to the front door.

Inside, the hallway is cold, musty and damp. Somewhere upstairs, in this warren of bedsits, a door bangs. Two chained bikes are propped against the wall behind the front door and a few foot-printed letters and circulars are scattered across the muddy linoleum.

There's no warning in any of this. Nothing to suggest Kate.

I flick twenty-odd letters with the toe of my wet boot, spreading them further apart, and pick up four.

The stairwell leading from the hall to the basement is dungeon-dark and stinks of cat piss and mildew. The timber in the bottom two steps springs down with a stifled groan, but there's no echo, and the sound is swallowed whole into some unfathomable depth.

Sometimes I wonder whether I've made this place, or if it's made me.

Dropping the groceries at my feet, I perch on the edge of the bed, rub at the carrier-bag handle marks chewed into my fingers, and watch Old Lofty stand by the sink and go through the pantomime of unpacking his own bag of provisions. One-by-one, he places each item on the draining board, and I know what he's got before they appear: his favourite length of rope, a packet of razor blades, a toy gun, a packet of sleeping tablets and a half-empty bottle of cheap whisky.

Is the bottle always half-empty these days?

'Sod off,' I say, and turn on the table lamp to banish the bastard, then glance at the soggy envelopes. Without opening them, I guess what they are: a bank statement, an invitation to apply for a credit card, a letter from *Reader's Digest* advising me that I, Thomas Passmore of 67 Albenry Park, Whittington, London, have successfully completed the first two stages towards becoming a millionaire and might like to consider how I'd prefer receiving my prize. The fourth envelope is hand-addressed, in writing I vaguely remember; redirected by my mother.

★ ★ ★

281

Dear Tom,

Thanks for your cards and letters of some while ago, and apologies for not replying sooner, but I'm not an over-keen writer of letters these days, as you've probably guessed. In fact, my friends tell me I'm the world's worst correspondent.

Anyway, I'm shortly moving out of the house I've been living in for the last eighteen months (the landlord is selling), and we're having a house-cooling party in a couple of weeks.

I was thinking it would be nice to meet up again, as you suggested once, and thought this party would be a good opportunity, so please come along if you're able and feel free to bring a friend or two.

The nearest tube is Ealing Broadway and the house is about ten minutes walk away. It's in the A-Z. (Details are on the reverse.)

Perhaps I'll see you soon.

Best wishes,

Kate

★ ★ ★

I sit down, read the letter again, focus on the bars outside the window, but don't know what to do next. Eventually, I stand, take off my wet trench coat, sit down and read it again.

282

'Well, fuckety-fuck,' Lofty says.

How will she ever recognise me? I've become a ghost.

'She won't,' he tells me. 'Forget it. Screw it up and dump it in the bin.' And he pokes a 'V' of two bony fingers in the air and claws them up and down, up and down at her letter.

'You did exist,' an alter ego reminds me.

'A long time ago,' I say to the room.

★ ★ ★

The night isn't icy cold. The moisture in my exhaled breath doesn't produce small funnels of fog. There's no ice forming on damp pavements. Instead, it's mild and more like a spring night than winter. And yet my fingers are numb, my teeth chatter.

Crossing the road into Kate's street, I walk past the house once before pausing, turning back and heading down the small front path. There's nothing more to lose. Nothing at all.

'I'm looking for Kate,' I tell the three people who answer the door together. Behind them a houseful of strangers are milling about: chit-chat, chit-chat, chit-chat. It's the first time I've spoken to real people in months. Music is bouncing forward from the back of the house.

'Kate? Anyone know where Kate is?'

'Still packing.'

'Try her room. Upstairs, far end of the landing.' And they point to the staircase.

On the landing I take a deep breath and knock lightly, but the door's ajar and moves to my touch. Straightaway, the murmur of conversation within stops and the door's opened by a girl I don't recognise.

This is a mistake.

'I'm sorry,' I say. 'Must have the wrong room.'

'Who are you looking for?'

Another figure stands and steps towards me.

'Tom.'

'Hello, Kate.'

She leans forward and kisses me on the cheek. 'You made it. Come in, have a seat. I'll move these clothes out the way. Sorry about the mess. I shouldn't have started packing until after the party.' She places a hand on her friend's arm. 'Tom, this is Wendy; Wendy, this is Tom — an old friend. Did you bring anyone with you?'

I shake my head, open my mouth, shut it again and sit down. One corner of her room is cramped with boxes, strewn with skirts, coats, t-shirts; several precarious stacks of books rise from the floorboards, waiting for an excuse to topple; other books have already collapsed across half-empty shelves; framed prints lean lazily against a wall; a stereo system spills out of a large box advertising *Kellogg's Rice Crispies x 24*. They're the furnishings and accoutrements of a Kate I've never known, and so I look for something I might point to and say, 'I remember this,' but there's nothing recognisable to cling to.

'No, I came by myself,' I say.

'You could've. Wendy's invited a thousand friends, haven't you?' And she seats herself on a trunk opposite me, but not so close that we could reach out and touch.

Wendy smiles and shakes her head. 'Well, I'd better go and start being sociable, I guess. I'll give a shout when Mick arrives.'

'Okay. Ta.' The door clicks shut. 'Mick's my boyfriend. I don't know what time he'll get here. He hasn't been over before.' She shifts her position on the trunk, tucks her hands behind her knees, looks at me and waits.

Her hair is the same lustrous brown, although a couple of inches shorter perhaps, and she's still undeniably Kate, even though her face is a tad thinner. But she's more guarded than I'd hoped. Maybe this is a test.

'It's not a difficult street to find,' I say. 'He won't get lost. I didn't.'

'Care to put money on that? He's got a

terrible sense of direction.' She smiles then, and presses her teeth against her bottom lip and shrugs — a gesture I remember — and relaxes. 'Well, how are you, Tom? It's been ages. Too long. I'm sorry about that.'

'Fine. Never better. You look well. I was worried . . . '

'That you wouldn't recognise me? I haven't changed that much, have I?'

'No, I meant that you wouldn't recognise me.'

She shakes her head and dismisses the idea. 'I'm glad you came, and I *am* sorry it's taken so long to get in touch. I never imagined life would be so hectic. And as for this year, it's been crazy — good, but crazy. How's your course, Tom?'

'I've deferred. I've taken a year off,' I tell her, and hesitate. 'It's a pity you have to move. This seems like a good place.'

'It is,' she says, 'but I've found a room in a great flat just round the corner from uni.'

At that, a car horn sounds in the street and Kate moves to the window. She pulls the curtain back to peer put and then lets it fall shut again. 'I thought that might be him.'

'And it isn't?' I ask, but am thinking about the bonsai sycamore perched on the window-sill. Here's something important from our past that I might mention. Should I mention it?

'No, not yet,' she says. 'He's probably caught in traffic.'

I nod. 'So what will you do when you finish your course?'

And we talk about Abetsby, her parents, about living in London, the over-development of Northampton, and hopscotch from one subject to another, wary of saying too much or too little, or so it seems. My sentences sound clumsy, with having shrunk from people for too long, and several times I almost let the words trail silently off towards a conclusion of their own, until I make myself steer them towards a full stop. Yet when her smile warms and she laughs at something I say, and when she gesticulates with her hands in a manner I recognise, or widens her eyes in exclamation in a way I've forgotten, I tell myself I'm doing well and can pass her test, whatever it is. I can do this even though I ache with sitting opposite and talking to her as if she's a relative or an old acquaintance met in passing — somebody other than Kate.

After about twenty minutes, there's a knock on the door and Wendy peers in. 'Mick's here.'

It's too soon. Way too soon. All the same, I stand to leave.

'You'll stay and enjoy the party, won't you?' Kate says. 'I'm sorry this is so brief.'

Picking up my jacket, I move to the door. 'Okay. I will then. Thanks.'

'It'll be heaving with people later. We might not get a chance to speak again. Not tonight.'

'I know. That's okay. I'll look after myself, don't you worry. I'll have a couple of drinks and a few dances. It'll be too crowded later to chat.'

'I'll write to you once I've settled at the new place. In about four weeks. Okay? Promise. We'll have an afternoon to catch up with one another. Not like this. Okay?'

'Sounds good. I'd like that. Thanks.'

She kisses me on the cheek and I pull the door shut after me. On the landing, I take a deep breath and let her boyfriend come upstairs before heading down into the fog of small talk and pounding music.

The house is bulging and I'm a stranger among friends. Do I really want to stand in a corner nursing a drink, pretending I'm not alone?

Forget it, I tell myself. Turn round and get out.

'Have a drink,' a less familiar voice coaxes. 'You promised. Let Kate see you talking and dancing, but don't become the party drunk

— not at any cost.'

Edging towards the kitchen, towards the drinks, I reach the doorway, but no further. The kitchen's a sardine tin, packed with people, shoulder-to-shoulder, fin-to-fin.

A possessive voice dribbles in my ear: 'Bugger this for a night of fun! You don't need this crap. Get the fuck out of here!'

'Stay,' another urges.

Old Lofty lifts my wallet and drops it in my hands. 'Here, you weak bastard. Buy a ticket for the Dream Bus. Been a long while.'

There's pressure at my back and I inch towards a bench crammed with bottles of wine, beer, lemonade, cider, shoulder-to-shoulder, neck-to-neck. A small group squeezes out, clutching drinks, allowing a ripple of movement forward, and I slide into a gap. There's giggling behind.

'Is this it?' someone on my heels asks, and I half-turn.

'Sorry?'

'Is this as close to the booze as we're gonna get?'

'Yeah, for the moment,' I say.

'It's a bit crowded.'

A voice from behind, peering over the first one's shoulder says: 'Should aim for an entry in *The Guinness Book of Records*.'

'I reckon.'

'Five-hundred people packed in a shoebox-sized kitchen,' she says.

'Booze, booze everywhere and not a drop to drink.'

With that, comes another ripple of movement and another gap, which places me in reach of the bottles.

'What'll you have?' I say, reaching over other reaching arms and dragging at a bottle. A bench full of bottles and cans.

I pour drinks into plastic beakers, grab a can, but am stuck. 'Cheers,' I say, trying to turn. 'Is there a way back?'

'Turnabout and follow the leader, I guess,' says the one in the middle. 'Come on, Jo, it's your turn now.'

And the slow shuffle begins all over, until the three of us are standing in the corner of a room adjoining the kitchen, where the wall vibrates to the music's bass rhythm. I try not to notice Kate dancing a few feet away with her Mick, but she catches my eye and smiles, and I hold my drink up in salute. It's alright though because her dance with him is different — less exotic, less poetic — to any dance we ever shared. And I refuse to laugh at Lofty, who jiggles an inch behind Mick, and who, with each exaggerated pelvic-thrust and each wiggle of hunched, bony shoulders, makes a travesty of his dance.

Smile politely, I tell myself, and don't flinch at the banalities of small talk.

'I'm Jo,' one of the girls says.

'I'm Elin,' says her friend.

Straightaway I forget which is which.

'I'm Tom.'

'Are you a friend of Peter?'

'No, I'm an old friend of Kate's. Tonight's the first time I've seen her in . . . ' I shrug. 'In ages. I don't know anyone else.'

'Didn't think I'd seen you at uni,' says one.

'Well at least you know us now,' says the other.

Small talk, rolling in from all sides. An evening of it. Dance, talk, laugh, I remind myself. Look relaxed and sociable, within sight of Kate — but don't search her out. Dance, dance, dance, but don't drift too far.

12

The steps to Whittington Underground stink of urine and shit. London's a toilet. Its streets are paved with dog turds, its walls streaked with night piss. There's blood smeared across the tiles of public toilets, and newspaper-coated bodies crouch or curl in dark corners; grey fingered, they cosset short-necked bottles in brown paper bags. And I'm slipping into it.

Hurtling station-to-station, the tube fills with Saturday evening revellers. Like moths drawn to the West End lights for a night of frantic fluttering against the glass, they'll dance and glow there, but in the narrow confines of the tube they're lonely people with emptiness in their eyes. And so much safer to stare at advertising strips and graffiti-smothered walls than risk connecting with anybody else's empty eyes. Anything to avoid acknowledging the existence of another anonymous moth.

Shaz, BOMBERS, alpo, wanker, Be alert — Britain needs Lerts, National Front kill wogs, Fuck U 2, BASTARD, Steamin' Blue, PRICK, RS 4 NG 4 eva, CUNT.

Changing trains at Embankment for Wimbledon, I'm ready to turn back. I should've stayed huddled in my bedsit, away from such emptiness . . . until I see Kate.

She runs across the platform, dashing towards my carriage, and I stand to greet her, but then the doors hiss shut. There's a shout from the guard and the doors open briefly, presenting an empty platform, and then close again.

Two stations later, I spot her sitting in the adjoining carriage — can make her out through the dirty glass — but the partition door's locked and she's facing the opposite direction. This is good though. We'll walk together to the party. Maybe we'll link arms, hold hands. She's got rid of the boyfriend and has stage-managed the invitation from Elin and Jo. Really the invitation's from her.

At Sloane Square, I race out my carriage along the platform and into her carriage. Standing in front of her, I take a slow breath to get my wind back and begin saying: 'Hello, Kate; thought it must be you,' when I see it isn't. All I say is, 'Hello.'

Up close, she's thinner, younger and wearing a ton more makeup than Kate would ever wear, but the hair — that dark chestnut brown — and the shape of her face are sort of similar.

Beyond any initial bemusement or anxiety, she clutches her handbag tighter, sits upright and sneers: 'Piss off, creep.'

This could never be Kate. She's never been ugly.

'It's alright,' I say, turning, looking for a seat further down the carriage. 'Thought you were someone else.' As I move away, I'm aware of a hundred eyes avoiding me, preparing for the worst: a mugging, an assault. Always the worst.

Old Lofty dribbles his slime of words into my ear: 'Hey, Creepy-creep, where's your flasher's mac then?'

The girl gets off at Putney Bridge. Trying not to look at her, her reflection slinks across every window and she's greeted by someone on the platform. They embrace, kiss, and then she points at me, and her partner turns, stares, places an arm around her shoulders and steers her towards the exit.

★ ★ ★

The front door to Elin and Jo's house is opened by a drunk. He grins, slaps me on the back and insists on shaking my hand before waving me through.

'I know you, don't I?' he slurs. 'Seen you about the traps, ain't I? Never forget a face.

Where do I know you from?' He holds up a bottle to silence me. 'Don't tell me; I wanna guess.'

Pressing his face so close to mine he grows squint-eyed and has to blink. His breath is a cloud of beer and curry fumes.

'Don't think you do,' I say, taking a step to the side. 'Do you live here?'

'Nah. Never set foot inside this fine abode before. Never set eyes on the place either. Professional gatecrasher; that's what I do. I know you, don't I? I know I fuckin' do.'

'Probably,' I say, prising free. 'Maybe I saw you at the last party.'

'Yeah, that's it. I knew I fuckin' had. Never forget a face.'

The place is packed and I edge my way from room to room, but there's no one I recognise. No Kate, not yet. I'm less sure by the minute what Jo or Elin look like and, invitation or not, doubt they'll recognise me either — not after one night. And I'm buggered if I want to stand around watching strangers dance, hug and get pissed.

Then someone taps me on the shoulder.

'Tom. Been trying to catch your attention. We were hoping you'd get here.'

Jo. She's cropped her hair. It's so short I look for the safety pin hanging from her ear, and find it. She's exchanged her copper-coloured page-boy for closely-cut, glossy black spikes, which define the contours of her skull. I'd like to stroke a hand across to see if it's bristly or soft, but remember the creep on the tube and resist.

'Your hair — that's pretty radical. Tonight you're a punk.'

She runs a hand through her spikes; smiles. 'Thought it was time for a change. Wanted to be someone else.'

'You're into punk?'

'Too right. Nothing but Johnny Rotten and the Sex Pistols tonight.' She screws up her nose and smiles. 'Not seriously though, eh? I hate jumping up and down to music. It's okay for a couple of minutes, but not all night. Next month I might be a skinhead.'

What a great idea. Being a chameleon is far better than being a ghost. 'You could be a bikie,' I offer. 'Black leathers and a two-fifty cc parked out front.'

She considers, then grins. 'Yeah. Definitely. Whoever I wanna be.' She runs a hand through her hair again. 'Didn't you bring anyone with you? You could've.'

I shake my head; shrug.

'That's great. Elin'll be . . . Elin'll be back soon. She had to dash to the shops. Someone dropped a bottle of Martini and a bottle of wine across the bloody kitchen floor, and we forgot to get Bitter Lemon.' She sighs in mock exasperation. 'Parties, eh?'

'Yeah, parties.' I look across the room. 'Shall I get you a drink?'

'No, I'll get you one; I'm the hostess. I can see how the kitchen's handling the crush. Beer? Wine? I know, you can try some of our Punch. We spent the afternoon concocting it. You can join the row of victims.'

'Think I've already met one.'

Leaning against the edge of an old, battered sideboard, I catch my fingers on a loose strip of veneer; two of its four drawers are missing and there's a spatter of paint stains across the top. It's the sort of junk landlords dump in properties so they can advertise them as furnished, to raise the rent, to protect their eviction rights.

Jo hands me a drink, holds her plastic beaker against mine and screws up her nose in what's evidently a habitual smile. 'Cheers.'

She's flirting with me, I tell myself, but wonder why; feeling more inclined to accept the view of the Putney Bridge couple. Maybe Kate'll walk in and see me like this — the new easy-going me — not stoned, not drunk but sociable, gregarious and . . . and she'll ask me to dance again. 'You've got a crowd and a half here,' I say.

'Yeah. Not everyone we asked, mind. We're

competing with some major college event, but there's always something on. If we hadn't gone ahead this weekend we never would.'

'Is that right?'

And I wonder if Kate'll be here after all.

'Dance,' she says. It isn't a question or a request. She takes my beaker and puts it on the sideboard with hers, but then reads the panic on my face. 'Don't worry, this is a slow one. Slow ones are the easiest. Unless it's punk, and then we can jump up and down. But you can't come to a party and not dance.'

'I suppose.'

'Definitely. No two ways about it. It's the law.'

The rhythm is strong enough to sweep me along. It draws me closer to the down on the nape of her neck, the softness of her cropped hair, the smell of her, and maybe that's all I need. Her femininity might be enough. Maybe that's all any guy needs to begin with. Besides, I might find Kate in dancing with Jo — that is, the Kate I once knew — and, if not Kate, then someone else instead. Anyone who, in time, might become Kate. More than anything, I need to be drawn away from the worst of myself, if only for a while. A person flounders in too much Self.

During our second dance, Jo pauses and reaches out to touch the shoulder of someone who's weaving between the dancers — a swathe of blonde hair, the colour of ripe corn.

'Elin's back,' I hear her say.

I turn and there's Elin holding a couple of bottles in the air.

When the dance finishes, Jo puts her hands on my waist and speaks. It's the first time I've been really touched in aeons, but, with the music cranking up, I've got to lean closer to hear her. I drink in the scent of her, am ready to swim with it, if only for a while, but then miss a stroke or two completely. Clearly I've misunderstood her.

'You should ask Elin to dance. She loves dancing too. Better not keep you to myself. Ask her to dance, Tommo.' She winks, kisses me on the cheek and leads me to where Elin is talking among a small group.

What's happening here? What game are they playing?

'I'm glad you made it,' Elin says. 'Did you bring a friend?'

I glance around the packed room, but there's still no Kate. 'No. Not tonight,' I say. 'It's a fine party you've made.'

'We've been planning it for months, haven't we, Jo?'

'Since we moved in at the beginning of the year,' Jo says. 'That last party, where we met you, made us finally get our act together.'

She's looking about; I'm no longer in front of her. 'Anyway, I best mingle, check out the booze, make sure everything's hunky-dory.' And she smiles at that.

'Make sure everyone's behaving?' I suggest, wanting to hold her a while longer.

'Yeah, sort of, within reason. But not too well-behaved, eh?' She's still looking around. 'Not much point in partying otherwise, is there?'

'I guess not.'

She ruffles Elin's hair and winks again. 'Well, kiddo, dance till you drop; party till you pop,' she says, and bounces away.

'Didn't have any problems finding us then?'

'No. Easy.'

'That's good.' She sips her drink, looks down at her beaker, then up at me and away again.

Perhaps she too is waiting for someone else to arrive or had planned on talking to someone different until Jo dragged me across.

'Do you want to dance?' I say. 'Or are you one of those people who need to be pissed — '

She nods and puts her drink down. 'Love to.'

And so it begins. I try keeping in beat with the music for an hour without pausing, but keep a weather-eye open for Jo and who she's moving with, just as I keep an eye on the door to see if Kate'll arrive late.

When I wake fully-clothed the following morning, I'm lying next to Elin, on her bed. I double-check to see whether Elin is Jo, but she's not, and she hasn't turned into Kate either. Bruised by my own fickleness, I tell myself it serves Kate right. She should've been there. And it does serve her right, until she writes.

* * *

Dear Tom,

New address as promised. Won't be here for a week. Please give ring or drop line after then. Hope you're well. Was great to see you again. Sorry this is so abbr. but must dash to catch coach.

Take care,
Kate

* * *

A night of unseasonably-late snow transforms the heartless old bitch that's London into something quiet, clean and beautiful. The trains stop and the buses crawl to the edge of the road, then stop. Morning traffic slews to a halt, and even the clocks are silenced. Any lingering dampness is snap-frozen into a sharp crispness, and it makes me stir, blink and try wiping the ice from inside my window.

I cook porridge for breakfast — hot, sweet and milky — and blow steam into the room as I eat. 'This'll melt the icicles,' I mutter, intrigued by how good the air smells and even by the sound of my voice. Snow-light floods between the bars of the window and the room's brighter than it'd ever be under the strongest of bulbs, and I notice stains I've never spotted before.

Tying my boots and fastening my coat, I prepare to crunch my way to the shops, to breathe the air, to drink its freshness in. But the snow is blinding when I drag open the front door, and I catch at the railings to keep from slipping down the steps. I'm met by a needlepoint brightness that pokes at my eyes and transforms the world into an over-exposed photograph. All the same, once I've got used to it, even the derelict houses at the bottom of the hill are no longer an eyesore, and the snowdrifts have blanked out the newspaper hoardings outside the parade of shops.

There's something about high-stepping through snow, staying upright on patches of ice and finding the hidden kerb when crossing the road, that reminds me of childhood and ploughing to school through banks of snow shovelled to one side of the pavement. And of a memory I never knew I had: of helping Dad scrape snow out the driveway and off the path, and of building a snowman, and having snow-caked gloves and snow slipping over the tops of my gumboots, freezing my toes. And he picks me up and swings me round and one gumboot flies off my foot, smack into the hedge, shaking a flurry of snow down. The memory is an antidote to where I've placed myself and reminds me there might be something else I've lost or forgotten, if only I could remember what. Perhaps it's something I once intended to achieve or someone I wanted to become. And the idea that there's something I've left behind begins nagging at me, poking me, worrying me, until Lofty appears.

The afternoon post brings a new letter.

★   ★   ★

Dear Tom,
    Hope you're well. As you can see from the address, I decided to head home for the holidays. Jo's staying with me until Saturday.

303

I appreciate Cornwall and rural life far more since I left for London than when I lived here. Human nature, eh?

I enjoyed the party and the time we had together, and wondered whether you'd like to meet after I return on the 22nd? Perhaps for dinner — something cheap and cheerful — or head to South Bank for that Aborigines, Convicts and Explorers exhibition I was telling you about.

Perhaps you could write while I'm here. I love receiving letters. (Hint.)

Best wishes,
Elin

★ ★ ★

I drop the letter on my bed.

'Don't you know what you're flirting with?'

'Perhaps she does,' another voice says.

'Perhaps? How about a few fucking certainties?' I wipe the condensation from the window and stare up at the street railings.

'A few absolute truths?'

'Yeah.'

Silence from the other voice.

'What about Kate?'

No answer.

Using the edge of a tea towel, I polish the window harder and catch a reflection of myself peering back. The figure I see, though, has deflated cheeks, shadows instead of eyes and a hollow grimace.

'Fuck off!'

* * *

Next day, to escape the confusion, I walk. Traipsing slush-swamped streets, under railway bridges, past abandoned shopping arcades, through an ugly cemetery, across an industrial wasteland, I stop when I realise my socks are saturated and my toes are beyond that initial numbness. To my right stands the entrance for an estate of large, rectangular warehouses; unit after unit of drab grey breezeblock and corrugated iron, too uniformly spaced across a barren, concrete landscape of loading bays and lorry parks; each contained within a barrier of chain-linked fences, garlanded with razor wire and security cameras. Next to the entrance is a large job board, empty of vacancies except for one: *WAREHOUSEMAN — APPLY REGENCY FOODS, UNIT 15.*

I stamp my feet, then wait and listen. The sky is empty. I'm on my own.

The reception counter is unattended, but there's a bell to ring and it brings the depot manager out of an office. We talk for five minutes and he offers me the job, starting next day. That simple. Absurdly simple, given the unemployment rate. Simply absurd, given my philosophy.

That evening, I sit on my bed and write replies to the letters. First to Kate, and then to Elin.

★　★　★

'I'm glad you wrote,' Elin says.

We're sitting at a sticky table in the Hayward's cafeteria. Steam rises from two cups, spilt coffee has slopped into our saucers.

'Wasn't much of a letter.' Pushing a hand through my hair, I try catching a glimpse of my reflection in the glass. 'I scribbled it in a hurry. Otherwise it would've arrived after you'd left.' Had a haircut before meeting Elin and nearly joined Jo with the punk look, but bailed at the last moment.

'Doesn't matter. A letter's a letter.' She folds a serviette and places it under her cup. 'When I was little I'd send for holiday brochures — you know, all those coupons from *The TV Times* — just so I'd get wads of mail. It was probably because I grew up on a farm, without older brothers and sisters to play with. I created my own links with the world.'

'Holiday brochures, Elin? Tahiti, Morocco, Spain? That's a bloody exotic world.'

'Why not? Maybe I was compensating for the bleakness of the farm. Didn't you ever do that sort of thing?'

Placing my coffee cup on the table, out of the saucer, it leaves a wet ring. 'I used to play at farms,' I tell her. And I imagine her standing on a Cornish cliff, with a raging, rock-pounding sea below and bleak moorland in front; dressed in baggy overalls and clod-hopper gumboots, but her blonde hair a crazy tangle in the wind, and laughing — Jo and Elin always seemed to be laughing. 'I thought you liked Cornwall.'

'I do now. Now I've left. For years, I couldn't wait to get away. How about that? If I could get a teaching post in Cornwall I'd be delighted, but it won't happen.' Absent-mindedly stirring another teaspoon of sugar into her coffee, she pauses and shrugs. 'It's harder to get a job in the country than in the cities. Who knows where I'll end up?'

'Did you like the exhibition?'

'Yeah, loved the paintings, but I get bored with stuff in glass cabinets. Give me inter-active stuff any day; those big displays you walk through and press buttons — get the models to move and tell their stories instead of having to read long explanations.

I'm just a big kid really.'

'You want to be involved?'

'Hands-on; too right. I was hoping to use something in my next teaching round. Get the kids to make those dot paintings of animals, weave baskets, cook damper — that sort of thing.'

'Sounds good,' I say, and imagine a full-scale diorama of two Neolithic men chipping flint against flint, with a toolkit of points and side-scrapers spread out. They'd be leaning against a tree, with a small fire in front and the odd billow of smoke from a smoke machine; there'd be the sound of wind blowing in trees, the guttural exclamations of an on-going Neolithic conversation, and an area with stones for visitors to try knapping points themselves.

As twilight descends, we cross the Thames and wander to Leicester Square. We go for a Wimpy and when we come out it's dark, except for the fluorescent glare of cinema hoardings feverishly pulsing half-a-dozen new Hollywood releases. Bud lights strung among the leafless trees imitate a galaxy of stars, but the night sky itself is displaced by the orange glow of the city — no Plough, no Pole Star, no Orion. There's a flow to the day and it draws us round the square, ignoring the drunks, down-and-outs and buskers, until we decide to buy tickets for a film.

And, after the film, we look even more like a couple among the thousands of other couples heading towards the Underground escalators of Leicester Square or Piccadilly Circus or Charing Cross . . . all talking the same talk, all feeling to find a way into the moment, which will, of course, feel like a going forward, but which is often the same moment over and over again. Quite natural. There's nothing to tell us apart. Two by two by two by two.

There'll always be bodies arching and arcing in the night, like rainbows spanning dusk and dawn, solitude and companionship.

★ ★ ★

In the morning, for the second time, I wake up beside Elin, but this time our clothes are on the floor. She offers me breakfast, but I claim I'm not hungry, and bolt back to the bedsit to try outrunning whatever might happen next.

I spend one evening with Elin, one with Kate. Trail anxiety behind me both times, like the smell of something I've stepped in. Life's starting to resemble the sort of French farce I've never found funny — one hundred per cent cringe — diving in and out a series of wardrobe doors: in one with Elin, out another with Kate; in one with Kate, out yet another with Elin; Jo sitting on a settee, stage left, apparently oblivious to the opening and closing of doors. Maybe I should sit calmly alongside her until the next act, when I can tell Kate that I still want to be with her. Only her. I want to spend my life with her. Always had, always would.

All the same, I watch events unravel with the uncanny sense of having become detached. I'm a marionette, scripted to walk in one direction, but dragged the opposite way. I'm a spaceman drifting at the end of an umbilical cord, attached to nothing. I'm a child whose remote-controlled plane is flying by itself; up, down, flying around, looping the loop, playing the clown. Nothing happens the way it should and there's sweet Fanny Adams I can do. Sweet fuck all.

★   ★   ★

Kate says: 'So, you're working in a ware-house, Tom? That'd be tiring, I imagine, but good to have a real wage.'

I can't believe I'm standing next to her again. Undoubtedly her face is thinner, her cheekbones more defined, but it suits her, and she's more reflective in the measure of her words. It's easier to see the woman she's becoming.

She'd suggested I come to her flat; thought we might stroll through a local park, get a takeaway meal. She'd be going out with friends later. So I cancelled a date with Elin, without explanation — unwilling to lie to her, unable to provide the truth ('I'm meeting someone I can't fall out of love with') — and began rehearsing the evening.

'It's not much of a wage,' I tell her, 'but at least I'm getting fitter again. Haven't been fit since I worked on the market . . . in Northampton. And it helps pass the time, even though it's mindless. But I'll be glad to get back to uni and start using my brain. What's left of it.'

'You plan on going back? When? This September? That's great.'

I nod. 'How many years have you got left?'

She shows me her flat and the tree outside her bedroom window, and then we walk a maze of streets and follow a genteel path through the park, alongside a boating lake, and start hopscotching again from subject to subject. But it's all too stilted. Why can't we relax and start discussing the things that matter, the things we're passionate about? And there are questions we're not asking, truths we're not speaking; stuff that needs to be said, or at least acknowledged before we can move on, but that we're unsure how to broach. What is it that has to be done or said first?

There are ducks on the lake and young families throwing chunks of bread, but no swans — no moonlit garden of swans waiting to watch over us. And maybe that's the problem: London's too prosaic for us, and short on miracles and mysteries.

'I only deferred,' I tell her, returning to the subject, needing to reach out and hold her hand as we stroll towards the Chinese restaurant she knows. In the movies it would've been an easy gesture, that reaching across and brushing of fingertips, but there's too much at stake between us. 'Come September, I reckon I'll be more than ready to give it another shot. It was all too wanky last year.'

Why can't I just blurt out: 'I told you I'd always love you and I do'? And yet the reason's obvious: because if she doesn't want to hear it, she'll tell me goodbye — in the middle of the park, in the middle of the street, in the foyer of the restaurant — and it'll be the last I ever see of her. She'd say something like: 'Oh, I thought I'd given you time to move beyond that. I thought we could be friends, Tom, but obviously I was wrong.'

Can't she see she's got to give the first sign?

Maybe I should ask her to dance, right here in the middle of the park. ('Will you dance with me once more, that I might get to know you again? Will you breathe the life into me once more, but stay for all time?') We'd raise our arms and throw our heads back and pirouette until the sky washed us off our feet.

We pass a middle-aged couple sitting on a bench and she digs her hands into her pockets. 'I've heard some Arts courses are a bit of a wank from beginning to end,' she says. 'Won't you feel the same way once you're back?'

'Don't think so. My perspective's changed, Kate. I know what I want to do now, whereas I didn't have a clue before.'

'You do? What?'

'I want to put exhibitions together for museums. You know, interesting, hands-on stuff to replace the boring rows of glass cabinets. I want to design displays that people can walk through and press buttons and have exhibits talk to them — that sort of thing. Have stuff to eat and touch and smell.'

She smiles. 'You were always into history, weren't you?'

'I guess I was.' And I remember the time we watched the mummers play together.

'You do like Chinese, don't you?'

Just before we start eating, she stretches and then tucks a strand of hair behind one ear with the fingers of her left hand. The linked gestures bring with them the memory of a bedroom and the sharp angle of an early morning sun slicing a blade of light across a shared pillow. I recall the yellow wallpaper with its faded pattern of roses, her calico curtains, the silhouettes of pot plants on the windowsill, and the scent of her. I recall the sensuousness of our shared nakedness and the way her hair fell across my shoulder — so that I never wanted to move from that time, but for that moment to lie there with us forever.

'This looks good. *Bon appétit*,' I say, but have lost my appetite.

When we finish our meal, she says, 'I'm meeting some friends in forty-five minutes. We have a night together every couple of weeks or so.'

'That's nice.'

'I've enjoyed catching up with you, Tom.'

'Me too . . . with you.'

'Perhaps we could go to a concert sometime?'

'I'd like that,' I say. 'When? What would you like to go to?'

She folds her aluminium meal container in half and drops it in the carrier bag. 'It's a bit crazy at the moment. Mick and I are going through a rough patch.'

'Okay,' I say. 'Fair enough.' And it's all I can do not to cheer.

'I'll write to you. We'll arrange something. I promise.'

'Good. I'd like that.' We're interrupted by a cacophony of sirens. The traffic pulls to one side of the road and a police car and two ambulances scream across the junction, and then the sirens fade into the distance again. Kate shudders and I say, 'So much noise, so little time.'

She bites her bottom lip and nods.

'I'll walk you to where you're meeting your friends.'

'That's alright. Thanks, but it'll be easier for you to catch the tube from here.'

And we kiss each other's cheek and say goodnight.

★　★　★

More sirens. Sticky tyres on a wet road. Screaming. An ocean crashes, folds in upon itself and swells again, wave after wave after wave, until the rush of the ocean drowns all other sound into silence.

315

In search of simplicity, I try detaching myself from Elin, ready to wait again for Kate. Maybe, she'll split with Mick and let me know about it. It's a smart plan, until Elin knocks on my door one Sunday afternoon.

'I thought I'd surprise you,' she says. 'You don't mind, do you? Such a beautiful day. Thought we might go for a walk on the Heath. What d'ya reckon?'

For a moment I say nothing, then let her in. 'Hello, Elin.'

I concentrate on washing and drying yesterday's dirty dishes, but am aware of her movements behind me. She paces up and down twice, removes her blazer and lets it drop with a clink of keys and coins on the bed, and then sits down.

'You don't know what you're missing.' Picking up the book I've been reading, she flicks through the pages. 'Can I have a glass of water, Tom? I'm gasping.'

'I'll make tea if you want me to.'

'Thanks, I'd love one. Can I have both? I need something to quench my thirst. I got hot just walking from the station.'

I give her a glass of water and prepare tea. There's nothing to say, so I make no attempt,

316

and Lofty raises his eyebrows and pretends to yawn.

The silence thickens. It grows into a silence to cut with a knife, then to hack at with an axe. While the kettle boils and the tea brews and the silence grows, I tidy away the dishes, clean the sink, fold the tea towel, empty the bin of rubbish. Elin returns to the book, feigning interest in the blurb and cover design.

Then, having turned to see what she's doing, and in being trapped in this second of contact, I offer half a smile that is also half a frown. I almost regret it, but the damage is done and I'm glad, and Old Lofty pats me on the back. For a few moments she says nothing, but it's coming, the breaking of the silence.

'Are you alright, Tom?'

'Fine, thanks. How are you?'

'You're very quiet,' she says. She says it quietly.

I shrug. It's in me now, the will to hurt and be hurt, to get it all done with and scuttle our relationship quickly.

'Have I disturbed you? Would you rather I hadn't come? I thought it'd be a surprise.'

Lofty whispers: 'Show her the door, you idiot.'

'Don't be silly. I'm glad you came. I love

317

surprises.' I tense my jaw, disappointed by my weakness. Surely there's a way to tell her straight without being a bastard.

She's silent while I pour tea.

I pass her a cup and say: 'Tea. Milk, no sugar; not too strong.'

She holds the cup without drinking. 'You don't want to go for a walk, I take it?'

'Perhaps not.'

'Haven't seen much of you this last couple of weeks,' she observes. 'Not since you cancelled that last time.'

I go to the window and tug at the handle, knowing it won't open. It never has. Outside will be the stink of rubbish thrown down from the street.

Lofty nods encouragement and rubs his hands together.

'What do you want to talk about then?' But in such coldness I recognise something of my mother.

Cupping the mug of tea between her hands, and silent, she looks from me to the floor and back. Then, in one sweeping movement, she puts her mug down, grabs her blazer and opens the door. Turning to face me, I see she's crying.

'Sorry I disturbed you, Tom. Next time I'll wait for a written invitation before I impose on you.'

I need to let her go, but can't. There are people I never want to become.

'What are you talking about? What have I said?'

Her exit is checked.

'Come off it! Do you think I'm stupid? That I haven't got feelings?' Her cheeks are wet. She leans against the door to find her handkerchief and it latches shut again.

For a second I'm relieved, then surprised at feeling relief. 'Come on, sit down, Elin. Don't go. Not like this.'

She stays by the door.

'You know your problem, Tom? You're so wrapped up in your own little world you can't see anyone or anything else at all. You're blind. Why don't you open your eyes? You need to open your eyes. It's not healthy. It's like you're frightened of getting too close to other people.'

'I know. I'm sorry,' I say. 'Sit down, Elin. Have a drink. Please.'

'Why? Why should I? If there's nothing between us, then I might as well go. I need to know. Just don't piss me about. I hate that. I hate people pissing other people about. I need to know if there's anything between us.'

I swallow. 'There is. Of course there is.'

'Is it something I've said, or maybe I've done something?'

'No, it's me. My problem.' I sit down and straighten the blanket. 'Won't you sit down?'

She blows her nose, turns from the door. 'Shit, it's cramped in this room! It's a poky little room. I hate it. Just being cooped up here makes me feel uptight. I don't know how you stand it. And that hallway . . . '

'It's a shitty room,' I laugh. 'Slums ain't what they used to be. Makes me uptight. Would you rather go for a walk?'

'Yeah, I think I would. I'll just wash my face. Have you got a flannel?'

'Somewhere. I'll find one.'

★ ★ ★

Even so, any romance with Elin is bound to go the same way as every other romance, but by then Kate might be ready to be with me again and, well, second time around . . . In this manner of thinking, May and June pass. The days are longer, lighter and warmer. I phone Kate once and she suggests we go to the concert after her exams. It seems we've almost moved full circle.

'We'll get together soon,' are the words she uses, and I interpret them in all kinds of ways.

Patience is paying off and I see how it might play out, until one Saturday morning and what begins as an urgent tapping on my door. It begins soft and hurried, but soon becomes a loud pummelling — a fist flailing against timber.

Fearing some mad-drunk bastard, I'm putting my foot and knee ready to shove the door shut again before unlatching it to peer out, when it catapults open and Elin falls into the room.

Her eyes are red and swollen, her hands hover in front of her mouth, and my first thought is that she's been attacked. Only last week a schoolgirl was raped near Whittington Underground. She's pale and beneath her eyes are the shadows of half-moons. Her voice begins in a hoarse whisper, but turns into a strained croak.

I can't understand.

'What's the matter?' I say, putting an arm round her. 'What's up? What's happened?'

'She's dead,' she groans, gasping each word. 'Jo's dead.'

What?

I lose my balance.

'What?'

'Jo's dead!'

Sobbing with each breath, she tries to swallow air, but the knowledge chokes her. I hold her tight, cushioning her. She folds onto the floor, onto her knees, and I go with her.

The door to my room is open, and from the hallway the stink of mildew is stronger than ever; I hear footsteps and laughter on the pavement outside, and a car starting.

'No. Say *no*.'

'She's dead! I saw her. Oh God!'

The sobbing fuses into one long wail.

'When? How? Tell me, Elin.'

It's the deepest grief.

'How, Elin?' I persist, trying to calm her. 'Talk to me. Tell me.' I clamp her shoulders between my hands, make her look at me, make her speak.

'Last night,' she pants. 'Motorbike accident ... on the way back ... I went to the hospital. She's dead! Why is she dead? Her parents ... '

The day caves in as Elin tells what she knows. Her grief sends waves crashing around the room, so I put aside my own shock and cling to her, to stop her from being washed away. I can't abandon her, can't just let go and watch her drown.

We lie on the floor and cry, and I hold her tight as the day passes. Elin lies there, staring into a corner, barely blinking, no longer hearing me, and I stare at the ceiling and stroke her hair.

And more than Jo has died.

This is what death does. A piece of the

world falls away. We spend the afternoon, the evening, the following days and weeks, placing our hands in the hole that's left, trying to name our surprise; picking at the scab of our grief, unwilling to let it heal over. Elin's closest friend has died, and something in her withers and is in danger of dying too, and if I leave her so I can be with Kate then it'll certainly die.

She'll be lost in grief, and I'll be lost in being a bastard forever.

I'd like to see Kate though, to explain why there has to be a distance, why I've stepped back from our plan to spend an evening together, why Elin is fragile and mustn't be hurt, so that she might understand and might wait a while — just in case. She'd understand if only she knew and, indeed, I know too well she'd despise the cruelty of any other response. She wouldn't forgive me. Not ever.

★   ★   ★

London summer, like most of that city's seasons, exists distinctly as summer for a fleeting moment only. There's merely a token beat or two from a long-forgotten rhythm; a clumsy step from the old dance, with no accompaniment and no further knowledge. Just two or three days of unsullied summer

323

heat and a ripe, juicy sun, and Elin and I sit in the park, soaking it up, trying to heal. However, the freshness quickly wilts, the days grow stifling and the city smells of cooked concrete and carries the throb of an over-heated engine.

And then it rains, and the rains last five weeks and summer is forgotten . . . until autumn, when a lost summer is mourned. Jo's ashes, shaken to the wind from a cliff top in Kent, have sailed and sifted and settled by then.

One September Saturday afternoon, cutting through Piccadilly Circus on our way somewhere else — pavements up, roads half-closed, generators chugging, jack hammers pounding, and even Eros removed for renovation — we happen to meet Kate. She comes from the opposite direction, walking quickly, accompanied by two girlfriends.

'Hello, Tom. It's been a while.'

'Hello, Kate,' but then I don't know what else to say because there's too much that needs to be said; so I introduce Elin. 'You remember Elin. I met her at your party.'

Kate smiles and says to me: 'It's good to see you. You're looking well.'

'You too.'

What else can I say? How can I tell her that in order to remain faithful to what makes me love her, I can't abandon Elin? How can I let her know, as we stand facing one another, that because we've been pulled in opposing directions for so long, it's proved beyond me to find my way back to her without more help?

'Are you off somewhere special?' she asks.

'Getting books for the start of term. How was your summer job?'

'Finished, thank God.'

'When do you start back?' I ask.

'Two weeks.'

'Me too.'

There's nothing else to say. Not now, not like this. She presses her teeth against her lower lip and adds, 'My parents would want to be remembered to you. I told them we'd caught up with one another. They were asking what you were doing these days. They occasionally ask about you.'

'Thanks. That's nice. Give them my regards, will you?'

'I will. I'll do that.'

One of her friends looks at her watch. 'It's almost time, Kate.'

She nods. 'I have to go. Sorry.' To Elin, she says: 'Nice meeting you.'

'Have a good weekend,' I say.

'Yes. You too.'

Elin squeezes my hand and we walk on. And I wonder if I'll ever see her again.

★ ★ ★

I turn to look back, but the pounding of the jack hammers abruptly stops and Kate and her friends have gone. Everyone's gone. Vanished.

'What time is it?' I say, but no one's left to answer.

No Elin, no workmen.

And I will the world to start working again.

13

The world starts working again. There's a knocking breaking in on my world. A series of short reports, one after the other. Not so much a jack hammer though as the hammering of a builder constructing the frame of a house, or the rhythmic flapping of a shredded tyre on the highway, or, or, or . . . It's followed by the chime of my mother's doorbell, and I fall out of sleep, grab my pants and struggle with one leg as I stumble across the landing. My left foot's still asleep and I almost fall down the stairs.

The postman hands me a plastic envelope. 'Express Post,' he says. 'Happy Christmas.'

'Ta. You too.'

I expect it's for my mother, but it's addressed to me, and I think I recognise the writing. I've seen the loop and flow of these characters recently, and some things don't change so much.

Inside the Express packet is a white envelope and inside the white envelope a Christmas card. The illustration is of a cartoon Father Christmas (red-robed, white-bearded), perched on the branch of a massive

Christmas tree in a forest of Christmas trees. Norway spruce. Perched next to him is a squirrel, a couple of birds and a mouse, and it's snowing. The idea is that they're decorative baubles on the tree, with a star shining above them.

Inside the card, she's written:

Tom. Will be in London 21st Dec. If you're able, I'll be at Café Lyons on Euston Road (near the station and Euston Square) at 11:00. Best not contact my parents again — they get anxious. Kate.

She's written to me. After twenty years she's written.

Now I'm sure it was Kate who phoned two nights back. I'll see my mother today and let her know not to expect me tomorrow; I'll phone Annette and promise to take her out for lunch another day.

★ ★ ★

'I thought you'd flown here to see Mum,' Annette complains over the phone.

'I did. I have. But she says she doesn't want me sitting there every minute like a vulture, waiting to pick over her bones.'

'That's just the way she is. She doesn't mean it.'

'Well, I thought I'd give her a break from

vulture-watch for the day. Besides, I've got a chance to catch up with an old friend.'

'Who?'

'An old friend.'

'I'll have to take the day off work then.'

'Course you won't. Give the woman a bloody break, Annette. And we'll have lunch another day.'

'Forget lunch. That doesn't matter.'

I say nothing.

'How will you get to London?' she continues.

'The train,' I say. 'I'd be no good driving. I don't know the roads.'

'The trains aren't reliable.'

'Well, I — '

'I have to go now, Thomas. Someone's at the door.' And she hangs up.

She is my mother's daughter.

Rain and gale force winds have kept the morning dark when I park outside Castle Station. The platform's crammed with commuters dressed in dark suits, wearing dark overcoats, carrying black briefcases and black umbrellas, and the news placards chained to the small booth declare: *SCROOGE TOMPKINS, MINISTER FOR UNEMPLOYMENT* and *TERROR THREAT WARNING*.

The same news is mirrored outside Euston

Station: *BRITAIN ON TERROR ALERT* and *BLEAK XMAS FOR NEW JOBLESS*. Next to these placards are lighter side-dishes: *RIGHT ROYAL MESS — PRINCE LASHES OUT, SOAP STAR'S SEXY PIN-UP POSTER*, and *WORLD'S RICHEST BACHELORS*. The umbrellas, briefcases and suits scurry onto escalators to catch underground trains, or jostle for taxis or disappear into London streets busy with signs, advertising, shops, offices, apartments, parked cars, congested traffic . . . busy, busy people. The wind's less icy here, but no less fierce, and the sporadic volleys of rain are grapeshot to pepper the morning with holes.

I glance at my watch: quarter-past-nine. Having allowed for delays that didn't happen, I'm almost two hours early, so decide to locate Café Lyons before heading to the British Museum, where it'll be warm and dry. And within a couple of minutes, there it is, the place for our rendezvous, the shortest of walks from the station. Kate chose well. Its burgundy paintwork and gold lettering, coupled with the façade of French Windows, which'd be drawn open in summer, give the place a continental look. Maybe we'll get croissants and decent coffee here.

I figure I can kill an hour in the museum before returning to Euston Road, and still be early for Kate. This time I'll be waiting for her.

The wind comes howling towards me with a fresh barrage of rain and I begin hurrying to the Underground. Except something happens.

I'm caught and I'm held by the sight of a car bursting into flower twenty-odd metres ahead. Stopped and mesmerised. Early spring on Euston Road. Orange and red flowers blossoming huge towards the memory of a distant sun, green doors sprouting out and across the road. Petals of twisted metal.

Beautiful.

Can only watch.

Stunned.

Winter one moment and spring the miraculous next. Then back to winter: the windows of small shops, apartments, offices, freeze and shatter into hailing shards of ice. The bleak season. A storm of glass, icicles, dust, sand.

Bleak and bitter.

The rending of metal.

Close to the car, an elderly man wearing an Abercrombie and a bowler hat, of all things, vanishes faster than a magician's rabbit . . . along with three or four other pedestrians. *Abracadabra!* And a pregnant woman pushing a pram, who wasn't there before, appears for a second and then disappears again — magically. And a man on a bicycle, his trousers tucked into his socks, a bike-clip over the top of each, grips his rearing bike, cartwheels backwards and flies upside down — still pedalling.

Then: more than a shimmer, more than a ripple, the streetscape disintegrates in the wake of an invisible tsunami. But silent. Every sound is sucked out of the day into something quieter than the tick of a wristwatch, the beat of a heart. The silence of it picks me up and blows me backwards. A bench catapults into the air. A news placard spins, like a giant frisbee, towards me. Flying. Magically.

So jetlagged. To be picked up and washed into a welcome sleep. It's the strongest of currents. Strong enough to pull the sea flat until it's the mirror of calmness, the smoothest of glass. So still. Not a ripple. Not a breath.

★   ★   ★

I'm standing on a rock, staring at a sea flat enough to walk upon and clear enough to sleep below. The temptation is to lie down and tug its turquoise blanket about me, to place a shell in each ear and drift.

'All mine,' I say to the beach, wanting to plant my footprints in the sand, but know that's not true. I belong to the sea more than the sea belongs to me. I whisper words which are grains of sand on the end of my tongue: 'I belong to the land more than the land belongs to me and,' looking up, 'I belong to the sky more than the sky belongs to I.'

If I strike any of these surrounding boulders with the edge of a stick they'll flower into bushes of fire. If I lay the stick on the sand it'd slither away to the nearest apple. This day, this place, this moment, is a waiting almost complete.

Why?

I don't know.

A flock of stones roost in the shallows, mesmerised to stillness with their watching. I might shout and wave my arms and make them spread their wings in raucous flight, and the commotion would end this moment, but I need to hold it, and so I sit on a hump of rock and stroke its pitted, volcanic hide.

There's a splash against the rock; a few droplets of sea bead on my knees. I look down and the rock winks at me with an eye that is wider than the span of my hand.

Remembering a childhood fairytale, of a man turned beast, riding on the back of a giant fish, I know what'll happen next and won't resist it. The magic and mystery have been rationed too long — rationalised, minimised, reduced — and so I'll go with the flow.

There is a flow. I can feel the tremble of it. So much so that for a moment I believe I'm observing a parting of the waters, a pathway through the ocean, and I stand. It is, however, the gradual rising of the rock I'm sitting on, far more submerged beneath sand than anyone could have known.

'Sit down!' a voice tells me. Gruff.

Not a rock, but a whale.

'No fishing boats,' I say, scanning the horizon. 'No trawlers.' I think of nets, harpoons, the squealing terror of my mount, and how I might not survive. I think of myself. I look for a piece of fin to hold onto, or a couple of barnacles.

'Shut up and enjoy the ride,' the whale says.

Travelling for less than a minute, but more confident of my grip, I glance over my shoulder, expecting to see a crowd gathering on the shoreline, marvelling at my departure. How will this be written in tomorrow's newspapers? Land, though, is nowhere in sight; only a vast flat ocean. Time must be travelling fast today, or slower; I can't work out which, and it doesn't matter now. The sea

334

is silent and smooth as syrup, and not a trawler or net buoy in sight.

We glide without effort, out, further out, without doubt beyond all that is out.

Apart from this whale, whose power and silence is beyond me, I suspect I'm the only living, breathing thing on the face of the world. The earth is still, the clouds can't move, the sky is vacant. If I could find the sun it'd be a broken egg yolk, spilt and caking over. If I could fly, I'd discover trees turned to statues, lifeless, silent. Perhaps I've inherited the world.

'You?' the whale spouts, catching me with spray. 'You're wrong. So wrong.'

'Where are we going?'

'Have you forgotten your appointment?'

'Appointment? What — ?'

Before the question is finished, a speck on the horizon appears. It may be fifty miles away or fourteen; two hours or thirty seconds.

An oil platform, I tell myself, or a small island.

Neither oil platform nor small island, it's a Victorian weatherboard cottage with boat-house attached, freshly painted in heritage colours — Indian Red, Cream, Brunswick Green — and conveniently located for the middle of the ocean. It sports a return verandah, enclosed by handrails and turned newels, and is decorated with authentic period fretwork and corner brackets.

As we glide closer, I notice half-a-dozen sets of small tables and chairs under the shade of the verandah. (There's shade there, but still no sun out here.) A banner is stretched between the gable finial of the cottage and the gable finial of the boathouse; it reads: *BOATHOUSE CAFÉ*. There's a ripple in the water and a murmur of voices lapping across one another, a soft slapping against the side of the timber decking. A cappuccino would go down a treat, but I'd settle for someone to greet me.

Halfway into the dark of the boathouse, the whale stops. Two steps lead onto the decking. 'Don't just sit there,' the whale says. 'I haven't brought you all this way for the ride, you know.'

My legs are stiff, but I clamber off and, in a blink, am looking at a row of empty chairs, empty tables. Should I sit down? Will someone appear with a menu? What's expected here?

I press my nose against a window, but it's impossible to see anything of an inside, and all I achieve is a grease spot: my sum total. Wandering to the end of the side verandah, there's no customers here either. It's a pleasant location for a café, although a little inaccessible, and I wonder how many more cafés might be dotted around the ocean, or if this is my only one.

At first sight, the rear verandah is also empty — except for the row of chairs and tables awaiting customers — until I notice a figure halfway along. She has her back to me and blends with the shadows too easily. I'll ask whether she's been brought here too and whether she can explain what's happening, but before the words leave my lips — quick as a blink — I know she's waiting for me. The whale has brought me to her.

There's something I might remember, if only I could.

She stands with a slight scrape of her chair, turns and smiles a familiar smile.

'Hello, Tom,' she says. 'I was concerned you might not get here for a while.'

It's Kate. She seems older than I've allowed her to grow in my imagination, but that could be because the fussy, floral, long-sleeved dress doesn't suit her, and the bonnet she's wearing belongs in a pantomime.

The table is laid for afternoon tea: lace tablecloth, china teapot, hot water jug, cups, saucers, tea strainer, a plate of scones, bowl of jam, tea plates, silver knives and teaspoons. She's here in front of me, standing, waiting.

'No greeting after all these years?' she says, stepping forward, leaning to plant a brief kiss on my cheek. A dead cold kiss. And I step back.

I peer closely at her, careless of appearing rude, and she twirls for my inspection, melodramatically drapes herself against a verandah post. A touch from a silent movie. Typical Kate. If I stare too hard she may shimmer and disappear.

'You want me to pinch you?' she asks.

'Is it really you?'

'Of course. Who else? Did I give you a turn?' And she laughs.

Stepping toward her, I say: 'Kate,' and want to hug her, but can't.

'Now, won't you sit down? You've had a long journey — years and years — you must be tired. I'll pour the tea.'

'How genteel.'

If the mockery in my tone is apparent, she chooses to dispense with it by adopting it for her own. 'Quaint, ain't it?' She looks at the teapot as if she wants to pick it up and pour but can't. 'I've been waiting for you,' she says.

Perhaps this moment has taken too long in the arriving and she can't move beyond it now. Maybe the tea is stewed.

'Am I too late?' I ask.

She chuckles in a most un-Kate-like

manner. 'Twenty years, give or take. But no matter, you're here now and that's all that counts.'

'Water under the bridge?'

'Lapping the decking? Yes, exactly.'

'You're looking . . . ' I begin, and don't know what to say.

'I'm looking my age. We both are. I'm not eighteen anymore and neither are you.'

'Seventeen,' I correct her. 'I was seventeen when we first met. You were eighteen.'

'That's right. You were so young — too young — such a romantic. Are you still?'

'I don't know. I don't think so.'

'Would you be here if you weren't?'

'I don't know why I'm here.'

'Really?'

'Really.'

'Good. A person can know too much.' She attempts a smile, but it's more a puckered grimace. 'You've been too hard on lots of things, Thomas: on yourself, on Britain, on me. You always thought too much. I always said you did. Remember?' She pauses. It's as if we've fulfilled some prerequisite of our meeting, and now her gaze returns to the spread on the table. 'So how have you spent the years?' she asks, achieving a different tone altogether.

'Surely you know already? You seem to.

How much do you know?'

'You should tell me yourself. I'd prefer that. Indulge me.' Removing the teapot lid, she picks up a teaspoon and stirs the brew. 'Real tea,' she croons. 'No tea bag muck.'

'Is it really you, Kate, or am I just projecting part of myself at a You I imperfectly remember?'

'*Questo tè è buonissimo*,' she replies. 'Or have you learnt to speak Italian too?'

The accent sounds impeccable. 'No. Sorry.' All the same, I think I know what she's said and, if I do, then she's used Holiday Phrasebook Italian on me, and I could've looked this up myself.

Sliding the teapot to one side, she shrugs. 'There's something missing. Sorry. I won't be a minute.' She stands and the chair scrapes once again, and she enters the building through a door I haven't noticed. As the door clicks shut, I lean back and peer through the glass, but still see nothing except a reflection of the sea. Within the minute she's sitting opposite again.

Real milk. So real it's yellow and thick with cream, fresh from the cow.

'I haven't seen milk like that since . . . our holiday in Yorkshire — that afternoon in Whitby.'

She claps her hands together, brings them

340

to her chin. There's something out of place about the gesture. 'How do you take your tea?' But her voice breaks into falsetto.

'White with one.'

She lifts the little jug and pours; reaches for the tea strainer, grips the handle of the teapot, juggles the tasks as if it's all she's ever done. She hands me a cup and saucer and says, 'This moment's been waiting all your life. Just bobbing up and down.'

'All my life?' It makes no sense.

'Every day of it.' Pushing the plate of scones to one side, she reaches across the table. 'Will you hold my hand?' she says.

'Why?'

'Because you can. Because it's time.'

Looking away, I see the sky is moving again. I'm not betraying Elin in being here; quite the opposite. I'm finally resolving the past and creating more room for Elin, I tell myself. The sea is still calm, but no longer syrup. I can smell the brine. Returning my cup to its saucer, I slip my hand over hers, but it's coarser and rougher than it should be, and I recoil. Both her hands are old, gnarled and masculine, beyond her years and femininity.

Instead of Kate, I'm sitting opposite Old Lofty in drag.

'You're not Kate, you bastard!'

'Hello, Thomas,' he strains out in his best Our Father voice.

'You're not Kate!'

'Indeed,' he says, pulling out the padding from the bodice of his dress: a silver goblet of red wine, a half-eaten loaf of bread, the stink of old fish. 'But I could be.'

'You're not even real. You're just an image I conjured up — my bogeyman, my Angel of Death. You don't belong here; not now, not anymore.'

'I do! I'll always be with you!' he shouts, standing, slopping gobbets of wine across the lace tablecloth, tearing a limb of bread away with his teeth. 'This is exactly where I belong!'

'No!' I shout back, but refuse to stand. My hand is shaking, but I lift my cup and sip tea nonetheless. Best china.

He sits again, leans forward and tries to suck me up with his hollow eyes. 'Particularly here, particularly now,' he spits. 'I'm more real than your precious Kate. Come with me, stay with me. If you want Kate, I can be Kate. I was doing a good job until you spoiled it. Come with me and I'll give you Kate.'

'Bollocks,' I say, wiping a fleck of sodden bread off my arm. 'You're a figment of my imagination — a fiction. I created you.'

'You've made me real.' He stands, unravels

his black cape from the shadows on the floor and clasps it around his shoulders.

'I'll unmake you,' I shout.

'Easier said than done.' He tucks the goblet of wine and chunk of bread inside his cape, then lifts his arms and flaps them back and forth, creating rushes of air across the verandah. 'Death!' he announces.

And I laugh. Melodrama makes me laugh. I crease at the middle with laughter and have to hold my sides, wipe my eyes, and even the whale joins in with squeals and ribbons of clicks, streaming laughter from the boat-house. And the more I laugh the madder he gets, and the madder he gets the wilder he flaps.

'One way or another I'll have you,' he declares. 'Sooner or later you *will* come to me.' He paces the verandah, flapping away — to and fro, to and fro — then turns and faces the sea.

'Never,' I say. 'Never, never, never.'

'I'll be back, and then you'll be mine. Forever and ever.'

He spreads his arms out, flexes his knees, leans forward and dives into the water. There's a small splash and then nothing. Nothing but nothing.

The manner of his departure is a surprise. I'd have imagined the graceless flapping of a gloated vulture, skywards, not the nimbleness of a circus performer's swan dive. Old Lofty has hidden depths.

But all this drama is wearing on a hot day, and I lean closer to the wall where the shade is deeper. The sea is emerald green and clear again, and a five minute nap on this table will set me right.

Sleep. Let me sleep. Keep the blinding brightness out.

'Wake up, sir.'

It's too short a nap after such a journey, and the whale needs rest too.

'Wake up, sir.'

Wrenched from my table in the Boathouse Café, I open gritty eyes to see a flight attendant leaning over me, rows of seats, open baggage compartments, the backs of passengers crowding down the aisles, clutching coats, luggage, passports, pressing forward. Among them, the backs of three figures are vaguely familiar: a businessman in an Abercrombie, a young mother cradling a baby, and a man wearing bike-clips carrying a unicycle. The attendant smiles and her smile is anchored in lip-gloss and eyeliner.

'I'll go back to the beach soon,' I say.

'Pardon?'

I shake my head.

'We've landed,' she says. 'Are you alright?

Did you take something to make you sleep?'

'Where are we?'

'London, Heathrow. Journey's end.'

'Where from?' I say. 'Where have I been?'

'Pardon?'

I've woken on a plane at Heathrow airport, at five-thirty on a winter's morning. Riding a whale to the Boathouse Café was more real than this.

'Would you like a hand with your luggage, sir?'

Poking out the side pocket of my flight bag is a white envelope with my name on it: Tom Passmore. 'Christmas card,' I say to the attendant, and she nods as if this might explain everything.

From the cabin speakers comes a tinny rendition of some old tune, but I can't make it out. At the cabin door, the flight crew smile and thank me for flying with their airline. It's night-dark outside and a rush of cold air stabs at me. The sunken eyes and flinty smile of one of the pilots reminds me of someone — and it isn't good — but I'm dopey with sleep.

'Enjoy your stay,' the bastard says. 'Night-night, sleep tight.'

I turn on him. 'What did you say?'

He looks at me with his lop-sided grin and says: 'Hope you had a good flight.'

In the Arrivals Hall, I dig into my pocket for my passport wallet, and a sharp edge of flint stabs the tender skin between my nail and index finger. Sucking on the graze, I pull out two flint points and, from the other pocket, a corn dolly. I show this collection of artefacts to the customs official who smiles reassuringly. I am Thomas Daniel Passmore. I am.

'I've been here before,' I say.

She nods, but says nothing.

'This must be a dream,' I say. 'It can't be real.'

She reaches across and places a hand on my shoulder. 'You can't sleep here.'

'What?'

She shakes me. 'You can't sleep here.'

One side of my face is pressed flat against a table and I'm staring at a waitress. The moment she realises I'm looking at her, she steps back.

'If you don't wake up I'll call the police.'

I pull myself upright in the booth and try working out where I am.

'Sorry,' I say. 'I keep falling asleep.' Looking past her, I recognise the style of French windows that form the street-facing wall of this long, narrow establishment and know that I'm inside Café Lyons. The place is empty, as far as I can tell, although it's difficult to see into some of the booths. I can't remember arriving here or having visited the British Museum. 'Can I have a coffee please? A long black.' And I hand her a five-pound note. Then I glance at my watch. Shit, it's stopped! Nine-twenty. But above the counter there's a clock: eleven-thirty! Shit, shit, shit! 'Wait,' I say to the waitress. 'Please. Have you had any other customers in the last half-hour or so?'

She stops, hesitates. 'The manager's out back.'

'I'm waiting for someone. I was supposed to meet them half-an-hour ago, but I'm jetlagged and keep falling asleep.'

'Jetlagged? Not on drugs?'

'I'm Australian,' I say. 'I only flew in . . . a while ago.'

This reassures her and she steps closer again. 'It's been busy most of the morning. This is the lull before the lunch-time rush.'

'A woman with long, dark hair?'

'No, not that I remember.'

'With short hair then? Or tied up?'

'I don't know. There was a woman by herself. She was sitting at that window table.' The waitress points to a table close to the door. 'She wouldn't see you from there. Must have left with the rest of the crowd, about ten minutes ago. You just missed her.'

Why did I sit so far back, and in a booth of all things?

'Did she leave a message or anything?'

'No.'

'You didn't see which way she went?'

'Get real.'

I pull myself out the booth, but my left foot's numb — my whole side's numb — and I'm dragging it badly as I make my way out the door. How could I miss her? I'm losing Kate all over again.

'What about your coffee?' the waitress calls.

'Get real,' I try to say, but the words remain a whisper. I want to shake my head, but it's not as easy as it used to be. And there's something different about this London street. It's to do with the light and the cyclone fencing.

'Can you hear me?' she calls.

14

Grabbing a bottom corner of chain-link fence, I tug it up and away from the post, and here's Elin squatting next to me, ready to scrabble through the gap on her hands and knees.

It's the sleepiest of Sunday afternoons when Elin and I break into the building site, and the rest of the world has vanished.

'Through here,' I say. 'Can you hear me okay?'

She nods and has almost crawled through when she stops and squints back at me and shakes her head instead. Except it's now Jo I see from this angle. She must have dyed her hair again: corn blonde. Until now I've never realised how similar they are, which makes me wonder whether they might've been the same person all along.

'It's alright,' I tell her, 'no one'll stop us. It's been this way for years. No one lives here.'

About eight houses on one side of the road are complete, but the remaining seven aren't much more than foundations.

'Careful,' I say, as we teeter across a

349

network of precarious planks bridging a maze of trenches. The number of trenches has increased since I was here with Gazza. Some are so deep I can't see the bottom, others are filled with an ocean of black water slopping backwards and forwards with the tug of an unusual current. 'Wouldn't want to lose you again.'

I knock on the door to one of the houses. The garden's a mess of builders' rubble, but Brian's car is parked out front.

Turning to Jo as I reach for the handle, I say, 'It's alright. I know whose house this is.' But she's no longer there. No one is.

The front door leads into the hallway at home. It becomes the home of my childhood, down to the pictures and carpets and wallpaper. However, although the house pretends to be empty of people, I sense someone waiting to jump out and wrestle bony fingers around my throat, or to charge down the stairs and push me over in order to get out — a burglar, perhaps. But nothing happens.

Whispers and muffled laughter come from the kitchen.

As long as I don't falter, the sound can belong to anyone I want in this dream. That's the power of the place. How lucky is that?

'Hello, Kate,' I call, and walk through.

But instead of Kate, there's a figure — a

man — who fills the kitchen with the many folds of a long, black coat. The coat's so large and dark that it swamps the light from the room, and it takes a moment to realise he's got his back to me and is holding the back door open for an escape, urging Kate to run away. Of course it'll be Old Lofty.

'Bastard!' I say. 'Ask her to come back. Why did you do that?'

He turns then, and it's my father. All this time Lofty and my dad have also been one and the same, and this revelation paralyses me. The kitchen door is open, Kate'll be scrabbling away beneath the hooked-back fence, and I can't move.

Though he stares in my direction, his expression never changes. He might be a statue or a photograph, frozen in time.

I want Kate back, but there's so much I need to ask him too. There's a question I have for both of them — Dad and Kate — and so I shout it as loud as I can. Maybe Kate'll return, maybe I'll unfreeze him.

'Why did you leave me?' I shout.

★ ★ ★

Andrew and Annette are still asleep when I ease my way downstairs. Each time I return 'home', the house is smaller in every

351

dimension, making me duck my head, squeezing me out, although I figure that won't matter much by the end of this visit. Sometimes it's hard to imagine how the place ever contained me.

Brian's in the lounge, engrossed by the morning news on his pride and joy: a brand new, large-screen TV. An outside broadcast shows a reporter and a policeman standing in front of a cordoned-off bungalow, where an eighty-one-year-old widow has been raped and murdered.

'Watching TV already?' I say.

He looks up from his chair, peering over his glasses. 'I'm waiting for the weather. It's after the news round-up. Unless you can tell me what the three-day forecast is?'

I begin walking away, then step back, make a show of looking towards the open French windows and the brightness of the summer morning, and announce: 'Rain, rain and more rain.'

In the kitchen, my mother enters through the open back door and she's carrying a colander of strawberries.

'You're up,' she says. 'Did you sleep well?'

'Not bad.'

She holds the colander out for me to see the crop. 'Thought I should pick these before the birds do.'

I reach out to take a couple, but she pulls them back.

'Not now. They're for later. You haven't even had breakfast yet.' And she begins rinsing them in the sink.

I make a mental note to buy two punnets of strawberries and a bottle of Asti spumante for Elin's birthday breakfast in a couple of weeks. We'll gorge ourselves in bed, not get up until midday, and enjoy every guiltless minute of it. And then I head out the back door.

'Where are you off to? Aren't you having breakfast?'

'In a minute. Thought I might have a walk round the garden first.'

But she'll know what I want to see. It was too late and dark when I pulled into the driveway last night.

Two weeks previously they phoned to wish us well in our new flat in Great Shentonbury.

'It's good,' I told Brian. 'Only one bedroom, but it's big enough for us.'

'That reminds me,' he said. 'Andrew needed more cupboard space, so we boxed up the last of your stuff and put it in the attic. There was only a couple of boxes — you might not even want it — it's been sitting in that cupboard for years, but you might want to go through it next time you're home. Old school books, reports, that sort of stuff.'

'Fair enough,' I said. 'What else is news? Got your holiday booked?'

'Your mum said to tell you we've taken the old tree down — got some men to come and saw it down and take it away. You should have seen the mess. The garden looks twice the size now.'

'Which tree?'

'That big old pine thing. It was pushing the back fence down. I spent last weekend putting in new fence posts.'

'The spruce? My Christmas tree?'

'Well there was only one, so I guess so. But hardly your — '

'Shit!'

'What — '

'You might have told me beforehand.'

'Why? It had to come down. The neighbours were complaining. It's not as though you live here or ever pruned the damn thing.'

'Okay. Alright. It doesn't matter. Don't worry about it, Brian.'

'I wasn't.'

So I kneel beside the sawn-off stump and place my hand on the remaining bark, pick at a piece of resin bleeding from the cut, sniff it and roll it into a bead. In the corner of the garden, tucked under a bush, several long cones lie like fat cigars, and I pick these up, pull back some of the cardboard-like scales and shake them until I've gathered several seeds. These I drop in my pocket, along with the best three cones.

I'm perched on a kitchen stool, with a mug of tea and a bowl of muesli, when Andrew shuffles in. His hair sticks up, his pyjama top hangs off one shoulder, and he yawns.

'You look like you haven't woken up yet,' I say, and ruffle his hair.

'You talk in your sleep,' he replies. 'You shouted one time. Woke me up.'

'You snore.'

'Don't.'

'Like a piglet,' I say. 'Oink, squeal; oink, squeal.'

The kitchen door's still open, and Kate's drifted irrevocably away from me. I haven't seen her in two years, and know that two will become five and five will become ten. We're following separate currents and it seems we'll never meet again. In a fortnight, I'll start work with the Wiltshire Library and Museum Service, and Elin has a teaching position in a small primary school. She'll have returned from her literacy conference by the time I leave Nenford.

When I finish my muesli, I take a sip of tea and make the announcement: 'Elin and I are getting married next March.'

There's a moment's stunned silence to savour.

'What? You're not? You're joking,' Mum says.

'Nup.'

'Congratulations,' says Brian.

'Really?' says Andrew.

'You're too young,' Mum tells me.

'Too young?'

'You've only just finished university.'

'I'm older than you were when you married Dad.'

'Things were different back then. We had to grow up quicker. Maybe we were too young as well.'

I stand up and push the stool against the wall. 'We've lived together for two years. We're getting married next March.'

'I still think you're too young,' she says. 'Twenty-two's nothing. You've seen nothing of the world — of life.'

'We'll see it together. Don't you like her?'

'She's lovely. But she's too young too.'

I begin rinsing my dishes in the sink and Mum pulls the colander of strawberries out of the way.

'The first week of the school Easter holidays,' I tell her. 'Thought you might be pleased.'

She says nothing, but reaches for a tea towel to catch the drips from the strawberries.

'Thanks for your good wishes,' I say, and step past Brian and Andrew on my way upstairs to the bathroom.

Annette's on the landing.

'What's the fuss about?' she asks.

I shake my head, intend keeping quiet. 'Nothing,' I say. Then: 'The same old crap. Some things never bloody change.'

'Mum! Dad! Thomas swore!'

★   ★   ★

That afternoon, I take the stepladders and climb into the attic. It should be cluttered with boxes, old toys and junk maturing towards antique-hood, but it's practically empty.

Close to where I perch, my legs dangling into the hallway below, sit two cardboard boxes with my name daubed on each, and only a little further away, protected by a dust sheet, the family Christmas tree: a two-foot-tall, ready-decorated, green plastic job. Apart from a few Christmas cards clustered on the sideboard, this is Mum and Brian's annual concession to Christmas decorations. Each year he'd lift it down from the attic, remove

357

the cover, sit it on top of the TV, plug in the lights, and there it'd be.

'Easy,' he'd probably say.

'Too easy by half,' I'd reply.

I haul my boxes down the ladders and sit on the bed to go through them. In the first, there's thirteen years of school reports, a biscuit tin full of badges, and several History exercise books with assignments written in fountain pen, using a careful script I no longer recognise. In the second box, there's a small, red tin containing two Neolithic flint points, a bag of marbles, a badly torn poster of The Stones, the black pretend-leather diary that Brian and Mum gave me one Christmas, and a wad of letters (green envelopes, green writing paper) tied together with a length of red cord.

Afterwards, I shovel everything into the boxes again and stack them next to my carry-all. Nothing will stay here; not even the stuff I'm gonna chuck out. And then I escape the house and walk a while. There's another, bigger argument looming and, having been bullied into avoiding the topic all my life, I need anger more than courage.

Walking past Gazza's old house, three streets away, I wonder what it'd be like to knock on the door and speak to his mum.

'You won't remember me,' I'd say, 'but I

was a friend of Gazza's, back at primary school. You showed us how to make doughnuts. You won't remember me, but I just wanted to say that I'm really sorry for your loss. It might be several years too late, but I am sorry. Really. I just didn't know it at the time when I read that he'd been killed, nor how to speak it. I just wanted to tell you this.'

And she'd look at me, with the front door half-open, and she'd either try to smile or she'd look blank, or stunned, or stung, or she'd begin crying and shut the door in my face. Or no one would answer the door in the first place. Or someone else would answer the door, like a young mother with a crying child on her hip, and I'd learn that Gazza's mum had moved away soon after her loss or that she'd died of a broken heart.

But I look at the house and the garden, at the peeling paint around the windows and at the uncut grass, and walk on. Too little has changed in some respects, too much in others, and the connection between yesterday and today is getting too thin to trace.

Two streets away, instead of crossing Northampton Road into Ald Lane, which once led to the River Nene, six lanes of ring road stop me. On my left, instead of a market garden, there's an enormous shopping centre, car park and petrol station. Further across, where fields once stretched to the horizon, stands three car dealerships, an electrical goods discount superstore, a carpet and flooring showroom, a McDonalds, KFC, Burger King and a cut-price furniture warehouse, surrounded by more car parks and another petrol station. A labyrinth of concrete and bitumen.

Close to the supermarket complex, a dark and fetid underpass leads to the other 'superstores'. It takes me away from Ald Lane, but to a less frantic stretch of road, which I dash across, before following a fence line to where I wanted to be in the first place.

How can anybody walk to the river these days? Where do kids make their hideouts or roast the apples they've scrumped on dull Sunday afternoons? They're rhetorical questions, answered by the smell of piss in the underpass and the graffiti across every wall in sight.

Ald Lane is still an unsealed bridleway leading to a farmhouse, next to the old mill — originally built in the Middle Ages — but is nothing without the hedgerow of hawthorn, crab-apple, elder, ash, cow parsley, nettle and burdock that defined it for centuries. In its place is a wire fence, complete with snagged plastic bags, a couple of shopping trolleys, a tyre, plastic crates . . .

Beyond the mill race, I come to the main artery of the river; still a popular stretch for anglers, who perch among flattened reed beds despite the drone of traffic bustling across the landscape from roundabout to roundabout. But two minutes later, I freeze. Across the footpath, some gun-happy, moronic bastard has arranged a row of dead birds. There are ten, all lined up to face the same way, from smallest to largest: seven finches, two starlings and a blackbird. The act of a sicko. I step back, scan the fields for some cretin skulking with an air rifle, and wish I could bury each bird down the bastard's throat.

It's then I see the dead swan.

Several metres up-river, its neck and most of its body is submerged, but part of one leg is on the surface with its head and bill, and a few feathers ruffle in the breeze.

How could anyone do this?

It's drifting with the current, and as I draw closer I watch its feathers ruffle again, except this time I hear them rustle. The rustle of plastic. It's not a swan, but a white, plastic carrier bag, partly submerged, with air trapped inside, caught in the fork of a branch. What I thought was part of a leg is a lollipop stick trailing next to it, and as I look at the markings on the swan's bill I realise there's a

361

printed banner in orange: *FRESH FOOD*.

I watch it drift.

Déjà vu.

Returning to the house, for an alfresco meal, the mood's become celebratory, almost apologetic, and I can't bring myself to break it. Not at first.

'Red or white?' Brian says, pointing to two wine casks sitting by the back step. 'Grab a glass from the kitchen.'

'Nice walk?' Mum asks.

I nod.

'See anyone?'

'No.'

There's little breeze here; just a calm summer's evening. The smell of a barbecue wafts from one side of the neighbours' fence and the sound of a TV washes in from the other. Bees and hoverflies drift around the flowers, even though the sun's dropping, and a couple of wasps drone around the border of rocks, exploring crevices. It's the calm before the storm, but I've shouldered her bitterness for too many years.

After dinner, when the twins have been sent to do the dishes and Brian's checking out the Saturday Night Movie, Mum says: 'We are pleased, you know, love. About you and Elin. She seemed a nice girl.'

'Hmm,' I say. 'She is.'

'A pity she couldn't have come back with you this weekend. It would have been nice to get to know her better.'

I watch an ant struggle to carry a crumb through the grass.

'There'll be other times.'

She takes a sip of wine. 'We don't see you that often.'

I take a sip of wine. 'Yeah, well.'

'What?'

I empty my glass. 'Nothing.'

She gets to her feet, holds a hand out for my empty glass. 'Well, this won't get my knitting finished, will it? I can't sit here all evening.'

'Why not?'

'I've got jobs to do, that's why.'

Pulling in a deep breath, I hold it, then exhale. 'Tell me one thing,' I say.

'What?'

'Tell me about Dad. Now. I want to know. I need to know.'

She doesn't wince or flinch, but turns away, then turns back; her eyes angry darts and her mouth pinched tight. 'Don't. Don't you do that. Why would you . . . why spoil a perfect evening?'

'Nothing's that perfect. I need to know.'

She walks inside, leaving me empty and outside. Two minutes later, she's shouting at

Annette for teasing Andrew.

The evening midges start to swarm, and I slap at a couple. It takes two commercial breaks in the movie before Brian comes out. He looks down at me, his arms crossed.

'Why do you always go out your way to upset your mother?' he says. He doesn't exactly whisper, but his voice is hushed; he doesn't want the neighbours to hear.

'I thought it was the other way round.'

'You're a self-centred bugger, aren't you?'

'If you say I'm a self-centred bugger then I must be, Brian. You're the expert.' I refuse to lower my voice.

He steps towards me and I'm ready to duck.

'Grow up,' he hisses. 'Stop acting like a schoolboy. Try thinking about other people's feelings for a change. It's always the same; after you've been home a few hours you can't help but stir things up.'

'Well you needn't worry about that anymore, Brian. It'll be a long while before I set foot in this house again.'

He laughs and begins heading back inside. 'Don't be so bloody dramatic.'

'It's a fact, that's all. If you and Mum won't accept there are things I need to know about my past — about my dad — then there's no point me being here. We've got nothing in common. What else is left?'

'Childish,' he snorts, and returns to his programme.

★ ★ ★

In the morning, when I go downstairs, Brian calls me as I pass the lounge door. Mum's still in bed.

'Come here a minute, will you.' He mutes the TV and nods at the settee. 'Sit down.'

I sit. 'What's this about?'

'Your dad. Your mum wants me to tell you.'

'Really?'

'On one condition.' He stands, shuts the door into the hallway, then sits on the edge of his chair.

'What's that?'

'That you don't mention anything to Annette or Andrew, and that you never raise the subject with her again — not ever. You have to promise that.'

I look across the room and realise he's missing his weather report. 'And if what you tell me doesn't answer my questions, what then?'

'I think it will. I'm sure it will.'

'But what if it doesn't?'

'Then you can ask me about it if you must. But not in anybody else's ear-shot.'

'Why? Why the big secret?'

'Some things are best forgotten.'

'Buried.'

'That's right.'

'Buried alive?' I mutter.

'What?'

I shake my head. 'Doesn't matter.' I wish he'd turn the television off.

'Well then?'

'Yeah. I suppose. What choice have I got?'

He sits back in his chair and it's my turn to lean forward.

'Your father hanged himself,' he begins.

'I know.'

'He worked for Elfords Glass.'

'Yeah, I know that too.'

'Apparently, for a number of months before your dad — before he died — they were looking at down-sizing the company, laying off some of the workforce. That stuff makes everyone fed up. From what I gather, he got a bit depressed.'

Brian pauses, as if he's finished.

'He killed himself because he lost his job? You're joking?'

'Just listen, will you. I'm trying to make this make sense. He didn't get laid off. In fact, a few days before — you know — he found out that he was one of the lucky ones. Even if there was a bit of a question mark hanging over the company, he still had a job.'

I twist on the chair, can feel sweat running down the inside of my arm, goosebumps on the back of my neck.

'But he did go and celebrate,' Brian continues. 'From what I gather, it seems he drank a bit too much with a few workmates at a Christmas party and, when he was driving home, had an accident.' He pauses, sighs, picks up the remote and turns off the TV. 'What you've got to remember is that the drink-driving laws weren't the same back then.'

I work my way through Brian's statement and realise he's understating a bigger truth. 'He had an accident? He killed someone? Is that what you're telling me?'

He nods. 'A child. A five-year-old girl. The daughter of someone your mum had gone to school with, except he didn't know that at the time. In a side street in Northampton.'

'Shit. But if it was an accident . . . '

'He'd been depressed for a while and things were looking up again, but he'd also been drinking.'

He's trying to tell me something else, but I can't catch it.

'I don't understand,' I say.

'He didn't stop. He could have helped the girl, got her to hospital, but he didn't stop. I

367

suppose he panicked, wasn't thinking straight. It was a hit-and-run. The media was screaming blue murder. The police had an idea of the car they were looking for. It would've only been a matter of time.'

I say nothing. Try to focus on the blank TV screen. Hear myself swallow air.

'It's what you wanted to know,' Brian says.

I nod.

'Two days later he went to work, clocked off, and well . . . '

'Clocked off,' I say.

'And hanged himself,' Brian says.

I nod.

'That's it,' he says.

I'm still nodding, and I sit in silence a while and Brian says nothing.

'A letter — did he write a letter? Didn't he leave some kind of . . . something?'

He raises his eyebrows and shakes his head. 'I don't know. I don't think so. There are things your mum won't even talk about with me.'

'Can't you ask her? There must have been a note. People don't just . . . '

'No. She won't. There are some things we never get all the answers to. I suspect he wrote something but she destroyed it. She won't talk about it. I doubt she ever will. You have to accept that. Forget it. You'll have to.'

I remember the words she uttered at the time, after the policeman called: 'Weak, so weak.'

I look up at Brian, who's looking at me and waiting.

'Are you alright?' he asks.

I nod again. I just have to get out of here, away from them. I need to get in the car and drive back to the flat. 'Thanks,' I say. 'Thanks for that.'

15

There's no two ways about it, I must see Kate's parents again. All I'm asking for is her address or a telephone number, to fix up another meeting. I shouldn't have fallen asleep, or sat so far back in the café. On the passenger seat next to me is a poinsettia loaded with red and green leaves, tied with a large Christmas ribbon, and in my coat pocket is Kate's Christmas card, to prove she'd invited me to meet her in London.

'Happy Christmas,' I'll tell them. 'It's no big deal; I'm happily married with a beautiful family. This is just for old time's sake. The last thing I want is to upset her life.'

Who knows, I might even find her in Abetsby on a pre-Christmas visit. Stranger things have happened. And then, over coffee or a meal somewhere, we'll talk and I'll tell her how I needed to make sure she was okay. Maybe I'll explain how things were all those years ago when I lost her, and redeem that part of the past, but we'll also renew our connection with one another.

A matter of letting go what's dead, embracing something new.

Turn, turn, turn.

At a T-junction in Abetsby, I watch a young mother struggle to carry a Christmas tree. She's steering a pushchair across the road with one hand while gripping her tree with the other, which is okay until she tries manoeuvring the pushchair back onto the pavement and it begins tipping and her baby starts screaming. The pavements are crowded with the busy rush of Christmas shoppers, but an elderly man with a walking-stick stops to help.

Pulling out from the junction, I don't see the bus overtaking a parked delivery van until it's almost collected me. I brake hard and the driver swerves, slams on his brakes and slides a window open. 'Happy Christmas, moron!' he shouts. Everyone on the bus stares and a kid on the backseat presses his nose against the window and gives me the finger.

Two minutes later, I turn into Kate's street and . . . and can do nothing but drift to a halt in the middle of the road. I sit, stare . . . stop. It's too big to comprehend.

Half the houses in the street have plywood panels nailed across their ground-floor windows and against the front doors. Not only this, but the unboarded houses are empty. There's no curtains, no furniture; even the Christmas decorations have gone. It's a street awaiting demolition. Impossible.

Standing in front of Kate's house, surely there's something that'll half-convince me I've turned into the wrong road, but over the porch is a corbel stone with a motif carved in relief: a face with leaves growing out the eyes, mouth, nostrils, ears, scalp. And it's only now I register that every tree in the street has gone; they've all been felled. All this in the space of a few days.

Kate would be distraught. The Kate I knew would be distraught.

The house is an empty shell. All the same, I knock twice on the front door and wait as both knocks echo back, the way abrupt noises will bounce around such hollowness. I knock again, then peer through the letterbox: the hallway and stairs have been stripped of carpets.

The door swings open to reveal several letters scattered on the floor.

'Hello! Anybody home? Mr Hainley? Mrs Hainley? It's Tom Passmore.' My voice runs upstairs and down again, and I shut the door behind me. The house smells cold and my breath fogs. 'Hello! Hello!'

The door to the lounge and the back of the house is shut, and maybe there's a murmur of conversation coming from beyond it.

But there's no one. Nothing. Even the gas

fire's gone. The kitchen's empty, the bathroom too. Tugging open the back door, there's only winter weeds dead in the frozen soil. A hundred white swans once filled this garden.

Upstairs, it's the same story. Almost. The front two bedrooms are empty, and my feet make too much clatter on the floorboards as I steal from one room to the other, but Kate's bedroom door is closed. And softly, I place a hand flat against it, as if I might trace some lingering whisper of life from it. Then I turn the handle and enter.

Her calico curtains are still hanging and, although there's no other furniture in the house, her bed is against one wall of the small room, where it always stood. I try tracing the pattern of the wallpaper, but the tangle of briar roses has faded to a bleak nothing.

This is the end of it.

'Kate.'

Positioning the poinsettia on the windowsill, I dig a finger into the potting mix to check it's not too dry and then close her curtains. There's no sheet or blanket, but the bed is more inviting than any bed I can remember, and I'm about to stretch out and claim the sleep I've been dying for when a loud bang echoes from downstairs.

Someone's there.

My heart's racing.

I mustn't be caught trespassing and am tempted to charge downstairs and out the front door, but what if I've conjured Kate's return simply by being here? I tiptoe to the top of the stairs, lean my head against the wall, place a hand on the banister, and wait and listen. But whoever's down there is playing the same game: waiting, listening.

'Hello! Anybody home? Mr Hainley? Mrs Hainley? Hello!'

Nothing. Silence.

Downstairs, I push the lounge door ajar and brace myself for an intruder to rush out — or to run myself. All quiet. Shoving the door fully open, though, sparks a flurry of movement under the window and I jump back. A starling flutters around the room, panics away from me and crashes into the window with another loud bang. I'm the only intruder. Dazed, it stands on the sill and regards me with one eye, and when I head over to open the window it panics again. From the muck by the chimney place, where the gas fire once stood, I can guess how it found its way in.

There's really nothing wrong with opening the scatter of post. It's an abandoned house. There might be some reference to where the Hainleys have moved, or even to Kate, but there's nothing. No suggestion at all. Two mail order circulars advertise Christmas Specials, there's a letter from *Reader's Digest* advising Mr Hainley that he's successfully completed the first two stages towards becoming a millionaire and might like to consider how he'd prefer receiving his prize, and three Christmas cards, but none contain the clues I need.

It's while I'm slipping the cards back into their envelopes I realise that, although no return address appeared on Kate's Express envelope, there should be a postmark to identify where she mailed it; something to narrow my search. Shit, I'm stupid. Why didn't I think of this before? Because I didn't know I'd miss her in London. Because I didn't know her parents' street was about to be demolished. But it's dustbin day in Nenford, with the envelope among the rubbish, and Annette asked me to put Mum's bin out that morning.

There's no time to call at the hospital, and even less time once I get snagged in the congestion surrounding Northampton's town centre. However, the road to Nenford's almost deserted, while heaps of nose-to-tail traffic heads in the opposite direction. It's like one of those disaster movies where the entire population is fleeing the site of impending doom, while the hero races against time and tide. Even so, I count three dustbin lorries during this short journey, each heading out towards the municipal tip, and my foot presses harder on the accelerator.

Turning off the main road and into one of the side streets that leads to Mum's house, several things happen one after the other. Firstly, the car loses traction as I turn the corner (the temperature has dropped and there's ice on the road); secondly, I notice all the dustbins lining this street have been emptied; thirdly, yet another dustbin lorry pulls out of another side street, and seems to be heading where I'm heading. I accelerate slightly to catch up, but as I'm negotiating a row of vehicles parked either side of the narrow road, a pale child in a nightdress steps in front of me.

Slamming down the brake, the car swerves, hits ice and skids sideways towards the girl and a parked car. I hold my breath, which is about all that's between us when I stop: a breath. She stares past me as though I might be invisible, then floats back towards a house with an open front door.

It's enough to sit still and breathe and be thankful I haven't turned into my dad, and then I drive slowly round to the house. The dustbin lorry isn't in sight and the bins haven't been emptied.

Dropping the lid to the ground, I drag out the topmost bag of rubbish and rip into it. The Express envelope is tucked down the side, next to an empty can of beans and a soggy teabag, and the dustbin lorry enters the street as I uncrumple it.

By now, I expect it to be date-stamped with a useless London postmark or illegibly smudged, but it reads quite clearly: AVE-BURY WILTS.

Letting myself into the house, I sink into a chair and the day stops.

It starts again in late-afternoon when the village sign for Avebury comes into focus fifty-odd metres ahead. Snow clouds have been hanging low over the landscape ever since I cut out of Swindon, adding a broodiness to the winter downs, and there's only the weakest suggestion of daylight left when I pull into the glare of the pub's car park spotlight. Throughout the journey, I've noticed a jittery insularity growing, with people rushing from place-to-place, and families in thick coats scurrying down driveways, laden with bags and boxes, into houses pulsing with the glow of coloured Christmas lights. It's obviously a day to abandon the bleak outside and be barricaded against the siege of a long night, to enjoy an open fire, mulled wine and mince pies and the company of loved ones.

Surely, it's not Christmas Eve already? It can't be. Time isn't flowing the way I'm used to. Has one day passed since I was in London, or none? I might've been in the UK for months, or even years. Anything seems possible at the moment. Maybe Australia was only a vivid, beautiful dream, along with my family and being the person I thought I'd become. I've always needed someone to anchor me steady to who I am. Perhaps I should phone Elin, so she can tell me about her day and how she walked along the beach and paddled in warm waters and felt the sand between her toes, and so I can hear my kids chattering in the background . . . except it's the middle of the night in their world and I'd only frighten them.

'G'day,' I say to the landlord.

I'm leaning on the bar with my overnight bag by my feet. There's an open fire crackling in the hearth; flames dancing, logs spitting and singing. The bar is a quarter full at most. It's a room of stone and oak, warm and dry, and stout against the winter. It'll do.

He smiles, nods. 'Australian?' he asks.

'Yeah.'

'Jeez, you're a long way from home.'

It's my turn to nod. Then I remember why

I'm here and glance round at the other patrons, but there's no one who could be Kate sipping on a beer or a brandy.

'What can I do for you?'

'Accommodation,' I say. 'I saw the sign out front. Have you got a spare room for the night?'

'They're all spare. We don't usually get visitors this close to Christmas. We weren't planning on taking guests.'

'It's a long way home,' I say.

'Give me a minute; I'll ask the missus. She's in charge of that stuff.'

The room I'm given is so similar to the one Kate and I shared in Whitby that I go to the window, half-expecting to see the onset of night in an east-coast fishing town. Instead, the view encompasses a sweep of huge sarsen stones glistening with frost: a parade of watchful ghosts.

Pint in hand, I lean on the bar and chat with Mick the landlord. He asks about Australia and why I'm in Britain at this time of year, and I answer him. In return, I say: 'So, how long have you run The Red Lion, Mick?' and 'What's the population of Avebury, Mick. It can't be very big, can it?' But it's harder than I imagined to ask the questions I need to ask, and a relief when he jumps into the subject himself.

'So, if your mother's sick in Northampton, what brings you down here just before Christmas?'

There's a tree dressed in silver standing in one corner, and thick garlands of tinsel tracing the beams and outlining the windows, and coloured fairy-lights behind the bar. The open fire has grown and now fills its grate; a stew of flames licking and laughing, feeding warmth into the room. More people are sitting at the tables than when I arrived; a few have left, but more have arrived. Their voices have the rich Wiltshire burr that reminds me of when Elin and I rented the flat in Great Shentonbury.

'I'm looking for someone, Mick,' I say, and take a gulp of ale.

'In Avebury?'

'Yeah. Or close by.'

'A relative?'

'An old friend. Someone I lost touch with years ago, who I'd like to catch up with before returning to Australia.'

'And he used to live in the area?'

'No. But she wrote to me recently. We were supposed to meet in London, but something happened. We missed each other. When she wrote she forgot to include her address — probably because we were going to meet — but the envelope was postmarked Avebury.'

Mick picks up a towel and begins drying a tray of glasses. 'Bit of a long shot,' he observes.

'Yeah, but the only one I've got.' I sip my beer, pluck a crisp from the packet — stop myself from rushing into the moment. I will him to ask and will him to know.

'What's her name then?'

'Kate.'

He shrugs. 'Kate what?'

'Kate Hainley. But she may have changed her surname.'

'You don't know whether she's married or what she does?'

'We lost touch. It's been a few years.'

He shakes his head, picks up another wet glass. 'I'd remember a name like Hainley. And I don't know any Kate either. But you might ask at the Post Office in the morning. Have you looked in the telephone directory?'

'Yeah. And the electoral rolls.'

'She'd be about your age?'

'That's right.'

'Sorry.'

And the front door swings open to admit two couples. They're laughing and loud; their faces are rosy, their eyes bright. No Kate. They bring with them a blast of icy air that makes the fire gutter for a moment before flaring and burning brighter than before. I almost expect to hear a glass being dropped.

★　★　★

Next morning, the sky over the downs is a steely grey and there's a stiletto-thin icicle forming in my throat. The downs themselves, dressed in their winter grasses and skeletal copses, along with everything about the village, are the thinnest wash of colour imaginable without turning transparent. The moment the postmistress flicks the sign from CLOSED to OPEN and lifts the latch, I enter the shop and follow her to the counter, where she sits behind a partition of thick glass.

'Yes?' she says, and I launch into my spiel about finding an old friend called Kate Hainley.

Almost before I finish, she lowers her eyes, pulls across a rubber-banded wad of dockets — pension stubs — and begins counting.

'Do you know anyone like that?' I ask.

'Couldn't tell you even if I did, duckie. Privacy laws, don't you know.'

'I've come all the way from Australia.'

At this, she stops counting and looks over the top of her glasses at me. 'Australia, eh? Internet romance, is it?' And laughs.

'No, she's an old friend. We were supposed to meet, but something happened. All I have is this Express envelope to go on.' I unfold it

382

on the counter, but she ignores it. 'Her brother's dying,' I add. 'It's important I find her before it's too late.'

She pushes her glasses onto the bridge of her nose and sits upright. 'Suppose there ain't no law against telling you what I don't know,' she says, 'and I don't know no Kate Henry.'

'Hainley. Kate Hainley.'

'No Kate Henry nor Kate Hainley.'

'What about a Kate? Any Kate? She's probably changed her surname.'

From a storeroom to one side of the counter, a man appears. 'Whereabouts in Australia?'

'A town called Dungarvan. It's on the coast, a few hours from Melbourne.'

'We like to watch *Neighbours* on TV, don't we, Shirley? That's set in Melbourne.'

I try smiling.

Shirley turns in her seat and says: 'Do you know anyone called Kate? This man's looking for a Kate.'

He shakes his head and walks back into the storeroom mumbling and chuckling: 'No Kates, no Katherines, no Katies; there's only Shirley in my life.'

'You better believe it,' Shirley calls after him, and returns to her pension stubs.

'What about someone posting this Express packet a few days back?'

'You're joking, right? Give it a rest. Do you know how many people we've had coming through here in the lead-up to Christmas? I usually have these stubs counted two days back. What with the buses of tourists as well as the regulars, there's been a line to the door from opening time to closing.'

Today, the shop is empty and I haven't seen a soul in the streets or a single tourist snapping away at the stones.

'That's a 'no' then?' I ask.

Shirley raises her eyebrows and carries on counting. 'I can sell you a stamp,' she offers. Then adds: 'The woman you're after was probably a tourist passing through. Have you thought of that?'

On my way out, I pass a carousel of Christmas cards, and am halted by a familiarity in the style. Flicking through several designs, I pull out one in particular. The illustration is of a cartoon Father Christmas (red-robed and white-bearded), sitting on the branch of a massive Christmas tree in a forest of Christmas trees. Perched next to him is a squirrel, a couple of birds and a mouse, and it's snowing.

'This is the card,' I say, waving it at the postmistress. 'The exact same. She must have bought it here.' Pulling Kate's card from my pocket, I hold them side-by-side for her to compare.

Again, she shakes her head and again her husband appears from the storeroom. 'Almost every shop in the country sells this brand,' she says. 'We even got sent one of those, didn't we, Ken?'

He grins, and I can't understand why they're not trying harder. I'm ready to pick up the carousel of cards and shove it through their bloody plate glass; I'm ready to tell them what arseholes they are, but I slump and take a step backwards instead.

He says: 'It's going to snow.'

She says: 'I'll believe it when I see it. People blab on about white Christmases every year, but it's only happened once that I remember.'

He says: 'It's gonna snow.'

Outside, the cold steel of the sky presses even lower and the insipid wash has almost frozen. I cough to clear my throat, but the icicle prods my lungs, inspecting each in turn. There's little left to do except walk the silent streets and hope that Kate, if she's here, might look out a window at the moment of my passing. I'd rather do this than admit my loss and head back to Nenford, and there's no betrayal in it. My mother doesn't need me; she never has. If I eat lunch at the pub, I'll get back in time to visit her this evening and to phone Elin too.

But the tiny windows of each cottage

remain empty, the streets abandoned.

After lunch, I close the door on The Red Lion, throw my bag in the car and realise I'll have to buy another can of antifreeze to dissolve the ice. Instead of walking to the shop though, I cross the road to stroke a sarsen stone or two first and walk some of the circle. I've come too far not to. Winter or summer, these megaliths are the roots of shadows, binding past, present and future. There's a part of me that belongs to the land — this land . . . what's left of it.

Wandering from one stone to the next and to the next, I trace a segment of their pattern across the landscape, and feel that Elin might almost be standing next to me, as she once did in this place a long time ago, and as of course part of her still is and always will be. The stones know the nature of time beyond any other knowing. It's one reason we're drawn to them.

And then, for the heck of it, I pull my collar up and strike out along Stone Avenue. One step and then another, on and away I walk, until, with Silbury Hill on my right, here's the road Elin and I once followed towards West Kennett. Crossing this, I notice a grass track leading back onto the downs.

A little further, I tell myself. I'll walk a few more minutes and then turn back.

The track would be muddy if it weren't semi-frozen, and it's semi-frozen despite being sheltered by a hedgerow and trees (hawthorn, ash, hazel, elder, horse chestnut and oak). Like the child I once was, I dig the toe of my shoe across the skin of an icy puddle to crack it, which is when, upon looking up again, I first see her.

She steps onto the path a hundred paces in front and takes the same direction I'm heading. To begin with, I figure she's thirteen or fourteen, and it's strange to see someone this age walking alone on such a track. Maybe she's meeting someone — a boyfriend — or walking a dog. I'd hate her to think I was stalking her, so slow my pace and consider turning round, but she slows her pace too and the distance between us remains the same.

Tucked to the side of the track, where she first appeared, is a fence stile linking with another path, and I wait here to let the distance between us grow. The temperature is dropping, and I'd do better to hurry back to the heater in my hire car and drive away, but am even less ready to do this now than before. There's a momentum to this day, to this place.

When I turn onto the track again, she's no further away. In fact, I can see her more clearly now, as if she's closer. And not only is she older than I first thought — maybe eighteen or nineteen — but there's something familiar about her walk.

She wears clogs, which always shape the way a person walks, and a calf-length olive green skirt with gilt embroidery along the hem, which somehow manages to catch fragments of the piss-weak winter light. For a coat she has a short maroon cape with a hood that's lowered despite the growing cold, and her hair is dark and long.

'Kate!' I shout, and immediately regret it. She's only eighteen or nineteen, so it can't be Kate. I stop, wave an abrupt apology at the girl who's turned to face me, and decide I have to scurry away to the car. 'Sorry,' I call out. 'Thought you were someone else.' And I too turn.

'Tom!' she calls after me.

16

We stand facing one another, a middle-aged man and this nineteen year old girl, and I want to reach out and stroke her face, to put my hands on her shoulders — to make sure she's real — but can't. Of course I can't.

'Kate,' I say. 'But it can't be.' She has the widest eyes of glistening burnt umber and a flow of chestnut brown hair that hangs loose across her shoulders, and her lips, which have the fulness and glossiness of polished olives, are the pink of rose petals, even now on this winter afternoon.

She smiles, breaks into a short laugh and sighs. 'You found me, Tom. You searched and searched. You spent twenty years looking, but you found me again. That's bloody incredible, you know. I can hardly believe it.'

I step back to look at her more fully, in case it's a quality of the insipid and grainy afternoon light that makes her seem so young. 'But it can't be you. You can't be Kate. You haven't aged.'

She fans her fingers in front of her face, raises them to create an arch above her head, then sweeps them down again. '*Olé*,' she sings, accompanied by the castanet-click of her fingers.

'It's impossible,' I say.

She pouts. 'Are you calling me impossible?'

And then something happens with the weak, watery light, because, for an instant, she shimmers. I'm reminded of a mirage on a hot summer's day and wonder why no one's ever commented about the mirages of frozen winter days before.

'We don't have long,' she tells me.

'I'm sorry. It's just . . . '

'I know. But I assure you I'm the Kate you've been looking for. No one else. People aren't like snakes, Tom. We don't really shed one skin for another as we grow from age to age, and there's always a part of us that's the person we've always been and will remain. I'm just amazed you managed to find me after all this time, and here of all places, and today of all days.'

I smile, then laugh, then shrug. 'Kate. Kate, Kate, Kate.'

She reaches for my hand and we begin walking in the direction we were both heading before. Her hand is icy, so I draw it into the depths of my coat pocket, and we walk as we once walked over twenty years ago . . . by a river, or down a street, or through a park; swans or no swans. Except, our ages are all wrong, and the idea of this man (who I've become) walking with this girl (who she's remained) is too sad. My stomach churns and starts rising, until I swallow hard, let go of her hand and stop.

'If anything, I should be younger than you,' I tell her. 'You don't think I'm some lonely old loser, do you? Some sort of creep? That's not who I am.'

'We're here together aren't we, Tom?'

'Then why haven't you aged? It doesn't seem right: us two, here now. I'm old enough to be . . . and you're . . . '

'Life's fickle like that. Though it depends how you look at things, I guess.' She reaches her hand out again. 'You don't know how lucky you are. Take it or leave it.'

Nothing's changed about the shape or feel of her hands — her long, slender fingers; the smoothness of her skin; the cut of her fingernails — except she's icy cold and they're coloured with raw pink blotches. I rub each hand gently in turn, then bring them to my lips and blow warm air across her fingers.

'Don't you have any gloves?' I say.

We walk in silence for a minute or two, until two becomes ten and ten becomes a swathe of the afternoon. That we now say nothing isn't odd or unsettling. In itself, this reunion is too big for words, and there's more integrity in remaining silent and soaking up the fact that this is happening than in risking the irrelevance of prattle. But it's also as if we're moving towards an even bigger moment, and she's leading me to that point.

Only once do I nearly forget who I am — who I've become — and begin easing her hand out my pocket to kiss her wrist and smell the scent of her skin, but she shakes her head to remind me that a lifetime has passed.

We walk across a landscape of interwoven earthworks — barrows, chalk figures, dykes, standing stones — and we're bridging the years, she and I. Emerging from the edge of yet another spinney, and skirting a hill, I recognise I've been to this place before and pause. Arriving at Grennard Hill, she ends the silence with a greeting.

'Hello, Tom.'

'Hello, Kate.'

It's a broad and frost-bitten landscape of skeletal plants and ice-burnt foliage. The moisture on fence wires and the tops of posts and along blades of grass are beginning to set with an opaque whiteness. The bleak season.

'I'm not just Kate,' she says.

But I must've misheard her.

'Why are you here, Tom?'

'I needed to know you were okay, Kate. I needed to see you again,' I tell her. 'This probably sounds stupid, but I've had too many dreams in which you were . . . well, it's been hard not being sure that you're really okay.' Turning to face her, a strand of the corn dolly pokes though my shirt into my skin. 'I've brought something with me,' and I pull it from my pocket by one end of the figure eight. 'A surprise.'

'I remember that.'

'You gave it me. Instead of a ring.'

'I did. A lifetime ago.'

'Or yesterday.'

She takes it, examines it, then passes it back. 'To everything there is a season, eh?'

Turn, turn, turn.

'I guess the truth is I haven't been able to fall out of love with you, Kate. Not properly. For almost twenty years I've loved two women. At times I've thought about you almost every day and wondered where you were, if you were okay, whether we'd meet again. And there's been other times — weeks or months, perhaps — when I thought I'd pushed you to the back of my mind, only to dream you back again, even with Elin lying by my side.'

'You always set too much store on the past, Tom.'

'Maybe.'

'And you put me on a pedestal, didn't you?

I warned you against that, but you wouldn't listen. Always the idealist.'

'When I was with you I felt alive for the first time. I began breathing, and to know who I was and who I could be. And then I lost you.'

She nods.

'In London, after your party, I thought — I hoped — we might get back together, and it was everything I ever wanted, but something happened.'

'What happened?'

I tell her about Jo's death and how fragile Elin was, and how it would've been the shittiest of betrayals to cast her adrift, and I remind her of our meeting at Piccadilly Circus, and how we'd planned to go to a concert before that, but never did. 'I'd have been even more lost if I hadn't stood by Elin, but I lost you again instead.' I stamp my feet against the freeze and try wiggling my toes. 'All the same, I wish we could've kept in touch — the occasional Christmas card at least — it might've been easier.'

'Or harder.'

'It might've been harder. But it might've been easier. Maybe we could keep in touch better now?'

She raises her eyebrows. 'Do you think it's because you lost your mum and your dad — '

'My mother's still alive.'

'You lost her as surely as you lost him. But you were never allowed to mourn any of that, and you wouldn't let yourself mourn Gazza either. You never really learned to cope with loss and to move on — not in a healthy way — only to wallow in what's past and to live in anticipation of losing what you cherish. You've never fallen out of love with me — the idea of me — because you've refused to let yourself. That's stubbornness, not love. But it is only the idea of me; you can't love who I've become because you haven't known me for twenty years. You don't know me.'

'Except we're not like snakes,' I say, trying to remember her earlier words. 'We don't shed one skin for another. We don't change that much.'

'Perhaps. But I doubt whether our choices and values and tastes as teenagers remain unchanged after an extra twenty-odd years of experience, do you? That's what we're talking about here.'

I shrug, glance at her, then at the ground.

She says: 'Did you need me to spit at you? To hurt you? To make you hate me before you could let me go?'

'No,' I say. 'No.'

'It's time to let go, Tom. Forget those old promises we made one another. Release

395

yourself. That was another lifetime. You have to live in the present. Don't hold anything back from Elin and your children.'

'You always had the right sort of smarts, Kate.'

'You know this stuff too, otherwise I couldn't begin to tell you. Sometimes we need to hear our most important truths from somebody else though. That's one of the reasons you're here, I guess.'

'It's not because I love Elin any less than I should. If I lost her, I'd feel the same. I know I would. I know it now. She's a part of me, as you were. But how can you ever get over losing someone you absolutely love? You can't. It's not stubbornness, Kate. It's more a matter of faith. Perhaps it's because we invest our idea of love with so much significance — as children, as lovers, as parents, and probably as grandparents — that it ends up defining us, and so of course we cling to it, in the same way we cling to life and who we are. The death of that sort of love — well, it's almost impossible to bear. That's the way it is. Maybe that was my mother's problem.' And when this rush of thoughts stop tumbling out into words, I put my hands together from relief and discover my fingers are turning numb too, with pink blotches flowering on the backs of my hands.

When we speak, our breath is mist. It hangs from our words.

'We have to learn to cope with death and loss, Tom, and to make the most of who we've got while they're with us. There's danger in anchoring yourself to the past, fearing the future, ignoring what's present. We have to mourn loss, grieve it, be angry and fight it by all means, but then we've got to move on and know that nothing's ever entirely lost. There's always something left to grow with. We have to make the most of what there is.' She pauses. 'You know, there's no other meaning in life except the meaning we choose to make for ourselves. It's that simple. It can cripple us or fortify us.'

I cup my hands together and blow on them. What she's saying is as clear a truth of life as I'll ever get, and I shrug, smile, nod.

She places her hands on my shoulders and leans close, and I think she's going to kiss me. 'Tom, Tom, Tom,' she whispers; 'turn, turn, turn.'

'What?'

Taking a step back, she fans her hands across her face once more, shakes her hair down, then brings her arms above her head in a dancer's arch, and she turns. My nineteen-year-old Kate dances as she danced only one big yesterday away. She spins once, twice, three times, more, until she's creating a ripple in this world and until the sky starts spinning and shimmering as well.

'Turn!' she sings, and so I stretch my neck up to the lowest of skies and, on numb feet and across rough ground, begin spinning too.

Round and round and round.

I fall to earth first and she follows suit.

Shimmering.

Like a child I'm laughing fit to burst, but I'm panting like a middle-aged fart. 'Out of condition,' I pant.

'Me too.' And her voice is different, and her hair's a shade coarser; less lustrous. She's different. Something's changed. She pushes a strand of hair behind one ear, and I see she's turned into an older Kate — a woman close to my age.

'Kate. You're you again.'

She places a hand against her face to feel her skin, wraps her arms around herself, then begins to stand, but stumbles, and I reach out to steady her.

'I've always been me. This is who I am. But I'm not just Kate.'

'What do you mean? You keep saying that.'

'Why are you here, Tom?'

'I told you. We just talked — '

'Why are you really here? Now and like this? How did you get here? Do you know how to find your way back?'

The freezing dampness in the air slides down the neck of my coat, wheedles its way into my socks and licks my ankles, the backs of my legs.

'Can't you remember? Where are you going to, Tom? Where are you heading?'

The trees are leafless and, but for a pinching iciness, the air is momentarily scentless.

How did I get here?

This is the place I once camped with Elin, with the spinney I gathered firewood from just fifty metres away; on a day of shadows, stones, trees and earth. At the edge of the spinney I notice a large Norway spruce — *Picea abies* — which must be about fourteen-years-old. I grew that tree from seed, raised it on the windowsill of our flat in Great Shentonbury, and must have travelled back here one day to plant it, as I told Elin I would.

'I . . .'

She puts a finger to my lips and says: 'Ssh.'

The steely grey of the sky has given way to thicker snow clouds banking up, but through a gap in the clouds there's a full moon rising — a small, brilliant moon, brighter than any bauble — and we hobble down towards the wood.

'You're limping,' I say. 'What's the matter? Are you alright?'

'You're limping too,' she points out, but rasps each word.

'I can't feel my toes.'

Her fingers are slips of ice, and she's sickly pallid in the fading light. Her lips have lost their colour and fullness — less like olives and more like pits — and her eyes are sunken and dull; even her hair hangs limp and dry. 'You're not well,' I say.

'It's almost time,' is her reply, but her voice is a husk. 'Time to let go. Little is ever entirely lost.'

'What's the matter?' I begin, but she winces and I stop.

She shakes her head and her chin is almost on her chest.

Twilight is collapsing and evening begins pulling a shroud tighter around us. I figure the trees might offer some protection from the wind that's picking up. Sanctuary.

'Please,' she mumbles.

And though I place an arm round her shoulders, she grows lighter, frailer, more gaunt, more ashen, with each clumsy step, until it's easier to carry her than prop her. By the time we reach the edge of the spinney, her cheeks are hollow and resemble the gargoyle cragginess of Old Lofty.

'What's happening to you? Why?'

'Don't,' she rasps. 'Don't be afraid. There's nothing . . . to be afraid . . . It's nothing. I need to lie . . . down.'

'What's nothing?'

Dragging a breath, she says: 'It's what . . . I came for . . . and . . . ' The sentence peters out, so she gulps another breath. 'It's what . . . you're here . . . for . . . '

'No. It's too soon. I've only just found you again. It's too soon.'

The moon disappears behind thick cloud and all trace of the twilight that was with us a minute ago vanishes. So absolutely has it fallen dark, it could be any hour of night. Long night. The longest. I'm sitting with my back against the spruce and Kate's lying against me, her head in my lap, except she's almost completely a gargoyle now, and I don't recoil.

'Remember . . . what we . . . said.' And she begins coughing. Each cough rises from her lungs and shakes her entire body; dry, rattling coughs that sound like bark being torn from trees. Her skin has the coarseness of dry leaves. She gasps then. 'Don't . . . it's nothing . . . really.'

'It's too soon,' I cry. 'Please don't.'

She mutters something I can't make out, and manages to smile, but the smile freezes and the light disappears from her eyes to leave a deeper darkness.

This is why night is the colour of death.

★   ★   ★

If I keep her warm, maybe she'll revive, so I cradle her in my arms. But her coldness seeps into me: brittle crystals of ice.

Letting her head loll on my knees, I reach wide to scoop armfuls of leaf litter and fallen pine needles until I've created half a nest for her to lie in, but it isn't enough. Shuffling backwards, I ease her head off my knees and draw in more leaf litter until I've fashioned a soft pillow for her, and then begin crawling round in the dirt, heaping forward whatever I can find, until the nest is complete and I've tucked in her legs and feet.

I lie with her then, whispering her name, but the bitter crystals grow. I touch her lips with my fingers, let them lie there, but there's no tremor and no warmth.

'Kate, Kate. Come back, Kate. Wake up. Don't go.'

She's still too cold. It isn't enough. Struggling to stand, I begin stripping thin branches of smooth-barked rowan to blanket her with, start layering young branches of

402

spruce into a thick coverlet, until only her face is visible.

At the very least I might believe she looks peaceful, as if she's sleeping, but she doesn't; she looks withered. Her eyes are sunken beneath dark, knotted shadows; her cracked and pinched lips reveal a mouth of broken flint.

Raising my arms to the canopy of branches above and beyond to the night sky and the universe and infinity and the vast permanence of death, my shout should shatter the fucking lot, and bring it crashing down like breaking glass to become ashes and dust on this miserable patch of dirt.

'NO!'

But nothing moves and nothing will move, even when I stumble in circles, so I slam a fist into the trunk of a tree — oak or rowan, spruce, birch, beech, chestnut, ash, hazel or almond — and then the other into another. Falling to the ground, I crawl snivelling to Kate. There's bark and blood in the air, pain bursting out my knuckles.

Face-to-face; she's lying on her bier in front of me.

There are seeds of death in all of us, as well as seeds of life. Have I never realised this before?

To begin, the moaning grows from gusts of

wind working the boughs of trees, backwards and forwards, to and fro, until I realise it's me — draining from the pit of my aching guts. Even so, the winter wind joins in, cutting down from Grennard Hill, nosing at the edge of the spinney to start with, but soon slicing between the trees and splitting the air in half. Branches sway, creak, complain, and an icy rain sweeps down on the heels of the wind and begins its stabbing. I'm howling and sleeting, and the night is blacker than ever before, and the knives of ice multiply into a torrential onslaught.

If I could become the night, I'd rewind each of these last moments until we were meeting on the track — or further back — and nothing need ever change again. Backwards, backwards, to keep everything the way it was and always should be. But I'm frozen small and shrivelling to the seed of who I once was, and every icy dart I pluck from my eyes to hurl across the landscape drains the me-that-was-I smaller and smaller, even though the I-that's-become-me rages and howls bigger and bigger.

Rage and howl.

My eyes spit ice daggers, and when I open my mouth to swallow the night with a roar, flurries of snowflakes bellow out. Some fall on her face and my fingers brush them clear while every other part of me storms. Blizzards of snow, stones of hail, knives of ice . . .

For hour-upon-hour, if time exists; age-upon-age. A thousand years, or the blink of an eye. From rock to sand; from earth to rock. Time to learn how mountains are born, how beaches sift into shape, and how it all begins again. Turn, turn.

Until . . . until something in me pauses, or ends, and sees the gathering drifts and hollows and ledges of snow are lightening the dark, stealing its edge, softening the wounds. Beyond Grennard Hill, the motorways and pylons and housing estates and shopping malls will all be smothered in a sea of snow. And the dampness in the concrete and bitumen will freeze and expand and prise apart, and someday weeds will be harboured there to root and grow and prise some more. These things are clear.

But my eyes, nose, mouth, throat and ears are burnt raw from spewing this storm, and my icicle fingers are bone-numb and colder than claws. There's nothing left to vent, nothing left to give, except nothingness. There may be seeds of death and life in all of us, but I'm sapped to a husk and all choice is gone.

On my knees with the body of Kate, it should be easy to collapse forward and embrace her one last time, except my knees are locked and something rough in my pocket presses through my shirt and pierces my numbness: the corn dolly. Kneeling back, with fingers too frozen raw to manage buttons, and my coat too caked in snow to grip, I fumble and wedge my fist between the overlapping fabric until a button snaps off. My fingers won't straighten, but I manage to hook them through the loop of the figure eight and drag the thing out.

'Two rings,' my lips begin, except they're bark-dry and split.

Cupping it against my chest with one hand, the torn knuckles of my other clear a circle of snow and leaf litter and try scooping out the frozen topsoil until there's a shallow bowl of sorts to welcome back the plaited dolly. However, before interring it, and though my hands no longer fully belong to me, a sharp, scalloped edge of stone buried in the dirt slices a loose flap of skin off one knuckle.

Here's the polished glint of chiselled flint waiting to be noticed and picked up. Here's a Neolithic point that I'd turn in the palm of my hand, if I could. And, if I could, I'd draw its sharp edge across the fleshy heel of my thumb and let the blood drip like pæony petals between Kate's lips until she breathed again, if only my blood wasn't frozen.

Scraping deeper to dig the flint free, I force a claw beneath to prise it out, but it crumbles like old bone.

There are two more in a tin on a shelf . . .

Gazza and I broke into the building site on a dead dull Sunday afternoon . . . but I can't go there now. It's too late

Gazza might have said: 'When you die your whole life flashes before your eyes. In the time it takes for your brain to shut down, you've relived everything.' It might have been Gazza, or it might have been Kate or Daniel or Elin, but there's nothing more to give, no strength left to grieve. There's nothing — absolutely nothing — beyond the simple recognition of who I really am.

Death becomes me.

*　*　*

My lips are shredded paper-bark, glued together with dried blood; my eyes are swollen and sealed with the grit of soil and dried tears and torn wafers of old leaf, and someone is dabbing them, licking at them with a warm, moist tongue.

Something's happened to the me-that-was-I. If only I could remember who I was.

'Can you hear me, Tom?' the voice says,

like a shell against my ear. 'I have to believe you can.'

I try opening my eyes against a blinding light, which is beyond all brightness and which creases them shut again.

'Wake up, my love,' she says. 'Try and wake up. When you're ready. We're waiting for you.' The voice is not fully Kate's and not fully Elin's; it belongs to neither of them and to both of them.

'Who are you?' I say, squinting at the woman looking down at me. 'Are you Kate or are you Elin?'

She smiles and the day is a fraction warmer for a moment. There's a faint smell of ozone and the crash of surf. Enough to wake me further.

'Elin,' I say.

And she plucks a polished olive from her mouth and rubs my lips with the moist warmth of it.

'Kate,' I say.

She smiles.

'Or both?'

She smiles. She's leaning with her back against an oak tree, with my head in her lap; the softness of leaf litter is my bed. I know it's an oak tree because a twig with a couple of last year's acorns is caught in her hair. Or it could be a eucalypt with a twig of gum nuts.

Or a spruce laden with young cones.

'What can I call you?'

She smiles. Her eyes are hazel. They are the burnt umber of Kate's, blended with the blue of Elin's, to become somehow hazel. Her hair is that reddish auburn which lies between the chestnut brown of Kate's and the corn blonde of Elin. Her features have something in common with both, although neither shares the slightest resemblance.

'Katelin,' I say. 'Of course. Why didn't I realise?'

Katelin says: 'Sometimes the simplest truths are the hardest to recognise.'

I remember the storm and, attempting to sit up, find that every sinew, muscle, bone and organ in my body aches beyond all aching. As she puts her arms behind my back and eases me upright, I feel the air sink out my lungs, then hear the crackle and wheeze as they half-fill again. I'm wrecked.

'Shit. That hurts,' I say.

'Ssh, it'll be okay. We're with you now.'

'I thought I'd lost you.'

She shakes her head. 'I'll always be here.'

We're at the edge of the spinney by Grennard Hill, and the sun is a brighter disc at the back of a frosted sky and the earth a barren down. It's a landscape of watery greys and bleached browns.

She is naked and her skin is streaked with soil and the juices of berries and the verdigris smear of crushed grass. I am naked and withered.

'So cold,' I say, but the coldness is in me, more than around me. My mouth is ulcerated, my skin is sore.

'Don't give up,' the voice says, sounding momentarily like my mother. 'I've always loved you, you know.'

The snow has vanished, and I ask: 'How long?'

'It doesn't matter how long. When you're ready.'

There are two conversations happening here, and they almost meet.

'This isn't real, is it? Is any of this real?'

'We thought we'd lost you.'

Katelin reaches into her hair and unsnags the twig. Her hair straggles loose and leaves drop out. An insect falls onto her shoulder, walks along the valley formed by the prominence of her collarbone, and then flies free. She smells of peat and earth, rain and sunshine; she smells of moss and wood. Tugging at the twig, she snaps off the two nuts and, holding one to my mouth, says, 'Suck on this. It'll keep you warm.'

Up close, it's neither acorn nor gum-nut nor cone, and is like no fruit or seed I've seen before. It has whorls like a shell, but as she turns it in her hand there's no beginning and no end to the whorl.

'What is it?'

'It's alright.' And she pops it inside my mouth, then places the other inside her own.

The effect is immediate. A warmth diffuses through my body, but it's more than warmth. It's a delicious energy streaming through my veins, pushing away the cold and the hurt, and makes me feel as though I'm growing an extra layer . . . which, when I drag my arms up, I see I am.

From my knuckles and the tips of my fingers, where the warmth is strongest to begin, nodules grow; firm, bud-like calluses, each with a faint whorl of their own. With a prickle of heat, they rise to the surface of my entire body, and with their rising I need to rise too.

'That's it,' Katelin says, helping me to my feet and drawing me a few shuffled paces forward. 'From head to toe. You'll feel better now.'

We're standing facing one another and I hold my hands up to see what's happening. Each node has grown into a green bud, and each bud begins to unfurl, presenting the tips of two tender leaves. I would tremble with the warmth of it and the energy driving through

411

my veins, but she holds me by the shoulders and I'm rooted to the spot.

'Don't be afraid,' she says, and is all smile.

'I'm not. This is . . . ' But there's no word to describe it. Beautiful, magnificent, glorious, miraculous, orgasmic — no word could do justice.

'Life?' she suggests.

'Yes,' but it's bigger than that.

'Green?' she suggests, and is laughing now. 'Leafy?'

I nod.

The sun has brightened and reclaimed its ocean of sky. A sea of grass is rising and a wave of vegetation laps at our feet. An almond tree flowers and leaves unfurl and fruit buds swell; rowans and oaks, hawthorn, chestnuts, beeches, birches, spruce and ash follow suit. Honeysuckle climbs and mistletoe fruits and masses of pæonies flower — out of all season. And as each leaf unfurls, I hear a frenzy of leafy whispers, and behind the whispers are words that might be greetings or might be the retelling of old stories that I'd have understood from years back if only I'd known how to listen.

Looking past Katelin at the mass of foliage in the spinney, I notice what might be the outline of a face, and when I look harder I see a number of faces. I can't be sure, but one

412

looks like the memory of my father, and one has an expression that reminds me of Gazza, and maybe Jo's there too, and even Brian, and everything's okay and everything's falling into place now.

'But why aren't you . . . ?' I begin to ask Katelin, until two leaves sprout from each side of my mouth, from my nostrils and my ears and the corners of my eyes. It's no worse than growing whiskers for a beard, with each pair of leaves followed by a slender tendril, and each tender stem budding into more leaves.

Katelin steps closer to me then; face-to-face. She pushes her arms carefully through my foliage to embrace me, noses through the leaves until her nose is touching mine, her tongue stroking my lips, the softness of her breasts and the tickle of her berry-nipples against my chest, and her toes resting on mine.

'Delicious,' I say, but the words are a rustle in the breeze.

'Now,' she murmurs.

And I wrap two leafy arms about her.

She lifts one leg and wraps it around me, and every part of me enters her, grows through her, until the warmth that's running through me is rising through her body too, and it becomes pointless to consider that we were ever separate or could ever be separate again. And why did I never know this before?

'Forever and ever,' we think.

★ ★ ★

Turn, turn, turn.

New spring.

I know that we could grow here forever, and slip into the consciousness of wood and foliage, to drift through the seasons in a curious harmony that would be beyond all knowingness.

Or, I believe, if I try hard enough I might retrace my understanding of how I arrived here and then dream myself back onto a plane landing at five-thirty at Heathrow, or onto a train arriving at Northampton Station, or into a car, or waking in a bed from another dream, with a building site in front of me, or into a memory so vivid it might seem like a dream itself.

Or I could listen to the whispering of leaves and the lapping of an ocean, and make myself breathe to its rhythm until I'm ready to dive forward to meet it, and swim down for a while, to find this new current, before stretching out and up — up and up — until kicking free and breaking the surface again . . . to open my eyes and take a deep breath.

And return to the world I came from.

But I must choose. I've no choice but to choose.

★　★　★

My lips have been rough bark, glued together with dried resin and blood. My eyes were a splintered ache, sealed with the grit of sand and salt, soil and dry leaves, and for so long all I've wanted to do is sleep and keep both the fathomless darkness and the blinding brightness out. But the wind is a warm breath across my face and neck, and the whispering of the surf is also the singing of leaves, telling me it's a new day. There's a part of me that's numb, so I ease my fingers apart, stretch my toes, and feel a blanket of kelp drawn across me, strapping me down like driftwood on the beach.

I look at the sea and see it rise and fall, rise and fall, and its rhythm is the rhythm of breathing. A wave rolls in towards me and I watch it lift as the ocean takes a breath, and then, as it breaks and crashes, it exhales that breath in a long sigh. Breath after breath after breath.

Breathe in.

Breathe out.

Breathe in.

Breathe out.

This is why we're hypnotised by the sea. Cruel though it can be, it nurtures life; is more mother than smotherer.

Breathe in, it says.

Breathe out.

Inhale.

Exhale.

I listen to the suck and sigh of the surf, each rolling rise and soft crash sighing onto the beach. I take a deep breath to draw in the sweetest, nourishing scent of ozone, and I push the blanket of kelp away.

'Hello,' the flight attendant says. 'Welcome back.' She's all smile, uniform and reassurance.

'Have we landed?' I begin to ask, but have no voice.

'Easy,' she says.

It's then I notice the tubes growing out my nose, my arm, my hand, and the leads sprouting from my chest. I liked it there.

'Can you tell me your name?' she says.

If I can't I'll become driftwood. I see it in her eyes.

I try to nod, but blink instead.

'What is it?' she asks. 'What's your name?'

It takes a moment to remember and would be easier if I could show her my passport, but she's in no hurry to get me out of here, wherever here has become.

The moment I remember who I am is also the moment I realise where I am.

'Tom,' I whisper to the nurse. 'Thomas Passmore.'

When she moves to one side, I see a window and out the window the meagre light of winter dawn and, some distance away, the form of a large tree — a spruce perhaps. The early light hasn't drawn out its greenness yet, but the shape of each of its layered branches is highlighted by a coating of hoar frost, and for a moment I'm sad to have returned to this place and to have left Katelin behind, but glad the tree has stayed with me.

The nurse lifts my hand and places hers across it.

'Can you squeeze my fingers?' she says.

Another figure steps into the space behind her — two figures — a woman and a child. The woman is holding the child's hand. She looks tired, sleepy, until she realises I'm looking at her.

'He's awake,' the nurse says, and moves to one side so they can edge next to the bed.

'Tom,' she says. 'Tom.'

'Katelin,' I try saying, but only half the word comes out.

Tamsin steps forward and puts her hand out, but doesn't touch me. Elin kneels down next to where I lie. 'Kate? Did you say Kate?'

I try to shake my head.

'She was here with me yesterday. She was talking to you for a while. Could you hear us talking to you? You've been gone a while.'

'No,' I say, 'not what I meant.' The effort to talk is too much and only half my words are breaking through.

She holds a glass with a straw against my lips. The attempt to move forward brings an axe-sharp pain that buries itself across the front of my eyes, and I wince.

'What?' she says. 'What is it? What do you want?'

'How . . . ?'

'Why are you here? Is that what you're asking?'

I nod.

She looks at the nurse, pauses, then speaks the words. 'A car bomb at Euston, a few days before Christmas. Do you remember?'

I close my eyes and try. All I recall is a dream about a young mother pushing a pram one hot afternoon in Spain.

'You've been out ten days, Tom. You've been gone ten days. It's New Year's Eve. We saw it on the news, but you shouldn't have been in London. You shouldn't have . . . Annette's looking after Daniel and Elspeth. We all came straightaway. It's been the shittiest ten days of my life, Tom. I thought we'd lost you — we all thought we'd lost you. It's been hell, Tom. What were you . . . why . . . ?' Her torrent of words ends in tears, and then she tries smiling. She's angry and happy, smiling and crying at the same time.

A murmur of traffic reaches me, laps against me — comforting — and I focus at a point beyond them. I see a tree in a winter landscape, and remember something more.

'Elin,' I say.

'I'm here now,' she says, dabbing her eyes.

'Tamsin,' I say.

My daughter strokes my arm. 'You're awake,' she tells me, then puts her hand up to cover the round 'O' of her mouth.

For the last — however long — my life has been full of echoes. But the echoes are fading now and that's okay, and I feel as if I've finally caught up with myself.

Elin leans forward and plants a kiss on my forehead. Tamsin grips my hand. I take the deepest breath I can and try to focus on the scent of them, the touch of them, the closeness of them. And to hold onto it. To reach out and hold firmly onto it before this small pond of a room shimmers like a ripple across still water, and before the certainty of them shimmers too.

'You've been asleep a long while,' she says. 'Welcome back, my love.'

ACKNOWLEDGEMENTS

Like many stories, *The Snowing and Greening of Thomas Passmore* has evolved through a number of tellings, and a number of people have assisted directly or indirectly in helping me find its present form. Of these people, I owe particular debts of gratitude to my wife, Siân Burman, and to my publishers Keirsten Clark and Tom Chalmers.

To Siân, who has supported my obsession with writing at every stage of our relationship and who's acted as a sounding board for everything from scribbled ideas to final proofs, and who's nudged me along through some of the darker places in-between: thank you, thank you, thank you.

To Keirsten, for investing so much energy and enthusiasm in this novel, and for providing that wonderful quality of editorial insight which enabled me to see Thomas Passmore's story more clearly; and to Tom, for picking it up and bringing it to fruition: a very big THANK YOU.

Thanks to Lowri and Gwil for your absolute support and for letting me run ideas past you, and — well, for everything. And thanks also to Ivan Boyer and Annie Lanyon who courageously allowed themselves to be press-ganged into reading a very early and unwieldy draft of something which, in places, may or may not have resembled aspects of this story.

I'd also like to acknowledge my indebtedness to the manuscript appraisal service offered by the Victorian Writers' Centre, Australia.

The extract from Bede's *A History of the English Church and People* is translated by Leo Sherley-Price (Penguin Classics, 1979). The full text of Giacomo Leopardi's poem A *Silvia* can be downloaded from a number of websites. I primarily accessed http://www.ilnarratore.com.

We do hope that you have enjoyed reading this large print book.

Did you know that all of our titles are available for purchase?

We publish a wide range of high quality large print books including:
Romances, Mysteries, Classics
General Fiction
Non Fiction and Westerns

Special interest titles available in large print are:
The Little Oxford Dictionary
Music Book
Song Book
Hymn Book
Service Book

Also available from us courtesy of Oxford University Press:
Young Readers' Dictionary
(large print edition)
Young Readers' Thesaurus
(large print edition)

For further information or a free brochure, please contact us at:
Ulverscroft Large Print Books Ltd.,
The Green, Bradgate Road, Anstey,
Leicester, LE7 7FU, England.
Tel: (00 44) 0116 236 4325
Fax: (00 44) 0116 234 0205

Other titles published by
The House of Ulverscroft:

LOOKING FOR OLIVER

Marianne Hancock

While clearing through her late mother's bedroom, Emma finds a thirty-year-old newspaper clipping that her mother had kept, announcing the arrival of a new baby boy. Realizing that the baby must be the son she gave up for adoption, Emma finds herself vividly recalling the stigma of her schoolgirl pregnancy and the pain of her separation from the baby. She becomes transfixed by this link to her first-born, and sets out to search for Oliver, her adopted son — despite the fact that she now has a husband and two teenage children, who know nothing of her past . . .

NOVEL ABOUT MY WIFE

Emily Perkins

Tom Stone is madly in love with his wife Ann, an Australian in self-imposed exile in London. Expecting their first child, they buy a semi-derelict house in Hackney despite their spiralling money troubles. But soon Ann becomes convinced that a local homeless man is shadowing her — she spends hours cleaning the house, and sits up all night talking with a feverish passion. As their child grows, Tom senses an impending threat. Their home seems beset with vermin, smells and strange noises. On the verge of losing the house, Tom makes a decision that he hopes will save their lives.